CW00543483

A Conspiracy of Events

john brooks

Published by john brooks, 2023.

A CONSPIRACY OF EVENTS

First edition. September 5, 2023.

ISBN: 979-8223077756

Written by john brooks.

Also by john brooks

Incidents of Slavery
Incidents of Slavery
The first rays of sun
A Conspiracy of Events

Table of Contents

'A Conspiracy of Events'

By John Brooks
Index:

A Conspiracy of Events

by John Brooks

Prologue:

The intrigue that unfolds before us cannot and is not claimed by us as being totally factual, due to the immense about of incidents discovered through our research, we thought it correct to highlight the lives of the main characters who shone through those incidents and gave reality throughout that awful period.

The initial files were delivered to us, wrapped in a substantial brown paper parcel and delivered via a taxi to our offices, which clearly showed us that the full story and the many diverse facts were not fully public. The information discovered by us thereafter and which came to us via numerous politicians, civil servants and other interested parties around the world, all generated such a mass of conclusive information, that it was impossible to catalogue it all into any form of readable literature.

The accompanying note, which, was delivered with those initial files, simply said that written below.

———⚫———

DEAR SIRS,

"It has come to our attention via the enclosed copied files that a world disaster of great magnitude was adverted via a mixture of natural means, international scientific corporation and policing, plus sheer good fortune.

The full gravity and number of incidents of this nature that are occurring worldwide and not made fully public are alarming.

We believe it to be in the global communities' interest to be fully aware of all such incidents. Such instances occur and are then too often dealt with secretly within governmental, media and scientific circles; simply create scandal and the application of secretive laws appears to of reached an unacceptable level internationally.

Whilst appreciating international incidents similar to the enclosed are dealt with by unknown governmental departments, and within the UK, buried deep within GCHQ, then, as if by magic, evaporate from all forms of the media and public investigation and scrutiny is, once again, very concerning.

We must of course be forever thankful for the protection provided to us, yet, we wish to assert our belief, that the public must be informed, and there lay our dilemma.

When any incident incurs such an apparent threat and loss of life, with both material and social damage over so many borders, together with the enormous potential, to disrupt, the very existence and future of humanity, it is a huge global problem. Surely, our full awareness must be alerted so as to affect the actions taken on our behalf.

As well-intended or democratic as some of the decisions may be, they do not appear to be adequately or directly, safeguarding the existence of humankind and the environment.

Indeed, all our futures appear to be constantly at risk these days and the majority of the time we simply have no idea of the current facts and the ramifications that face us all. Representation without open and honest consultation is no longer happening, if anything, it appears to be reducing, maybe this is a new necessity within social control within the digital and internet age, or simply, the future in some other dubious guise, ultimately maybe a more secretive and yet harmonious system which is appropriate in the world of tomorrow. It may indeed be, after the environmental issues, the biggest problem currently before humanity – how do we move forward globally; with truth or deception and what is the acceptable balancing point?

———◉———

THIS WHOLE INCIDENT recorded in the initially supplied files is beyond our understanding.

How do such matters become so tightly controlled by governments and, ultimately, the media?

As a group of concerned citizens, we can only conclude, that many departments are existing within governments that the vast majority of us will never hear about.

The decision to leak this information for international awareness has not been easy and does involve great personal risk for many, including, moral and principled dilemmas.

The number of people and governments involved, together with the tragic and enormous amount of fatalities, crop failures and global financial disruption, make such an occurrence appear impossible to suffocate to the degree that it was; let alone, a new and deadly transfer between plant and mammal. All interwoven at the highest level, with sabotage surrounded by high-level corruption.

'The earlier incidents and various strains of Covid were successfully dealt with ultimately, but the science was a known scientific possibility. We have now entered an era of the unknown'.

That the facts and incidents herein, could be diluted by governments, and others, simply by misinformation, fake news and localised reporting alone, seems impossible in the age of the World Wide Web, and yet in this incident, it certainly did happen.

There is nothing further to add, hence, now having passed this material onto yourselves, neither do we wish to.

Our consciousness thus satisfied that the responsibility has been passed to yourselves, to take the appropriate and responsible action, on all our behalves.

We wish you luck and wisdom with whatever actions you decide.

Yours Sincerely, Interested Parties.

—

————●————

NO FURTHER MEANS OF contact from the source were forthcoming.

Endless collaboration of statistics and research appears to confirm that something exceptional occurred over those months, and only some of the horrendous facts were released. Part of the confusion, or indeed diffusion is created by the number of instances, many than only reported in part, the effect generating a patchwork of inconsistent and un-trackable information due to the enormity of the true events and those created to cover the truth.

Unfortunately, the nature of modern journalism and media allows fake news to be spread widely, without the due diligence of checking and confirmation. Therefore, we appear currently to live in a world where only headlines and sound bites have importance.

The story that follows, expands and gathers just a few of the confirmed incidents and uses them to their full potential for our international wisdom and awareness. We have attempted within this story to capture the essence of what happened during that period. Any added drama has been carefully vetted, to ensure it does not affect the investigated reality.

Most of the locations and incidents have been confirmed by our research.

The characters are fictional but represent directly those indicated throughout the files supplied, together with their journeys and involvement to add human reality.

The huge amount of fatalities over the recent past are known to most of us by the name of whatever temporary disasters or diseases fit locally. Other changes and events have been blamed upon anything from global warming, genetic modification and a thousand other possibilities. Some of those claims are in part, genuine in their association, but not the majority.

There are indeed many and increasing incidents happening around the world with no qualified explanations given or understood. All be it, to say that the changing climate and the continuing environmental disasters are still awaiting our full and serious attention by governments in the main.

The world population has drastically increased over the past decades, and no doubt, most of us are aware that reproduction rates within the Western Industrialised World continue to fall to unsustainable levels. In other places, they surge out of control. Maybe these substantial changes offer plus's and minus's for our civilisation, but it is impossible to predict. But, it appears very clear that we need to adjust and adapt our ways given the enormous weight of scientific opinion.

Migration generated by rising temperatures, sustainability problems and the growing awareness of inequality learnt via the internet, cause further major issues, let alone those growing concerns about the health of our planet which create all those issues. The prospects for future generations of humans and the many other reducing species are daunting.

Thankfully, to date our world still moves forward on its journey; hopefully, we can learn and grow in wisdom and take a little more care of this wondrous planet we call home. It is but a long challenging journey ahead and indeed, if there was ever a time to apply the generations of wisdom and scientific advances, that time is now upon us.

'The files supplied to us, are now with carefully selected and appropriate authorities, and we only try to present here the story based on those files, and our research. 'As the story unfolds, you will clearly understand how little factual news was available to you, the public.

For security reasons, we have needed to relocate our own lives, and we thank the publishers for their bravery in making available this short story. You disregard the information within at the risk of future freedoms, truth and our children, (indeed the future of humankind), together with the survival of our still beautiful planet. John Brooks

—

London: Early 1960s:

It was an unsettled period full of new visions, particularly in the Western World, a time of messy regrets, and exciting and new adjustments.

P ast disputes and war had come to their natural conclusions. Of course, nothing achieved a hundred per cent satisfaction but indeed what in the world ever did?

Aiming for a hundred per cent was good, but achieving eighty or eighty-five was excellent. As long as one achieved over fifty per cent, it was acceptable.

Michael Ramondi had achieved many eighty-fives, even a few nineties in his time, he was exceptional.

These were times when every day something seemed to be improving. There was new thinking, new fashions, music and foods; most important were those new personal freedoms and extra money in the pocket from somewhere. New freedoms meant new responsibilities; you could question, you could protest, and you could strike.

Whether or not these freedoms were real, was another issue altogether, but they seemed to be in those times.

Europe was beginning to leave World War Two well behind in social terms; yes, there were still many other conflicts around the world, actually far too many happening, and many new and serious issues developing. The world was changing, for the better, it seemed, but the real issues remained much the same under that surface shine we all saw.

Any system based on consumerism and production and, all be, it rapidly moved the world forward, long term it would have enormous unsustainable consequences.

The East-West entrenchment, which was up and down, was potentially serious, as it appeared to be continuous.

There was underlying and growing unrest across the muslin world and yesterday's third world countries which now were looking very much like tomorrow's leaders were just some of those issues underlying. Those issues, together with the foreseen shortages of fresh water, and questions concerning the future of oil and plastics were all deemed problems that were growing year after year in scientific circles.

Global warming, plus the ever-present realisation of needing to improve poverty levels and inequality, was to occupy the future in ever-increasing degrees. Nevertheless, internationally, minds were considering new and exciting concepts, socially, politically and scientifically, and indeed, they seriously had to.

The growth of computerisation and its control and dominance over society was beginning to generate an uncontrollable world initially, and we all knew that a day of reckoning could soon be upon us.

Michael Ramondi had enjoyed his life journey over the past decade and a half. He had been able to progress to head of the Department for Diverse Scientific Studies and Investment within the Civil Service, the D.S.S.I.

It was spring, and energy appeared to be lurking everywhere and in everything, the fresh pale green shoots of grass, the bursting buds upon every tree, the bird song, the forsythia - that wonderful splash of vibrant yellow heralding a brighter tomorrow, crocuses and little things creeping, crawling and busying themselves.

All things appeared full of promise and new splendour, indeed, most passers-by had that spring in their step, and a lighter and happier air surrounded them, but Michael was apart from happy thought, those rumblings and disjointed thoughts and memories in the head of Michael Ramondi were, more paralleled to a dull and miserable winter's day.

The projects within Michaels Raimondi's department had to be politically acceptable and financially viable, particularly in the 1950s to 60s and thereby hung the rub, the politicians had to win votes or they could achieve nothing.

There were many new projects and realisations, which could turn all excepted science on its head and some were in particular, on the effects of chaos, and in parallel were the possibilities of cross-species infection and mutation.

—

Michael Raimondi lifted his head and starred out across the park to the River Thames. He knew this strange mood he found himself in, must be gone. He reluctantly took tobacco from his pocket and rolled a cigarette. He knew he shouldn't smoke cigarettes and understood that one day they would be illegal everywhere but he still enjoyed the habit of a lifetime, although disapproving of his weakness in not stopping the habit. He lit his cigarette and took a deep draw, stupidly filling his lungs with smoke, but was to be the least of his worries.

Nevertheless, the cigarette made him feel a lot more at ease and he again took himself back in his memory to those missed opportunities when at the ministry. Opportunities that just might have changed the world for the better, the waste of those opportunities annoyed him immensely; the failure not to push harder with those projects, annoyed him so much. The short-term thinking of politicians and indeed scientists annoyed him.

Michael should have known better, but procedures are procedures, both main projects had then been cancelled, funding had been pulled, and the department restructured, and that was a true tragedy, for if it had been handled correctly, this could off become a great legacy.

In their unquantifiable wisdom, they had decided that he and his futuristic projects were too dangerous, too expensive and well before their time in history, therefore, achieved little for the real world in gaining votes in that particular period.

—

London: Late 2006:

The whole shape of the ministry was different nowadays. Michaels Raimondi's present, miserable reality, as well as his undignified retirement, were the things he had to worry about nowadays. No job, a past that had sabotaged the present and the future, had left Michael down and depressed, regardless of a good pension. He was a nobody in reality nowadays and nobodies tended to be overlooked in the greater scheme of things and given the thin end of life's wedge.

Luck was not on his side and any luck he still had was about to run out – permanently. For Michael, as for many other Londoners, fate, together with the essence of his past work was about to intervene in a way, that he had never imagined and make all his worries and past regrets pale into insignificance.

At Kings College, London, in a high-profile lab, two Petri dishes had mysteriously been disturbed inside the fume cupboard, assumingly as the result of a clumsy move by a lab technician, 'possibly'. No one in the laboratory had noticed the incident or understood how it could off happened.

It was not as if any of the cultures grown in the cupboard were intrinsically pathogenic or dangerous in their own right. But what none of the lab staff, or research microbiologists realised, was that the laws of chaos and chance, or indeed subversion had entered that fume cupboard along with those cultures. The one in several million or, indeed, billion, likelihoods that any of the innocuous microbial occupants of those dishes might conspire together or be added to, so becoming one very nasty little problem, was then in play. The disturbing dishes now made sure of that, mixing like evil dark shadows into the unbelievable and causing a pandemic of new and epic proportions.

—

Kings College, London:

"How's the paper going Liz?" Andy asked as he removed an earphone from his right ear and half-addressed Liz using one part of his brain while the rest of his grey matter remained immersed in the white noise that was some kind of death metal music.

"Do you want to now? I certainly don't want to waste my breath competing with that noise."

Liz lifted her head from the binocular microscope and nodded in the direction of the noise source, without moving her hands from the sides of the scope.

"Oh, yeah, sure I do. Sorry!" Andy fumbled with the other earpiece and the on/off switch of the MP3 player and entered the real world of the lab fully with a shake of his head, his long, dark, greasy hair taking on a fresh dishevelled style in the process.

Liz had already resumed her watch through the eyepiece of the microscope, her fine blonde hair falling gently to either side. The last light of evening through the window picked out the fine golden strands in a reflection of silken smooth colour.

"If you really want to know, it's bloody boring. I made the wrong choice when Dixon suggested this project. I honestly don't know where all these tests are going at the moment and part of me wants to give up and start again on something completely different; if only." Liz's eyes were firmly fixed on the microscope. "The only thing that keeps me sane is being able to look out across the park to the river for inspiration. Looking back, I should have looked into the effects of certain other parasites on large mammals; that was an option. As you know, micro-marine biology has always been my real interest, in the light of common sense, that would have been more interesting to me obviously, but not so relevant to Dixon currently and he is the one who sorts the money. Instead, I go follow his lead and start on mutant fungal and bacterial diseases of bees. At the time there seemed sound reasons and there appeared some obvious links to pursue."

"Why on earth did you choose that if it didn't grab you? You turned down and avoided some excellent offers last year so it sounds a bit of a dumb choice," he asked in his curiously rude and customary way, "Particularly being I had supported your brilliance numerous times".

The silence was very loud.

Liz mainly confined her work within the level three facilities, not through conscious choice but that was simply where the organisms she worked on at this time were classified and researched. Liz was the most talented PhD Professor Andy Gould had working under him at this time. She had been head down for the last five years becoming a world expert on vectors and transfer methods of airborne, water-borne and insect-borne pathogens – from bacteria to viruses, fungal spores, protozoa and algae, the latter algal work in the areas of algal blooms drying and then distributed by air currents and the wind. Now published in several respected scientific journals, Liz was only a final research stretch away from her doctorate and marine biology was still her love and ideal.

"Why? Arrr, the sound reasons you ask for; well do not repeat this to anyone, ok Andy, like you promise. No one." Liz's eyes were wide with a penetrating and urgent stare designed to elicit the desired response.

"No one. Promise." Andy was reassuring on the surface but not taking the look too seriously deep down inside.

"Because...you won't believe this truly scientific reason. Are you ready for this...Dixon had suggested it and I love honey! There, I told you. Tell anyone and you're a dead man and that's after the kick in the balls and the thumb screws, ok."

"You are shitting me, aren't you?" Andy was working hard to subdue a little smile and that was trying its energetic best to become a fully-grown laugh. "Honey! Ascosphera Apis. Streptomycin. Penicillin...just because the lady loves... honey! Wait till I tell Dixon...no, no, just kidding!"

"Look. Just forget it. I am joking, really, I am. I hate honey, just thought I would like to start there, but it turns out to be boring as hell. Now leave me alone and go do something useful *Mr Boss man*, you are indeed very horrid." She was trying to move the conversation on but Andy was having none of it.

He walked slowly around her lab bench until he was standing opposite the bench between them. "Honey, eh? Acacia? Clover Blossom or maybe Manuka! well, I guess they do have antiseptic healing properties so maybe you had better try honey on preventing culture growth. Now, actually, from a simple piss-take, that is a pretty good idea to get your reason for taking this on in the first place, involved in your study! Isn't it?"

Liz had disengaged from her observations and was now sitting back, her left elbow on the bench, her left hand holding her forehead, head nodding from side to side and a forlorn half-smile as she listened to Andy's ridiculous rant. Her hand twitched with both the reality of that ghastly choice of subjects doubled by telling Andy of all people.

"Ok, I can see from your smiley face that it's time for that useful something," Andy took the hint and moved off towards the fume cupboard. "You got some cultures in here too, haven't you?"

"Yes. Be careful you don't disturb their positions and don't forget to extract before you open," Liz cautioned.

"My dearest Liz, was it not you I remember sitting in at my lectures."

"Yeah, sure, you know. Floss before you brush, condom before you go out in the rain, extract before you open."

Andy was indeed, seen by many as simply brilliant and knew his subjects back to front.

In the lab, he reached over to the extractor switch at the side of the cupboard and flicked it upwards. The whir of the fan entered the still lab.

As he stood waiting before opening the door, Andy glanced inside and for the first time noticed that something was wrong, possibly badly wrong. Two dishes looked as if they had fallen from their positions, or been moved towards the rear of the cupboard and were obviously out of place and he could not understand how that could have happened. What was more alarming was that their contents had developed a mass of culture growth, an activity like nothing Andy had ever seen before. As he looked and thought, it was clear this disruption could have occurred days before because the growth was so extensive. Fungal, bacterial, viral or all of them, Andy was not sure at that moment, all be it, very concerned. He called out to Liz but after the second try realised she could not hear him above the noise of the fan. A thought that led him to wonder if it had been wise, in these new circumstances, to have turned the fan on without thoroughly considering all the factors, but in fairness, that rarely happened.

Those thoughts and facts, together with the later horrendous discovery of a damaged extractor duct before sterilization and filtering units which ran horizontally over the laboratory windows collaborated and unknowingly; the butterfly wings of the disaster had begun to flutter, apparently starting an almost unstoppable chain of events, social, scientific and ultimately, global.

—

Kings College, London, England:

The recently added high-level biohazard facility at King's College was a jointly run affair and had been highly controversial since it opened. Overseen by the Government's Centre for Disease Control, part of DEFRA, the new college facility was given wide rein to research and explore the frontiers of microbial sciences, from pure microbiology to virology, microbial genetics, parasitology and more – just as long as breakthroughs by staff and PhDs were partly or completely attributed to the Government's support.

It was, in reality, the level-4 research in the heart of London, which caused the controversy, with Brucella and Ebola investigations both condemned by several groups. "Deadly research in the City" was just one of the many headlines that had started moves to shut the facility down before it had even developed a head of steam. But now, some years down the road, all was relatively quiet on the media front and the King's Biohazard lab and its research kept a low public profile.

Within the medical community, findings were regularly published in the Lancet and the B.M.J. Even Nature, Scientific American, and New Scientist magazines sometimes carried more digestible articles about results from within the KBHL. Times were quiet, research steady and not exciting, with discoveries just out of reach.

Professor Andy Gould, unconventional, risk-taking, but extremely good and highly regarded throughout the scientific world of microbial genetics was the college's head of the K.B.H.L.

One of the youngest professors on campus, his headstrong confidence in his abilities – strengthened over the years by being right most of the time – gave him the right qualifications to keep the government side of the faculty happy. Yet, there was much more to him than that, and that was why Kings had no hesitation in choosing him as their head of KBHL. When it first opened, they knew that either they would have to tow a pure government line and play the nodding dog to Whitehall all the time, or they had to have someone heading their side who could not be bullied, and who knew their stuff.

Andy hated politics, politicians, Whitehall corruption, and his disdain for anyone in grey suits from the other side carrying a brown folder and thinking themselves important was often open for attack, fair game to Andy's ridicule and sarcasm and cynicism and, ultimately, being ignored as much as possible.

Professor Andy Gould was also one of the world's pre-eminent, if youngest, experts in the field of Microbial Mutation and had experienced the widest range of practical field scenarios and real-life epidemiological situations when Level 4 pathogens in the wild had shown characteristics both normal and expected, or abnormal and perplexing. On more than one occasion Andy has found himself in the middle of tropical Africa in full biohazard protective gear investigating Ebola or plague outbreaks and helping local authorities to contain them, only to be an "un-co-operative little blighter" that failed to behave in the normal way – if normal could ever be the right word in such scenarios.

This opened his mind to the possibilities of new treatments, and so he had given a glimmer of hope to those with fever who were still alive and many others in the future.

Yet a conundrum existed. Several people, over 100 in one village, who had nursed their relatives and had held them as they died, and who, by rights, should now, themselves, be very dead, were, in fact, very alive and relatively fit. In fact, so alive that they displayed no outward signs of illness and whose blood cultures revealed nothing abnormal. The occasional sickle cell, but no viral or bacterial infection. These people seemed immune to the sickness and Andy had simply been able to make copious observations and notes without any final deductions or observations – the Kigali labs still held samples, but the agony and ecstasy of those weeks remained unsolved. He was indeed a man of wide experience.

For Michael Raimondi sitting there in the park next to his regrets, where his final breaths were about to mix with thoughts about his son, loves and achievements, issues which; were unknowingly now unimportant.

He moved his hand down and touched a small scientific reference book, it was packed with the data he had always treasured and hidden within his inside pocket and let some small amount of satisfaction flow through his body. Throughout the world copies of that little book based on those earlier and cancelled projects were causing many to take chaos, random theories, and mutation in particular, very seriously. The mutation was the vehicle to explain the theories and it was beginning to change scientific thinking through the back door without political interference at last. It was simply a shame it had taken forty years to truly surface via a scientific colleague in Sweden.

Then it happened, the invisible cloud of microbes that had drifted across from the University laboratory buildings beside the park caught on the breeze and were so quick to close his respiratory pathways in the form of severe anaphylactic shock that Michael and many others suffocated in a matter of moments. No one in the coming days and months would be prepared for this new pathogen, its ability to mutate rapidly, or its ability to survive outside a host and travel by all means, to the four corners of the earth, forever changing its attack and causing disaster where ever it flowed. For all the treatments and attempts to stop its spread via the very latest chemicals and science, nothing was currently being achieved. All the answers to that unfolding nightmare had already been considered, against current scientific and medical knowledge...and ultimately then dismissed with a sad shake of the head and many a disappointed smile.

Plus, a cynical and very worried shrug of the shoulders.

Away from the public scene and behind locked doors, contingency plans on how to fight yet another disaster lay upon humankind. It was discussed and re-discussed and instantly reached the very highest levels across the globe.

Direct lines from president to president, from continent to continent began to burn around the clock. Great medical and scientific minds settled to apply themselves. Politicians conferred on how to control and manage the media and potential panic. Secret conferences were held.

Of course, history had shown that many such potential global issues suddenly and indisputably disappeared into the ether, the details of which were filed in the great vaults of secret reference and knowledge buried deep beneath the capitals of the world. At least, as far as the masses were concerned, such problems were resolved and under control, but something about this latest problem was very different. Its strange characteristics and its obvious ability to change its attack from animal to plant-based victims was something never experienced before.

Aid's was still with us but the developed world thought they had it under control; surely, they did? Only five fatalities every minute of every day and only six million recorded cases in India, let alone Africa.

The European foot and mouth out brake in 2001, and the subsequent slaughter of seven million animals, costing an estimated eight billion pounds.

The disaster of BSE, which had rocked parts of the world, had now been effectively controlled and the lessons learnt; well maybe! The incident factor of BSE is so very different from that resulting from AIDs.

Asian Bird Flu, essentially, just had not happened. Now fully reviewed, the odds were, and are, on our side, but can we afford to be complacent with so many risks?

The floods of 2007, and thereafter, were devastating and then the increasing number of hurricanes, terrorist attacks; disasters that just kept on increasing, everywhere. Also, the civil unrest that was currently accruing across the globe, *and mostly without warning.*

The ice melt of the artic. The thaw of the great lakes across Siberia releases copious amounts of methane, which is thirty times more dangerous for our atmosphere than CO_2 and subsequently speeds up global warming by that enormous factor.

The list just kept on increasing in both speed and number. There ultimately becomes doubt on cause and cure, and rational thought becomes a little rarer.

Yes, there were more and more disasters and strange mutations occurring, but mostly, unspoken of; leaps across specie, more air-born instances occurring. Conflict, man against man, via religion or race or simply politics polarising, resources reducing, and then hunger and the spread of deserts causing a slow but defiant drift away from those unsustainable areas towards the affluent regions further north or south of the equator. Disasters on unheard-of levels, which, our global systems are not geared to deal with, all be it, the United Nations and other groups repeatedly warn and advise

Yes, most, but not all were being reported to the wider audience, yet in part only, and somehow, everything in the day-to-day world kept on rolling along in a kind of controlled anarchy in which, strangely, people wittingly and unwittingly cooperated, all be it, there is an increasing quantity of doubts and questions.

In the United Kingdom, the eight sixteen commuter train still appears to arrive each morning at the platform at Orpington station. Folks trying to settle and read their sanitised newspaper, sitting, standing and swaying uncomfortably, compressed next to others like the obvious sardines they had been turned into, they neither knew they were being misled, or not informed accurately or fully, and, did not care, once an issue was apparently resolved – they just needed to arrive at work. Anyway, even if they did suspect being misinformed, there were no real means of true public expression or action they could take.

The media attacked everything and everybody, always searching for somebody to blame for the un-blameable; raising doubt and suspicion at every turn. The constant and serious undermining of society and community had been in process for some fifty-plus years now. Politicians had become confused and inadequate and ultimately; more than ever before in history, everybody was a spin doctor in their own right; 'sound-bites' everywhere. The free market was now beginning to appear very expensive and factually unsustainable. There was not enough control being applied to those major financial institutions and for all that political chatter that spilt out over the media, very little of major importance and in real time was being changed, apart from the rich becoming richer and nothing as regards future planning and serious problem-solving. There was the intent, but not the will or political bravery. At the great international conferences, future and mutual agreements of action were too often unfilled and drastically too slow considering the environmental threats.

The BBC World Service and all the other news sources chugged out a continual stream of apparently well-reported news and views, but in reality, they missed so much, lacked detail and contradicted each other far too often; vital stories never fully followed up or followed through. The chatter on the street or places of work remained active in both the legal and illegal bars and homes. Everywhere, there was only one topic of conversation now for the next generation, one disaster, after another disaster and another disaster. Just another killing somewhere which had no genuine meaning, only emotional hype. Constantly, there was another new threat to everyone's very existents.

The conversations were ill-informed, the media was confused about the facts, and the experts and politicians were also. How could it be anything else, there was only huge amounts of speculation. The world had never been here before, regardless of all the recent problems and discoveries. Granted; there was expert opinion but it was expert speculation nonetheless, which was simply added to the great snowball rolling down a large and dangerous hill.

Fifteen minutes of fame is preferable to honest or accurate reporting or comment. Reporters offer contradictory versions of every single story.

Today was the 2nd of March; the first fatalities were officially reported to the public on the 27th of February.

"Good Evening. This is the B.B.C. World News."

Earlier today the United Kingdom's Prime Minister, Blyar Prescott together with the government's Chief Scientific Advisor, Sir James Guest assured the country that earlier reports of the mutated fungal spores that tragically escaped into the environment last Thursday from the research laboratories at Kings College London appeared to have been contained naturally, *(that was not true)*.

Blyar Prescott went on to say he had already initiated a high-profile investigation into the incident and felt it inappropriate to comment further at this time but undertook to report to the nation and the world when the initial investigation was complete or before if appropriate, *(that never happened).*

The government gave their condolences to all the families and areas affected and assured the country that the isolation facilities provided together with localised security restrictions now being applied, should be short-lived. Adherence also provided the very best opportunity for recovery in the affected areas and the containment of this tragic viral disaster.

The closest contact, via police and military experts, was being maintained with the communities and families within the affected areas. The nation was asked to be patient and comply with all regional and local instructions, particularly where curfews had been applied.

It remains appropriate to restrict all non-emergency travel and it is recommended within the affected areas facemasks be worn in all public areas.

Sir James Guest expressed that it was the current view of the foremost scientific minds that the tragic and unfortunate release of the spores carrying the virus occurred at the peak of exceptional solar activity, which now appears to be subsiding and subsequently has greatly reduced the spread and risk nationally and more significantly, internationally. The rate of fatalities is reported to be rapidly falling, *(that was not accurate).* International fatality figures were currently impossible to calculate accurately, *(that was not true)*, but media sources estimated and expected that figure to be exceeding the one million mark.

Blyar Prescott, sounding weary, all be it, went on further to say that detailed information was being made available locally where appropriate. Currently, all local government efforts was being directed towards assisting services and areas worst affected in the southeast. Central and European Governments are acting rapidly to assist those countries at the forefront of the current weather system which appears to be causing and driving the spread of infection. Currently, Scandinavia and Eastern European countries were reporting large numbers of fatalities but thankfully, at a reducing rate, *(that was not true)*.

If conditions and circumstances should occur where military law is locally or nationally required for social stability; the government would not hesitate or fail in its duty; for the wellbeing of all.

—

London: May 2006:

Whilst an internal investigation at Kings College rapidly began, and which was initially simple and clear in its intent and endeavour, governmental departments instantly clashed and conflicted due to the required speed of the operation. Police and military control internally was confused and unsure. Political spin was indeed inspired, and more creative than ever before, indeed, it became a pure art form. Maybe not intending to mislead to the level it ultimately did, and possibly directed towards calming, but with such an instant situation following so many other climatically disastrous events, governments were failing. Being mainly used to courting mass opinion to guarantee their image and future re-election; there was indeed at this moment only 'sticky-plaster and drawing pins being used." All assumed that would be the situation until matters globally presented a clearer way forward.

Back in Kings College, Andy Gould and Liz Clement's quiet life was a sunder.

At great personal risk, the contents within the fume cupboard were investigated, as were the many victims of the disaster. The results found did not reflect the laboratories records. Neither, Andy Gould nor Liz could explain nor recognise the resulting pathogen and while other scientific bodies were undertaking the diagnostics, Andy Gould had been invited to lead the scientific investigation into the wider cause and the effects beginning to spread across the globe.

The campus had then suddenly become a military zone, and all but selected science personnel were hastily relocated. Entry and exit were impossible but for the few unknowns in grey suits. The working staff was now residential within the science block, and all were fitted with irremovable digital tags. Liz and Andy, plus another twenty high-profile scientific minds laboured with cause and effect. Certainly, some mutations were well understood, as they had been researched since the 1940s, yet all of those people involved knew that here and now, there was something quite new occurring.

At another location, great minds applied themselves to the solar quandaries that many appeared to believe, could off intensify the disaster and were adding to the known global environmental problems.

New, surprising discoveries had been occurring, almost daily. New knowledge that was possibly turning the accepted world upside down was being seriously reviewed and rapidly being absorbed and changing yesterday's scientific thinking; let alone the many new sciences that were also being created to contain so many new fields.

Andy Gould was a naturally gifted scientist, a child genius even, and now he was well overqualified and internationally respected. He shared his time and talent with a number of his favourite universities, varied institutions and favoured people. Yes, a little unconventional, off-the-wall and very hands-on, his flashes of genius allowed him his eccentricity and his position within the scientific fraternity.

Liz was one of his favourite people. Like himself, a little scatty and destined to follow a similar path as Andy but only if she would commit to one discipline for long enough. Currently, she was displaying her musical impression of tumbleweed yet again, but this was indeed a time for seriousness. Liz knew it. She was trying hard to correct the situation by finding that serious side of her brain and she needed to find it fast. She had joked with Andy that she had searched under every local bush, in nooks and crannies, and behind great cobwebs in the sky for her serious head; but nothing yet Andy, sorry about that, but it is out there somewhere, I will find it soon, honest!

"You are not looking properly Liz, you're hopeless, you are a Worrsel Gummage woman – go away you mad thing and only return when you have found the serious and professional Liz, she's needed badly by me and the world." Andy had retorted.

He had discussed these very matters with Liz only two weeks previously. Now she was to act officially as his number two and he liked that thought very much but they were both involved in these extraordinary circumstances. Andy Gould rarely felt doubts and reservations yet now they were appearing as Andy and everybody else had never experienced anything like this before; and he felt angry with Liz for the first time, as she delayed in assisting him.

She had been noticing Andy slowly winding himself into gear a little more each day. Watching the looseness fade slowly below the mountains as he battled with a thousand thoughts and quandaries; she understood, she was inwardly with him, just having to take a slightly different route and was quietly confident she would be there by his side very shortly.

The intensity around the campus was immense. Not only were those people dealing with the science but their families and friends plus the security issues together with worldwide death and disaster. All of which were falling upon their heads, at an increasing rate.

Behind all those major issues, was the confusing and scary problem of how did somebody infiltrate the security at the King's lab, and then place this unknown disaster into the fume cupboard. Did they also damage the ducting? Did they understand the horrendous effects this would create? If some organisation did undertake such an action. Who were they?

Andy felt responsible, but his schedule was now so committed he reluctantly had no option but to leave the answers for others to discover.

—

Brussels, Europe: June 2006.

A man in a dark suit sat behind his desk in an office deep in the heart of Brussels. He placed a red tick on the page marked "European Outbreak", as a teacher might mark a test paper with a positive result. The page exchanged hands with the other dark-suited man on the other side of the desk. The first suit closed the European folder and slid it to the left side of the table. Underneath were several other brown folders, the top one marked Africa. In the bottom right-hand corner of each were the words: *Bilderberg Eyes Only.* His hands rested on either side of the pile before he slid an index finger under the cover of the top file and opened it to reveal a page marked 'African Outbreak'.

There was no red tick anywhere on that page.

Such people were patient and had been waiting for the perfect circumstances to occur before their plan could, and indeed, would be activated, and now that moment had appeared.

In secret laboratories around the world their top scientific people had worked for years on everything from serious toxic substances, viruses and bacteria, let alone horrendous weaponry just encase their position in the current financial and social structures should need support. From their position and with good intent, *'Order must be maintained'.*

Now by good fortune, they had discovered something the world had not, and they were determined to re-establish yesterday's power and order by any means at their disposal.

—

Africa: The Zambian Situation, June 2006.

The air in the field research centre was stifling. Situated in the heart of Zambia, Mongu was not just hot at this time of year, but downright unpleasant without air conditioning. And with that luxury restricted to the centre's lab, paperwork was left to cooler evenings or, when it was urgent, often ended up blotched by drops of sweat dripping from researchers' heads, male or female – it wasn't true what they said about ladies sweating less. In Mongu, the effects of the heat were the same no matter whether you had testicles or ovaries.

Sam, the station manager, was at the centre early every morning along with other members of the team. An early start meant an early departure when the place just got too damned hot to work. An afternoon 'siesta bola," as they called it, meant they could work in the evening if they wished. It was a good time, cooler, and more productive and the atmospherics seemed much better for listening to the radio. The B.B.C. World Service kept them in the picture of world affairs and since the terrible news broke of a global pandemic caused by a new microbe released from a U.K. lab, everyone had their ears glued to the set whenever they could pick up a strong enough signal.

The centre's work on the Aid's virus combined with its search for vaccinations to counter several tropical diseases was important stuff, but then there was the routine stuff growing in cultures and helping the community with basic medical lab facilities. However, the Mongu field centre was merely at the end of a long chain in the country's scientific community when it came to funding and supporting work going on in bigger centres in Lusaka and Lilongwe. That is where they made the big moves and the big decisions and that is where the money goes. Mongu officially just verified and tried things out, just did all the donkeywork.

—

Africa: Zambia, July 2006:

The backpacker stepped off the bus and onto a dusty street on the outskirts of the town. Looking like any other rugged tourist, he thanked the bus driver and stepped away from the bus.

"Which way into..." he began.

The driver pointed somewhere ahead and right, not clear instructions he thought, as it drove off with its door open, leaving him bathed in a cloud of dust. He turned his head with his eyes closed and waved the air in front of his face, spitting the dust from his mouth.

It was well past midday as the stranger walked slowly into town, taking careful notice of his surroundings as he went. His heightened curiosity might simply have been that of a rather intense traveller. Only he knew, however, why he wanted to be as familiar with his new surroundings as possible.

"Hello there," said the stranger to a woman walking in the opposite direction with her arms filled with items that included a piece of carpet and an old cooking pot. "Can you tell me if there's a hotel around here, in town, somewhere?"

Another silent response consisted of an expressionless, disinterested face and a weak backwards gesture with her head nodding in the direction from which she'd come.

A "thank you" from the backpacker ended the brief encounter and he kept on towards Mongu's heart.

As he moved away, a curious sound began to fill the air, drifting on a faint, warm breeze and steadily growing louder. At first, it seemed like a buzz-saw in the distance, but as it increased, it became more like the voices of a thousand people all whispering as loud as they could. He stopped and stood looking around him outside a small grocery household store with items arranged in organised chaos outside the front of the shop. The noise now seemed almost on top of him as he looked to the sky only to witness what looked like a huge tumbling ball of smoke heading right down the road about 3-4 metres above the ground.

A firm hand took his elbow. He turned, reacting with the experience of someone very capable in self-defence and without hesitation as if he was half expecting something bad to happen. His clenched fist almost drove home but he realised in time that was not needed. The smiling black eyes met his startled stare and showed a friendly urgency that was not threatening. He was pulled quickly behind the safety of the shop's screen door. No words were necessary, as the two men watched the massive swarm of bees tumble, and seethe their way down the road in front of them.

"Wow, thanks for that. Dangerous out there, I guess. They those super bees? You know the ones from South America that kill people. Read about 'em in the papers." The stranger's sweeping mass media-based generalisation tarred all bees with his ignorance but was lost on the shopkeeper.

"Don't know those. Not here. Happy bees here and they keep us happy with Happy Honey." The shopkeeper drew the stranger's gaze away from the street outside to his shelves, stocked on one wall with what looked like jars of amber gold and labelled 'Happy Honey' – Produce of Mongu, Zambia.

The backpacker took his Ray-Bans from his face to get a better look at the golden jars. "So, they the bees that make this stuff?"

"Are, sure. Lots of forest hives and trees where honey hangs. From all kinds of flowers. Strong taste. Are you new here? Don't see you before." The man was interested in whom he had rescued from the swarm.

"Yeah, just packing around the whole of Africa. Great country. By the way, I'm looking for a place to stay, a hotel maybe. Is there one in town?" Of course, he knew where he was going, but that was not the impression he should give anybody.

"The Sleeptime Inn. Five minutes and you will have it on the right of this road."

"Thanks. Wonder if it's clear yet?"

"They gone. Busy doing what bees do, no time to waste. Not like people." The shopkeeper smiled.

"Be back for some honey. Maybe."

The screen door slammed behind him and his shape passed the window towards the town. The shopkeeper walked out after him and stood watching the man's back as he struggled along with his backpack and other luggage, his shape growing smaller in the distance.

—

London: Late July 2006:

In real terms, the global effort was intensifying, taking on shape, organisation and some kind of serious direction. Non-reported instances that appeared connected were staying under wrap. Reports of crop failures, random lakes suddenly and instantly polluted, the resulting effects, sucking the very life from all within, dead and dying fish and all freshwater life floating hopelessly, animals backing away and not drinking. These occurrences appeared mystically over a short period, causing immense dismay and further extending localised disasters, as the food chains broke down and communities disintegrated.

As information was gathered from all four corners of the world, some loose patterns seemed to be appearing. Not all regions or countries were affected in the same way. The effect on bovine, grass-munching livestock was almost non-existent everywhere, apart from not being able to drink the affected water sources which developed haphazardly and obviously had its associated problems. Yet such crops as mushrooms and others were being devastated along the pandemic weather front, which now reached deep into China.

Strange inconsistencies were now being recorded in many countries. Countries outside of that horrendous weather front now experienced their own strange happenings. Huge numbers of deaths in one region, and nothing in another; it was as if this enemy changed at will, mutated, and had a cunning and clever collective brain, determined to confuse. Any connection or thought of how is immediately unfathomable.

Serious thinking and head-scratching were the only positive activities. Many reports via the media were only grabbing for their moment of glory and fame, where they monologued pure fantasy, and fiction, their comments and reports then exaggerated further. At times, and to some, it was clearly ridiculous, and sad in the extreme.

World leaders pleaded with humanity for international self-control and unified thinking and actions, all be it, the full details of the happenings were not being given out openly and honestly. From political, medical, military and scientific professionals there were no

co-ordinated points of view, as in reality nobody understood what was happening.

From the Vatican, the Pope in a release to the press of the world had questioned the morality and direction of humankind, suggesting that could be the underlying course. He warned that the wrath of the almighty could soon be upon us. That unless humankind curbed his greed and sexual depravity, the holy threat of a doomsday could be inevitable. He called for global calm, confession, repentance and faith.

He went on further to call for patience about the almost instantly growing food shortages.

Mob rule was not the way Jesus would off chosen. The example of Jesus Christ would lead us back to tranquillity and peace.

—

London: Whitehall. August 2006:

Professor Andy Gould was passed a brown folder across a dark mahogany desk.

"Everything is arranged Professor Gould, you will be met by Miss Yoko Cheng in Beijing, she will take over from there.

You and Miss Clemence will get up to speed tonight and on the flight. We will meet here again next Friday, at the same time as today, please ensure you bring Miss Clemence along."

Andy was silenced by the assertive instructions for longer than he had ever been, he specialised in intellectual flipness with anyone, on all levels but on this occasion, nothing materialised. A long, long moment hung in the air embarrassingly. There appeared nothing for him to add or challenge, in reality, he had been told nothing, quite simply, he was expected to comply, and he also felt he had to comply, this went against all his natural inclinations, yet he felt obliged, it was so out of the normal for Professor Andy Gould.

In a vain effort to contribute something he stuttered out; *"I-is M-miss Clemence aware of the arrangements"*; he was immediately aware that what he had said sounded ineffectual; again, the moment extended to eternity while he again felt the embarrassment of asking the obvious.

He received no response from the grey suite who only responded with; "Good luck Gould, next Friday then. That is with Miss Clemence, good day Professor."

The door opened behind him, another was waiting to be ushered in front of the mahogany desk. Andy did not recognise him. Without a glance and with clear direction aimed to hasten his departure he heard, "Thank you, Gould, good day to you."

Andy floated insignificantly away from the desk, the office, the corridor and out into the streets of London. He had never felt so suddenly free and yet confused, he took a long and deep breath without replacing his mask. Once installed again upon his tired face he walked slowly towards Kings. The brief experience had strangely shaken him, and re-enforced something within him; he had never felt like a mere minion before; just a cog, part of a machine. This was indeed a new reality and he knew he would never be quite the same person ever again. 'One moment can equal a millennium', he thought to himself.

He stopped on the embankment for maybe ten or fifteen minutes, it was warm and the air was surprisingly pleasant and the streets quiet. Apart from a few people hurrying by, heads down in their masks, which was now the norm, and apart from those masks, just for a moment, London seems relaxed and as if nothing out of the normal was occurring. It was the first time for some weeks Andy had sat and enjoyed such a moment. Then an ugly creature disguised as guilt perched upon his shoulder and that together with the confusion of his undermining meeting, his instructions, and his current delightfully wistful position of sitting in momentary peace by the river Thames, clashed and tumbled around inside his head.

Suddenly, he jumped up, as the peaceful moment was gone and he strutted with intent towards the science block where he knew he would find Liz and some form of comfort.

After enduring the entrance security routines, he headed straight down the main corridor to the small laboratory at the far end on the right, not many folks ever went that far down the corridor, it was somehow private. His assumption was correct, there was Liz with two colleagues, all three bent over an endless printout of data in very deep conversation.

"Hi Liz, hi you guys. Sorry to interrupt. Will you be finished shortly Liz, it is important?"

"About five and I am all yours." "Really, how wonderful! Will that be five this afternoon or tomorrow morning?"

"Smart arse; five minutes, and no, another misunderstanding."

"Thanks. See you in room four."

Room four was a restroom with the standard 'mountain spring fresh water dispenser, coffee, tea and juice. There were several small tables covered with fresh blue gingham cloths with surrounding cottage chairs were at one end plus, at the other end some comfortable lounge seating where Andy or indeed anyone of his staff could snuggle down to sleep when called for. Andy could just about remember the days when room four would be full of smoky fumes, smells, ashtrays, alcohol and fun chatter; that all seemed quite a long time ago now.

Andy settled for the comfortable seating, opened his briefcase to reveal the very large brown folder box, and again took a deep breath, but the weather was warm, the atmosphere heavy and he was suddenly feeling very tired.

"Andy, Andy, come on you, wake up. Would you like a coffee or a juice?"

"Liz; my goodness how long have you been there, sorry."

"No problem boss man, only ten minutes."

Liz busied herself with the coffee machine while Andy slowly came back into the world. "Boy, that was a deep sleep." He sat forward and rested his head on his hands and yawned while realising he had forgotten to shave that morning. "Oh God, you did it again Gould", he thought to himself. Then stretch for several moments. "I must off needed that."

"Liz, I was ordered to the big office this morning. I have never felt so insignificant, it was awful and it was the strangest experience."

"That's a big statement coming from you. What did they want with you?"

"Us. We are off to carry out some discussions, field inspections and generally observe I guess."

"You guess. Please explain, what are you saying to me. That wasn't very clear."

"Sorry Liz, still trying to wake fully. That brown folder tells us all, we are off to Beijing tomorrow afternoon or evening to meet with a mysterious Yoko Cheng.

I have to report; no, we have to report back to the big office next Friday."

"What's in the folder and what big office?"

"No idea about the folder, I haven't had the chance to look yet. The 'big office', Whitehall of course."

"Andy Gould, you can be such a dam hippy at times, pass the folder over here."

The scantiness that was Liz had evaporated over the last few days, she was in tip-top form now and Andy had seen the change happen before his eyes. He loved her for it and was relieved. He needed her full support now, her ability to check his tangents and replace them with her own sound alternative views. When on form, she was able to speed through paperwork like nobody else; somehow, she made Andy feel secure and allowed him to "mind-wonder" with abstract and complicated thoughts.

It was a little like going out shopping with Mum when you are an eight-year-old, when all you needed to do, was hold on tight to her hand. Liz would not have liked the comparison with Mum, so Andy never mention this thought or indeed the vision of a giant Liz with a huge shopping basket, while he just dragged along beside her in a school uniform sucking his lollypop.

The brown folder was comprehensive. Bundles of endless data; up-to-date reports, and new contact details for anybody of importance. There was also a clear and precise agenda and itinerary.

Miss Yoko Cheng was no more than "Head of Scientific Studies at Beijing University and a world authority in a number of areas; Andy had not recognised her name initially but now his mental filing case was open and information was tumbling to the fore.

"*She is quite brilliant!*" he exclaimed from nowhere. "I have read loads of her papers, this is excellent news. You must have heard of her Liz, you must of."

"You didn't remember her up to two seconds ago Gould."

Liz was running her eyes over the data and information sheets, while Andy continued to enthuse over Yoko Cheng. "Yes, now I'm thinking, I have read some of her papers; to be honest it was a little beyond me at the time but I recognise what you're saying. She is brilliant."

"Andy, it appears after Beijing we are destined to visit an agricultural area in Fujian province where they have experienced complete destruction of their mushroom crops of all things, they supply some eighty per cent of the world's tinned mushrooms or they did, all very weird! Evidently, no human fatalities at all have been reported; boy, that is strange. Miss Cheng needs to discuss a mutation theory, which has been developing within Beijing, all the current data is here; my word, this looks complicated. Is this the paper you were looking at the other day, Andy? We are going to need all the time we have to digest the surface of this lot. She, Yoko Cheng, will also be returning with us to London together with a number of colleagues. On Wednesday week after our return, there is to be a two-day, conference, an international, face-to-face update, and of course, lots of discussions.

Gosh! Everything we could possibly need from this end is currently being compiled, all currently applicable research data, like bloody everything, wow!"

"Errrr, you don't mean in Room 4." "Andy, shut up and wake up you fool."

"Hey look, take one of these Andy; evidently it will keep us awake."

"Mmmm! pretty little thing."

"Mmmm! Yes, I guess I am. Aren't you lucky to know me?"

"No; no not you, idiot, the magic tablet. Boy, they seem to have thought of everything.

Andy, I suggest we go eat first, after that; we can bury ourselves in this lot for a while. Take-off is tomorrow at 4-40pm, it does not give us much time, does it?

Is that ok with you?"

"Nothing to do with me babe but don't you think this all seems a little crazy? Anyway, you have the instructions, let's go eat and then just get on with it."

The meal was fine, nothing incredible but Mexican always seemed a good choice. They both adored the hot and spicy set against the soured cream and salad. Liz ploughed into her veggie mode with Fajitas while Andy was more inclined towards the Enchilada Combo. An hour drifted by feeling more like five minutes, and they enjoyed a couple of Corona beers, probably too many. "It's that slice of lime that's to blame. We weren't called limies for nothing." Commented Andy.

Strangely, the issues or arrangements at hand were not mentioned, in fact for Liz and Andy, it was a very overdue quiet time. Both consolidated their own thoughts and inwardly started preparing for the nights and days ahead. The little tablets Liz had issued to both of them from inside their government package were obviously doing their job. Instead of becoming drowsy as their bodies were expecting to feel, both seemed gradually more alive and refreshed. They stroll back to the campus feeling thoroughly ready for a night's hard work.

By late morning the following day, they were happy with their understanding of the contents within the brown folder and agreed to a short rest period. Tiredness was not the problem, simply eye, neck and brain ache, they needed to move around and reconsolidate their thoughts, stretching and walking was the answer. As they strolled around the limited grounds of the campus, Liz slipped her arm into Andy's as they walked. Initially, he was a little inwardly taken aback, there had never been anything physical between them but it felt good and he was conscious of not allowing his inner thoughts to appear before Liz. More strange messages were appearing in Andy's head; *'like a married couple this', 'does she like me more than I realise', 'what should I do now',* 'just stay cool Andy boy she's a woman, can't trust their emotions.'

Liz interrupted his stupid chain of thought.

"Andy, we have one and half hours before we are picked up and that stroll was just what I needed, hope you didn't mind me hanging on, it just felt right somehow.

Come on, let's go and grab one more beer each then back for the lab stuff and our bags."

"I agree. That sounds good to me, no time to waste, let's go right now."

As they moved quickly towards the security exit, a well-spoken deep voice stopped them. They both turned simultaneously to be addressed by a tall and broad young man in a very nicely cut grey suit.

"Excuse me Sir, Miss; I am afraid you are not permitted to leave campus now."

"What! Pardon! Who are you?"

"Security Sir," he said displaying his authority card. "Please don't be alarmed but you are under 24/7 surveillance and protection, Sir, Miss."

"Since when?" Andy once again began to experience the feeling of being a minion. He had no adequate response to the situation and worse still, he had that horrid feeling of authority taking over his life. Liz now joined the abbreviated conversation. "Are you guys just watching us"? "Yes Miss, myself and Mr Browning here will accompany you throughout the trip you are to undertake, my name is Mark Gates and Mr Browning is Phil. I am sorry if this is a little bit of a shock to you both but it is the procedure and your file info did brief you on security measures and our details."

"Andy, I am so, so sorry but I must have missed it, I don't know how, I'm sorry, really sorry."

"Liz, Liz, cool down, it's not a big worry. I haven't really been with it much myself for the last few days and I did not see that info either."

He could feel and see emotion building within Liz. Possible pressure, the release of all those tensions, which, were possibly being denied inwardly by both of them, or maybe those little pink pills.

He wrapped his arms around Liz, he could feel her let go, she hugged him back for a second and then with one great sniff and a backhand across her face to wipe away the wetness, she appeared back to herself.

"So, so sorry everybody, I really do not know where that came from but it has now gone away and will not return, I hope."

"There is no need Miss, actually I should now call you Liz if you don't mind Miss. I understand you are both under enormous pressure, it may well be my turn next." "Phil, can you zoom ahead and go drum up some coffee in room four; four cups please and we know that we are leaving at four which is not too far away. Who's for it," he said with a broadening smile recognising the silliness of so many 'fours' within his sentence. All smiled simultaneously and the moment disappeared in the good humour.

At 3-15 pm Phil together with a very out-of-condition porter, sweating, puffing and wheezing badly, returned to room four with Liz and Andy's personal bags from their dormitories, they also had two further bags with localised information and equipment from the laboratories that Andy had organised throughout the night.

"If you are ready ladies and gentlemen, time to move."

The balding porter, Albert, lowered himself upon a nearby seat and placed his hands on his knees, "Gould blimey governor, give us a blow. Phew, I isn't any good for this game no more, not when it is on the double and surrounded by trouble. All this security stuff, stand up, sit down, show your pass, kiss me arse. Oh, sorry Miss but I'm sure it's driving us all mad!" Liz responded, "Albert, you wouldn't be here these days if you were not a very special chap." He smiled in appreciation and nodded toward her. "It's not like the good old quiet days Miss, that's for sure."

Mark and Phil grabbed the bags, all of them, and then with no commotion, marched off, indicating with head movements the direction to walk. Out of room four and down the corridor towards the entrance; halfway down they turned left through double doors that were normally locked. Andy had no idea what was down there for all the years he had known the place. Two flights of stairs and through more double doors and suddenly there was this Olympic-sized underground car park, brilliantly lit. Before them, the largest Mercedes limousine ever seen, shaded windows thrown in for good measure. The boot was already open, and it was approximately the size of the Albert Hall and was already half-loaded with many official-looking bags and cases.

"Gould blimey, didn't know this was *eer*," commented Albert with boggled eyes as he looked around and continued to pant heavily, albeit, he was only carrying an odd few coats.

"Andy and Liz jump in now please, this is a tight schedule and we must be on our way. Thank you, Albert, be sure to have those doors locked."

With everything feeling presidential, slowly the limo pulled away.

"Andy, would you prefer to be addressed as a professor, Sir or Andy."

"Andy is just fine, no problem either way around."

"In public anywhere we will address you as Mr and Miss or Sir and Madam; you will always address us by our surnames. You can, if you wish talk shop in our company, I doubt we will understand anything you say. In public, as you are aware you must censer whatever you discuss or say. We will politely interrupt if we note any straying from that particular rule which we all must observe."

"Can we ask you Mark, where we are exactly headed now?"

Liz was already practising her royal wave and in fact, as she continued her fun effort at waving to the non-existent crowds, Andy noticed what a refined wave she was developing, so quickly. Mind you, she did come from a good family, titles and money, although nobody ever guesses that of her. Andy thought he would not mention that nobody could see her from outside, through the shaded windows.

"Yes Andy, it is Heathrow, a military flight disguised as BA flight 196. There will be others on board forming a very full delegation, but it is unlikely that we will meet up with them as everybody will be discussing and dealing with their own areas of responsibility. This is how such matters are currently being organised. There is a section onboard designated for ourselves with all facilities and cabin staff at our disposal, you both have private sleep berths, plus a common area for us all."

"Mark, this all seems quite incredible, to be honest, we do not understand the treatment, is there something else we should know? Both of us are somewhat overwhelmed and it is all becoming increasingly difficult to concentrate on what we are possibly doing here, we are simply scientists and yet this appears so political. It is becoming scary and a little threatening. What else can you tell us?"

"Andy, Liz, please. If I were to ask you for confidential details within your security brief, what would you say to me? All of us are instructed what to say and what not to say and when. The rule is; that you brief everyone on what they need to know only when they need to know it, no more. I guess we live with that code and I understand it is a little new to you guys at the moment and that no doubt you are beginning to feel threatened. It is not sinister; it obviously makes extremely good sense with matters as sensitive as saving the planet, so to speak. I guess in reality you understand what I just said to you?"

Liz had broken from the conversation with Mark and Phil and was paused in thought. Then she turned and spoke quietly to Andy.

"Possibly another mutation with global impact, just like the scale of the accident in our labs, if indeed it was, but this time affecting crops; how can this be? Why do they want us, when there are so many other experts out there and when there is so much collaboration going on already?"

Andy turned and responded to Liz's question leaving the other question unanswered.

"I guess we are both experts in the field through some of our current research," Andy surmised, "But we also suffered that mysterious 'event', seemingly resulting in the current pandemic across Europe, Scandinavia and way beyond. Maybe they really need our input, too, like Holmes and Watson to the rescue. Mind you, I am not sure what your bee and honey research has to do with saving the world, Liz. "Thanks for mentioning the honey Andrew and sure, I'll take my magnifying glass and you take a pipe. Ho ho, chaps, or is that Biggles and the R.A.F." Liz then looked to Andy for his response. "No, I think it sounded like Father Christmas to me."

As they walked down the almost endless airport corridors, they both were considering the surreal events unfolding before them. One day, just two average professors researching new frontiers. The next moment, finding themselves at the forefront of the global pandemic, and politically involved, then being jetted around the world to help solve the awful situation, all be it, and admittedly, everything appeared to have originated from our labs and unfortunately, at a time when they were engrossed in their own lives and their relative own work projects. Now, whether suspects or potential saviours, they had been forcefully pulled in by the Government, along with the world community, to lead the investigation into the incident. The public needed to see the Government's responses, and fast. Governments were panicking due to the constant mutation occurring, leaving them with only limited controls they could apply, most had considered quarantining varied regions, but where and when. Quarantine hospitals were quickly erected and located, and in China, they were being built incredibly within weeks, all be it, their main problems were agricultural devastation, and those actions are taken more in an attempt to create public confidence. That appeared necessary as certain elements within the public were asking far too many questions that simply could not be answered, and even those that could be, were not helpful, hence governments everywhere were holding back to avoid unrest.

Andy and Liz were finding it all so unreal, that they, Andy and Liz, should be so key in this horrendous situation.

From relative public obscurity to notoriety on the world stage in such a short period. Was it plausible that this was how such matters were regularly handled? Something was indeed not fitting and the jigsaw puzzle was not yet complete, hence, they were now both becoming aware of the pieces of the jigsaw that were missing.

One of the only international flights being allowed at this time and they were on it?

With different thought patterns, Andy and Liz walked on with a growing sense that in the greater scheme of things, people at the top, seemingly charming members of the cabinet, might need a fall guy or two.

Who better than a pair of clever but politically innocent scientists who just happened to have been in the right place at the wrong time or the wrong place at the wrong time, depending on whom you happened to be?

"You know, Andy, I've got a bad feeling about all this," whispered Liz with classic female intuition. "I have been thinking over this situation, and both you and I are aware that we are really dealing with something very unusual. It seems as if every aspect of the social and biological threat is interacting, and yet, so many happenings just do not fit recognized knowledge and awareness.

—

Africa: September 2006:

"This is the B.B.C. World Service. Here are the main points - *Crackle, -ews.*

Crackle." The broadcaster's words faded in and out of loud white noise and interference. "...across Europe and beyond.

Those latest figures are at least a further 3 million deaths since the weekend and earlier reports of containment seem to.... *Crackle...* premature....*Crackle.... Crackle.*

The white noise drowned out the words and the car radio reverted to being an early-morning sensory nightmare. Sam switched it off with a gesture of irritation and focused on the dusty road heading through the centre of Mongu.

"Man, what is going on," he thought. "First, it's the U.K. then Scandinavia followed by Europe and now Asia, in particular, China. Never before had it been like this but now two outbreaks at the same time and completely different, possibly meaning constant mutation. Is somebody being very careless at their job? Not us microbiologists! Well, maybe not." He smiled to himself as he recalled numerous minor incidents in various labs to which he had been attached over many years. Yes, microbiologists were definitely fallible, so looks like chance has simply played a mean trick.

As he drew the white Hitachi pick-up to a stop at the intersection outside town, Sonny Ndumbo waved from the other side of the road outside his shop as he opened his shutters to the morning sun. Sam nodded his head in recognition and raised his hand from the window ledge. The streets were more or less empty at 6 am. A couple of dogs lifted their sleepy heads as the pick-up passed. Long shadows shortened with the rising sun, as Sam headed down the main street and passed the municipal buildings and the Sleepy Time Inn. A black cat chased across his path as he passed the Police, Fire and Ambulance station – an all-in-one, single-storey with a lean-to sheltering within it the multi-role Land Rover that supported all three emergency services.

Driven by the one and only first responder in town, Kanu 'Pete' Sitoli, that old, green long wheelbase had seen better days.

"Morning Sherman. Sun's high and the air is fresh my good man.

Let's do what we have to and end the day before our throats get too dusty and dry." Sam unlocked the outer door to the lab as 'Sherman' the team's tame spider monkey peered through the inner screen door at him as he entered, swaying from side to side in his cage in eager anticipation of the day's first human interaction.

"Hey Sam," the voice behind him startled him as he turned, half in and half out of the main door. "Thought I'd get in early and sort out the autoclaves.

Temperatures, were not right yesterday so better fix them before we need them." Winston Mbanwe was young and keen, recently attached to the centre in the hope of a long-term position and so far, doing everything right to impress Sam.

"Wow! Made me jump. Winston early? Guess that goes with your record! The autoclaves do need sorting but before you do that, I need some caffeine! How about you?"

"Certainly, need some, too," Winston made a gesture with his fingers to open his eyes, "or these will close on me!"

"Well, as you're here early you have the privilege, normally reserved for me of making the first cup of the day! Mine's black, strong, one sugar. And I don't think anyone got any milk yesterday?" Sam smiled.

Normally alone for the first 30 minutes of each day, his first cup of coffee was usually his own affair. This made a pleasant change, and he was not worried about no milk, either.

Sam unlocked Sherman's cage and the office mascot made a beeline for Winston's shoulder. When it came time for a cube of sugar to be added to Sam's 'lion mug',

Sherman took it from the box on the side and dropped it into the steaming black liquid with a plop. As Winston turned to rinse a cup in the sink for his own brew Sherman's mischievous games added a further four cubes to Sam's mug.

"Here you go," Winston said as he placed the coffee on Sam's desk careful to find the only spot clear of papers and microscope slides.

"He's taken to you, hasn't he," Sam said, motioning to the little monkey on Winston's shoulder.

"We have a bond. Deep, spiritual," tongue-in-cheek, Winston continued with more realism, "I'm just a walkover source of food, that's all."

"You know what they say: Weak with animals, weak with women. Be careful or they will have the shirt off your back...Yuccchh! What the! How many sugars you put in here, 50?" Sam broke off as he took the first gulp of his very sweet coffee.

"One. Just one. Seriously." Winston emphasised the point with his hands and the initially sceptical look on Sam's face turned slowly, in unison with Winston straining his neck. Both men set their eyes on Sherman who twitched knowingly on Winston's shoulder and suddenly jumped for safety amongst the files of an upper shelf, sensing the men's accusing looks.

"Bad radio reception this morning. Can you try the set? Don't think you'll have any luck but seems from the little bit I heard that the epidemic across Europe has flared up again and several million more have succumbed, the pattern of this thing seems quite mad, people, crops, water, wind or air, scary stuff. Just hope and pray the winds don't turn this way, not that they would," Sam knew there was little chance of a European infection coming their way with the prevailing winds as they were.

"No good, just static. I will try later. What did you hear, anyway?" Winston asked.

"Just that containment reports had been premature.

Cannot remember how many millions they said died. Sun was in my eyes." Sam's reasoning seemed strange. Sun, eyes, hearing. Not mutually exclusive, Winston thought, but he said nothing and went about his work.

Fixing the autoclaves would be a pain in the backside but it had to be done as they'd all be needing them before long, otherwise, the lab would be like a kitchen running out of clean cutlery, and sterility in a lab with ugly bugs was, maybe, a little more important than risking a zippy tum at a restaurant.

The screen door swung open and a tall figure was silhouetted in front of the morning sun.

"Goooood Morning Monguuuu!" In a poor attempt to mimic Robin Williams" "Good Morning Vietnam" Arnold Harris – his real name was Joel Undama but he'd wanted to sound and be like his favourite Hollywood stars, Arnold Schwarzenegger and Ed Harris, men of action. At six feet six inches tall, Arnold could certainly stop the crowds in their tracks with his imposing stature. But, when it came to 6.30 am, he was as sleepy and in need of a caffeine fix as any other lab technician in Mongu.

"Noise, noise. Do you have to? Why so happy? Water's off the boil and there is no milk. Maybe that'll do you in?" Sam said with a look of pain in response to Arnold's early morning greeting.

"Milk I got. Sonny was open early when I went by. Got some honey and bread, too. It is my birthday. Toast anyone?" Arnold never had breakfast before reaching the centre. He was a desktop breakfaster and as today was his birthday, he was going to enjoy himself in any little way possible.

"Sure, forgot. Happy birthday!" Sam was genuine.

"Me too," Winston's voice floated from the next room.

"21 today?"

"I wish." Arnold's 30 years placed him at the centre of the team, chronologically. But as a chief lab technician, he was low down the theoretical pecking order although, at Kabwe, there were no heirs and graces. Team meant team – if not family.

–

The Cessna 402 pitched and yawed as it flew just below the few low-hanging white clouds that speckled the sky over Mozambique's Sofala region on its way to its destination in the skies around Mongu. Flying between 1,000 and 3,000ft the little plane was nearing the final leg of its fateful journey and pretty much below radar detection altitude. Occasionally flying higher to avoid obvious ground detection, which might have raised suspicions, the pilot was prepared to risk the occasional momentary blip anomaly on an air traffic radar screen. There one second and gone the next, most control staff would not even make a note in their logs. Since leaving Madagascar and crossing the Mozambique coast at Chinde under cover of darkness, the single-minded pilot had kept himself amused most of the time playing his blues harp, kept in place by a chrome neck brace. Upbeat blues rifts competed with the noise of the twin engines.

The 402 was typical of its class and instead of a small 8-passenger payload, this journey carried a freight consignment packed in cardboard boxes in the compartments on both wings and on either side of the nose. Inside every two layers of 24 sealed glass conical flasks, each containing a cloudy white-green soup. Several more boxes of culture occupied the vacant seats inside the simple cabin strapped in to ensure they had a 'safe flight."

The only other anomaly to this particular Cessna 402 was the laser guidance device on the underside of its belly. Not something usually associated with this aircraft, or any other for that matter. But somewhere along the line, it had become separated from the laser-guided bomb, which it would normally have accompanied to its target.

Ahead, the early-morning sky glowed with the first streams of sunlight. Rising behind him the sun cast an ominous shadow of the Cessna on the underside of the clouds, which themselves were growing darker as they billowed in the seething sky.

A sudden downdraft jolted the little plane vertically and it dropped as if it had just stepped off a cliff. The mellow blues of his harp stopped for a moment as the pilot adjusted controls.

No sooner had the plane stabilised and the next upbeat rift had begun than two updrafts in quick succession sent the plane pitching violently. At this low altitude with less than 1500 ft. between him and the treetops Craven knew he couldn't afford too much of this kind of trouble. He also had no desire for his cargo to sustain any breakage until it had reached its destination.

"Steady girl," Craven said as he gripped the throttle in his right hand and the steering column in his left, settle down."

The Cessna responded and the sound of glass rattling behind him subsided. A bead of sweat dripped from his forehead onto the harp that sat in the brace around his neck. Craven wiped his furrowed brow, checked his instruments and then gave a sweeping, steady glance to the skies around him. "We're fine baby. We're just fine," he said soothingly to himself and the 'female' plane.

On any other flight that little bit of turbulence would not have even raised high blood pressure at a single point. Craven had flown Cobras during the first Gulf War. His worn and pockmarked complexion, topped with sunken, dark eyes had seen their fair share of terrible things over the years and his heart had become immune to what man could do to a man. Having worked closely with Special Forces and unnamed operatives on several occasions, he had gained a reputation among his comrades for tough, focused reliability. No emotions. After leaving his uniform behind to try his hand in the real world he had been approached by an intelligence operative – a guy in a jacket and tie at a Howard Johnson's road stop - for an international organisation with government affiliations throughout the Western World and N.A.T.O., so he had been told. His reputation for getting the job done – any job no matter what – had led to the approach.

When he kept asking questions, trying to find out more before committing to work for just anyone, he had been silenced by the size of the remuneration involved. No one could turn down those sums. So, the questions stopped and with some vague reassurance, plenty of partial answers but no route into the inner circle. True to form, he just got on with the job at hand.

Several covert ops around the world since then, not to mention the ever-improving health of his bank balance and here he was, on what he had been told would be the last time he'd be needed. 'Time for a well-deserved retirement' he had been told. But Craven knew this was not your traditional agency stuff. The people Craven had climbed into bed with were something else. They were all over the world in little pockets, particularly heavy with Europeans. Inter-Government stuff, Craven had wondered. New World Order if you were into conspiracy theories. But Craven was not. Whatever it was he was involved in it was highly unlikely that any of his escapades had ever been sanctioned by Washington or Brussels, or London or Paris – by themselves at any rate, or even as an official collective.

'Maybe it was better that he did not know too much, certainly, the truth could be dangerous' he'd told himself that on many occasions. He had once had a 'briefing' weekend at a chateau on the banks of what seemed to him, like a lake in Switzerland. Once he had reached Paris, he had been met and the following lengthy journey was aboard a blacked-out S.U.V.

The briefing involved partial orders, just enough to get the job done but never the aim, objective or reason for any particular actions. Just that this, whatever 'this' was, was morally justified. Always morally justified. Made him feel better, not that he believed it. Then expenses upfront, technical and equipment requirements and instructions if out of the ordinary and most importantly, contingency plans should something go wrong. Game end – you are on your own; we do not exist.

The handful of people he found himself working with were equally in the dark about who it was they were working with. As true professionals, no one talked about it and no two operatives worked together more than once ensuring that no bonds were formed. Once a job was over individual orders meant going separate ways.

Craven's peers came from all over the world and their only common feature was that the operational language was English.

In the run-up to this latest and seemingly final job, Craven had been briefed with only one other operative around. Tranter, a Brit, would be undertaking the ground segment of the operation, after which the two were to make an exception and head together in any direction from the so-called 'point of closure' as long as it was opposite to the prevailing winds. But until that time, this was a solo job, so he had thought, 'and that was fine by him.'

The route to Craven's start points in Madagascar, however, had been the most cautious and convoluted he had ever experienced so he knew this was something 'they' wanted to remain hidden at all cost. Something big!

In the Cessna, Craven was playing the blues again and thinking, 'so far, so good'.

But the clouds around the Cessna were growing darker.

Some of the travelling guests at the Sleepy Time Inn were waking as Winston drove past in the white Hitachi on his way to Mongu's scientific field station.

One guest, in particular, stirred in his bed and reached into his rucksack at his bedside for a cigarette. Tranter, half-naked in his boxers and wet with perspiration despite the room's central fan, lit the Camel at the wrong end and swore as he dragged on the filter. "Shit," he growled as he threw the stick away. He reached for a half bottle of Jack Daniels, already open and half consumed on the floor beside the bed and washed away the taste. He lit another, this time with his eyes wide open. Tranter's day had now begun and he knew what he had to do.

—

London: Heathrow Airport:

R egardless of growing doubts within both Andy and Liz, they completed endless procedures and together with Mark Gates and Phil Browning were ushered in the direction of the 219 flight. Neither really noticed much due to their minds being occupied now by unusual and confused thoughts. Each directed step they took heightened the feeling of threat, and menace that was growing deep within them.

At one stage, Liz could not deal with the growing menace that she felt inside, *'fuck'*, what is going down here; her frustration exploded and converted into a physical response, the likes of which Andy had never before seen.

She violently flung down her shoulder bag to the floor and planted herself upon the bench seating edging the corridor along which they had strutted behind Mark and Phil. Her knees pressed tightly together, her hands cupping her face. While Andy quickly took in the situation, he could not help noticing that she looked rather attractive when angry. *'I don't think I'll mention that right now'*, Andy thought to himself but inwardly he allowed himself a small smile.

Mark and Phil continued down the corridor without taking notice of the scene behind them.

Andy addressed the situation. He knew he must, and he wanted to help Liz through her crises.

"I understand Liz; I am feeling much the same. Take some deep breaths."

She thrust her hands into the pockets of her red and blue Nike jacket and found a single cigarette; she was not a smoker really but asked Andy if he had a lighter or anything similar. "I never knew you." Liz interrupted his flow abruptly,

"Just fucking light this for me Andy." "Sorry Liz but-." "For god's sake Andy!"

She threw the cigarette across the corridor void, unwittingly hitting a no smoking sign and got to her feet and walk off down the corridor with attitude. Andy gathered up her shoulder bag and magazine with a nervous hand and walk behind her not knowing quite how to deal with her outburst. This was the second time Andy had been surprised by Liz recently.

Liz suddenly stopped dead, staring down at the floor. "Sorry, Andy." She turned and walked slowly back to Andy's position, flung her arms around him and hung there for a moment breathing heavily. Andy stood motionless. "You ok now, are you getting there?" "Yes, sorry, I am getting there. Yesterday I knew what this was all about, now I have no idea, it's all ridiculous, this trip, what seems to be happening everywhere, the bloody secrecy, the rush here, you must get that done and this done, whom are you please madam, I just hate, hate, hate all of this."

"Me also Liz, these are extraordinary times. We have an enormous amount of extra responsibility on our shoulders. *Imagine being Blyar Prescott these days.* For us, we just need to follow our brief and leave others to take care of theirs. Once we gather enough material and info to start annualizing properly, we will be ok."

The instant passed, Liz regained composure slowly and the journey continued.

The flight was not as expected. A stop-ingover came and went and sleep and drossiness were the constant companions; little was discussed between the four travellers. Andy found himself providing a comfortable shoulder for Liz as she came and went from deep, deep sleep to a dozy-half-awake state with occasional mutterings. It was a little undignified; mouth wide open with occasional high-pitched snoring.

The food, was excellent, it also came, was consumed, and then the remnants cleared away efficiently. Staggering and swaying trips to the little room included repeated washing and brush-ups in an attempt to generate a refreshed outlook on the world. The bending of knees and the circling of hands and feet to check they still performed their function. They all seemed destined to fail. The bodies remained in hibernation.

Suddenly, as if an internal alarm had sounded Mark stretched and checked his watch with purpose.

"Only a couple of hours guys, who cares for a beer?"

The suggestion sprung them all into movement; a simultaneous nod indicated total approval and all dragged themselves into upright positions in preparation for their joining the real world once again.

Liz displayed her new body language; which Andy was noticing with interest, by laying slightly on her side and bending towards him. She did not apologise and Andy's body displayed an approving response. He felt comfortable in this new supportive role. He saw nothing special about the changes, they seemed appropriate. Only now, Liz needed that extra comfort, and indeed, what kind of friend would not be able to offer such comfort when it was obviously needed? Particularly in such unusual circumstances.

He had always avoided any thoughts beyond friendship; he had never allowed Liz to enter his dreams, well not too often. When on odd occasions she stood on the edge of entry, he closed down that line of thought and changed direction so as to exclude her, usually in his dreams making her walk away while saying to him, 'you enjoy yourself Andy darling, I'll see you a little later', or something of that nature.

"Well that was one hell of a sleepy journey" commented Phil as he gulped at his cold beer and looked like he had been asleep for a hundred years.

Mark interrupted. "Phil, we must spend fifteen to get back up to speed, Andy, if you two would start to gather yourselves, I need to talk you through the next stage of this little mission."

—

China: Beijing, September 2006:

The landing in Beijing was smooth.

As Andy viewed the first glimpses of China he was excited, Liz was leaning over his shoulder with similar feelings, neither had visited China before, and this was a first for both of them. Suddenly the air of adventure was upon them and beginning to worm its way into their souls. They were both filled with anticipation, somehow, they were aware their knowledge and their science would not fail them, and they knew, as much about the mission as there was to know. Now new confidence seemed to occupy their minds and spirits.

Liz stepped slowly into China and glanced around, flight 219 was over and adventure was ahead of them. Absorbing all her eyes fell upon, she followed her group of three, feeling nervous every time a shoulder nudged between her and her companions she continued to repeat to herself, *'not a time to get lost Elizabeth, act like a professional'*. Hence, she tried her best to walk with her head held high and confident.

Andy was looking around for a vision that might match his brown file photograph of the famous Yoko Cheng. Simultaneously, his thoughts were now flicking from datasheet to datasheet, pre-thought tangents and possibilities he had been working on and thinking through and re-accessing his rejection of certain cause theories, he doubted now any connection with the sola theories while simultaneously sharpening his own conclusions and theories; questioning and exploring every aspect.

All of the party of four had passed and all nodded at the others upon flight 219 as they departed in different directions. There appeared to be nobody to recognise, certainly no dialogue of relevance had been entered into throughout the whole flight, just distant social politeness. As they disembarked, they realised exactly what a large delegation they were part of, it was yet another view of the enormous issue they were dealing with.

The initial stages of clearance were speedy and efficient. Mark moved with great expertise through everything presented to his small group. Phil co-ordinated the collection of numerous cases belonging to them all and suddenly there they were standing in a great hall, feeling extremely small and awaiting further guidance.

Liz was first to notice the board held high above the swaying heads, 'BA Flight 219, Gould, Clemence, Gates and Browning'. Actually, not spelt correctly, but clear enough for the group to recognize.

Mark took the lead, as was his position, raising a hand in recognition of the name board.

The small reception group moved towards them, the board holder continuing to hold his board aloft as they weaved their way. While introductions, bows and courtesies were observed and exchanged, the little call board remained held overhead and acted very much like a fan as it wobbled back and forth.

When Yang, both the board holder and a translator came to shake hands all hell broke loose. Possibly, he was not one of those intended to shake hands, but following the general flow of the greeting and whilst still translating furiously, he let go of the board with one hand, to courteously undertake the now appropriate and continuing shaking of hands. The board slipped, then smacked him firmly upon his head and slipped further down, which initiated much juggling by those close at hand and finally crashed to the floor amongst them. Andy realised it was a glorious moment as all

scurried to regain the troublesome board and dignity, heads, arms
and shoulders intermingled and clashed as they all attempted to
recover the dropped board. The faces reddened as attempts were
made to reassemble with some of that missing dignity. Much
embarrassment appeared on stern and serious faces. The momentary
silence was followed by further confusion. Both Liz and Andy
suddenly and simultaneously roared with laughter and were then
joined by Mark and Phil; followed thankfully by the complete
Chinese party.

Dignity was regained with an instant bonding between all, with
only poor Yang still bowing and muttering deep apologies. The party
marched across and out of the great hall to the awaiting transport.

As they sped towards the centre of Beijing in a very splendid
silver Mercedes, Andy, in attempting some further easing of Yangs'
disgrace was expressing a burning desire to know when he and Liz
would be able to meet with Professor Yoko Cheng.

Yang, regaining a feeling of usefulness, explained Yoko would
dine with them that evening if it were convenient. "She too also most
pleased to meet with you, Professor. Please, I say nine o'clock is a
good time."

"That would be a privilege for both Professor Clemence and
myself, thank you Yang."

At last, Andy felt back in familiar territory; he was now
beginning to talk and think his language and felt the real purpose of
their mission was about to start. Hopefully from here on Mark and
Phil's world was to be in the background, apart from their obvious
ability to speak fluent mandarin.

Liz, sitting quietly and listening, turned towards Andy, now
looking at herself once again and she smiled softly.

It was good to be experiencing a rare relaxed moment.

Most of the party appeared capable of speaking English to one level or the other and elongated conversation crossed back and forth in a nervous but light-hearted manner, even a joke or two were managed by Liz, that even if not fully understood, caused much superficial laughter.

The party appeared to consist of the standard political observer, a security official, Yang of course plus two of Yoko Cheng's assistants. Their qualifications and standing, even with Yang's assistance appeared unfathomable

The Emperor Hotel was a dull structure, uninspired, yet once inside, consisted of an enormous entrance and reception hall, spartan by western standards but instantly with pleasantness and grandeur. Booking in procedures completed, all were pleased to be led away to their rooms on the sixth floor, 601 to 604.

Seven o'clock seemed ages off when refreshment was to be taken in the huge lobby area.

Andy still felt exhausted by the circumstances and immediately located a bottle of water from the small fridge in the room, then threw himself upon the very ample bed. Prior to entering the room, he felt fine but two seconds of solitude was all it took for the effects of the flight, conversation and circumstances, to bring on the drowsiness.

A knock on the door disturbed his moment. Liz shuffled in; "I can't settle, my head is buzzing all over the place again, just need to work out exactly what we are up to here. There is no real sense in all of this, is there Andy."

"Oh, please Liz, just try and let it go for a moment. Sit or lay, go or stay Liz, we'll be dealing with things we understand very soon."

Feeling chatty, she chose to lay upon the bed to which Andy had already returned.

Andy had set a small travel clock for 5-30pm. He closed his eyes and again felt relatively relaxed. "Just try and relax Liz, we will need to be on the ball soon."

He felt Liz staring at him with those penetrating green-hazel eyes but remained as he was; not wanting to disrupt his mood or state of mind.

Suddenly and surprisingly, an arm was laid across his chest; it was comfortable and fitted into his mood.

Then a head snuggled against his shoulder, that too was comfortable and fitted into his mood.

He understood it to be friendship and the need for support, security and comfort; he was more than pleased to oblige.

A hand slid inside of his open shirt. This raised suspicion within his mind that something else was happening, and he became a little nervous. It broke his concentration.

He still did not move or possibly, now he felt he could not.

He now noticed the rhythm of his heart had increased, he felt hot and had no idea how to respond.

His head, heart and body felt in conflict, there were certainly no thoughts of science.

Desire, together with affection entered the frame of circumstance.

The hand slowly ran across his lightly-haired chest; 'oh my god', a soft finger touched him, as if by accident; his body tingled and responded, in his confusion he attempted to stay calm and in control.

Soft full lips, wet lips, closed over his mouth. A sweet breath.

His eyes remained closed. The moment was exquisite. He did not want that moment to fade, not yet; he also knew this could be a problem, one he had not yet catered for in his understanding and thinking. His mind floated and his body continued to tingle from head to toe. He was now eager for this moment to continue and somehow, he found some words.

"Are you sure about this Liz? It may get complicated; get in the way of our purpose."

"Andrew, hush please, say nothing. I think we need a cuddle, both of us."

He obeyed her wishes but turned his face and opened his eyes a little.

She was without a doubt, beautiful, and glowing, but he had always thought that.

He understood, he should not move, she was driving this moment; it was very much her game. He watched her swing her long legs to the floor. He watched her round and soft shoulders and the wonderful curves of her back, her hands and her fingers. The roundness of her bottom. He melted into the moment; it was but a haze of wonder.

She removed her top, then leant forward and slid her trousers off. He watched her intently, enjoying every moment, every angle her body took, her breasts hanging and he was filled with wonderment and delight; she was far more beautiful than he had ever realised.

He was fully extended with anticipation, leaking excitedly, his heart beating rapidly.

She climbed back onto the bed and passed one long leg over him, then slowly and expertly engaged him in a long, long kiss full of passion and loving.

Her mouth moved to his neck, then his shoulders, moving around him slowly and elegantly. Andy watched and relished every movement. He noticed her graceful ankles and feet; her long beautiful fingers, he loved all of her, everything about her. She shuffled further down the bed and along his body. Then very slowly began to seduce him fully. Moving up and down on him in steady movements, again and again, and then again.

His own mouth in turn could not resist her pale white flesh as he kissed her continuously, completely out of control, his mind a whirl. He moved her position, turned her around, head down, bottom up, and now she was kneeling before him, then both were so wet with enthusiasm, excitement, desire and heart-beating love.

Time then began to vanish, as did any hint of inhibition.

Andy could not hold back any further, he wanted to explode, inside her. Reaching towards her and holding her waist firmly, then swinging her onto her back.

Her legs automatically and naturally spread widely and she arched her back, her feet flat to the bed pushing herself upwards towards Andy's view and access. They were as one, totally entangled and breathing hard.

He entered her instantly, there was no more foreplay, and then, with a great thrust, he pumped in and out of her for what seemed an eternity. Groans of pleasure filled the room as Andy filled Liz with every drip of his sex juice. Liz demanding harder and faster between great groans of pleasure.

Then, before he wanted, or indeed expected, their bodies began to tense once again until for a second time, eruptions of ecstasy and necessity flowed over the both of them.

The sounds of pleasure filled the room. She was noisy.

Their love juices mingled. She gushed with the excess of Andy fulfilling his lust.

The lovemaking seemed to be lasting forever and ever.

The release of all their tensions mingled with strangeness and happiness, as slowly they subsided and then both collapsed, naked and entwined - relaxed and exhausted all in that wondrous single moment in time with feelings of love and devotion.

Andy gently kissed Liz's mouth and face; enjoying the smell and taste of her soft skin while his arms continued to embrace and hold her, feeling the softness of all her curves, her back and her bottom; her legs, shoulders and feet.

The moment eased a little and they rested for a short time, just kissing gently. It was not long before their bodies once again called for satisfaction and loving.

They made love twice more with equal intensity and affection before the bell of the little alarm clock shocked them horribly back into reality.

'Bloody hell you.' That was all Andy could manage to say, softly and repeatedly.

"It took me by surprise somewhat Andy Gould. I wasn't wrong though was I Professor Andy Gould."

"No. That was wonderful, just the best, and you miss Liz are, without a doubt, truly beautiful, I just never truly expected you to want me; to go beyond friendship I mean. There you are all sort of beautiful and young, and here am I, scruffy and old."

"I guess you are right, scruffy and old, but I also thought that just being friends was enough Andy but something else has taken over now and we'll never be able to return to yesterday. We have spent so much time with one another. We have had to share so much and I don't really know whether that was about passion or mechanics."

"Liz, where ever this leads and whatever happens, promise me to always stay friends. I never want our friendship to fade or be lost."

Liz leant forward and they kissed symbolically confirming something that had not been clearly expressed verbally, then she stood beside the bed looking concerned but still looking unimaginably gorgeous. Andy reach up and lovingly squeezed her hand then delivered a sharp smack to her small creamy buttocks.

"Come on you, we must put a move on. Remember we have to save the world this week." "Could we not just do half the world this week? That seems more than reasonable."

After wiping herself on her blouse, Liz pulled on her clothes. Suddenly there was an air of panic and awkwardness. She dashed towards the door only half dressed.

"See you in ten minutes, Mr Gould."

Andy was already on his feet heading towards the shower. It is a strange moment when you have to rush after a sexual and emotional event; it was as if it had never happened. If only there had been more time available, Andy thought to himself.

The sudden rush had also confused Liz; she also needed time to absorb the event; to wind down from such a wonderful experience. As she dashed into her shower, the whole matter seemed like an illusion, unsatisfying yet exciting. Standing there in the shower, she could still feel him inside her. She could feel his hand upon her bottom and found herself placing her own hand there as a replica; she cuddled her arms around her body, then pulled at her own breasts feeling erotic and exotic and still very sexual. Then very reluctantly, let the warm water slowly wash away her love and desire, her confusion and her glow.

With no further time to consider such thoughts they found themselves strutting along corridor six heading for the lifts and refreshment or perhaps they knew it would not be very refreshing after all; whatever it should be officially; once again, they would be playing and acting like professionals. Only they could see and feel the other's body sitting across from them, nobody else would be seeing them as if they were naked, her with her legs wide apart, him thrusting himself deep inside her. It would be hard to concentrate on saving the world for a while.

They entered the great reception area and stood for a moment taking in the surroundings. The area did not look quite so spartan this time around. Some twenty to thirty enormous chandeliers decorated the ceiling area. Possibly lanterns were the correct term, alternating red and mauve with tassels at the sides and from the bottom. Around the white marble flooring were many groups of exotic plants and trees; like small tropical islands, in fact, it was definitely not spartan on the second viewing, it was powerful and had its own very distinctive style.

They looked around for signs. On the far side, they noticed Mark waving a beckoning hand. They entered a comfortable seating area diagonally across from the reception desks; wicker chairs and tables, with lush exotic plants forming those tropical islands to either side of where they sat.

A quick look passed from Andy to Liz. It was a look that expressed that their lives were not their own. "Hi, Phil. Nobody else here yet?" Then Mark interrupted. "I gathered that someone was to be here but it doesn't matter, I am starving, no doubt you guys are, let's just get organised with some drinks and a light snack, shall we?"

"Sounds really good to me, I'm famished", responded Liz. "Yep, I guess sleeping is exhausting Liz." She turned towards Andy with a private smile.

The area was busy with small groups; nodding to each other, chatting, laughing, dealing, and haggling; nevertheless, there was a kind of peace. They decided to move elsewhere and wandered through the area trying to locate a space large enough to accommodate the potential party, then realised the area extended into an open terrace, which was ideal. They settled overlooking pleasant gardens and ordered long cool fruit juices, awaiting the platters of mixed delights that Mark had arranged.

After a few minutes of no real conversation, Mark placed a document on the table. "Sorry to disturb this moment of peace but we must discuss the schedule."

Liz and Andy were not keen, they knew they had a nine o'clock dinner arrangement but assumed that from there on, they would be led through a pre-arranged schedule. One paralleling what they had been informed of, including the visit to the Fujian province. There to observe the mutation effects on crops and the great lakes in that region, together with the effect it was having on the whole of those communities. This, together with some planned experiments at the Beijing Uni, thereafter, discussions with the Yoko Chengs team were scheduled. It was not to be an easy few days, but with luck, by the time they and Yoko returned to London, new theories might have been discovered and facts realised, or even proven and those old and rather foolish theories dumped and buried. Being able to rid themselves of those redundant theories was currently as important as discovering a real and convincing direction forward.

Mark ran through his schedule and polite nods of the agreement were given, unfortunately not much was being retained within Liz and Andy's memories.

The only item generating a response was that throughout their stay, no professional or social event was to be undertaken without prior agreement, or an accompanying security officer.

It was still really difficult for Andy or Liz to concentrate; their minds kept flashing back to thirty minutes earlier. Every now and then, there was a burst of magnetism pulling them together, and it definitely had to be resisted somehow, particularly in these circumstances.

Yang arrived to join the group passing on apologies which were explained away by work pressures. That was all very acceptable. At eight o'clock Liz excused herself and disappeared to dress for their nine o'clock arrangement, followed ten minutes later by Andy.

Mark and Phil were somewhat uncomfortable with the looseness and style of both Liz and Andy. They were not the norm and neither had experienced the necessity of this level of security before. As they returned to their rooms, they discussed the issues that concerned them; they knew that a close and discrete eye was going to be required.

On the sixth floor, they approached their rooms to observe Liz leaving Andy's room and in turn, Liz observed them both entering room 603.

"See you guys in ten minutes," Liz commented as she disappeared into 602.

Female intuition rang some bells in Liz's head for some reason; had they been talking about her, was there a problem?

She dismissed the feelings but moved them into her reserved memory for further consideration at a more convenient moment.

It was not long before they were all gathered once again around a large low table within the reception, awaiting Yoko and her colleagues.

Andy had recharged his enthusiasm for meeting Yoko Cheng and was observing the too and throws of guests and visitors within the reception. His eyes hung for a moment or two upon a beautiful woman entering the reception area, there were indeed a number of attractive women but none stood out like this particular woman. Most of the male's eyes unavoidably turned in her direction, some obviously, others more discretely. She was dressed in black silk trousers with a matching jacket displaying rich colourful embroidery and accompanying accessories. She moved with style and grace.

His eyes returned to her repeatedly, they could do nothing else; she was magnetic.

Inspired by this vision, Andy suddenly found himself approaching the woman, who was now standing before the reception desk, something was telling him it was Yoko Cheng; yet he was not sure whether he was applying wishful thinking and the vision did not match the memory created by the photograph in their master file.

His companions' eyes swivelled to follow him towards the reception desk, all a little surprised by his sudden action. Nobody commented.

"Yoko; Professor Yoko Cheng?" Andy enquired standing face to face with the vision.

"Yes, I am, and you I know would be Indy Good?"

"If only I was; it is Andy Gould actually. I am so pleased to meet you, Professor. If I may be so bold as to say you look quite stunning." He never intended to speak so directly, it was not his style either if the word style was even appropriate. To top the situation, he thought he noticed a flushing on Yoko Cheng's face. *'Oh my God, how embarrassing.'*

In an attempt to soften his upfront compliment, he spoke small talk about Yoko's outfit and then asked her to join the group around the table where they had settled.

Again, Liz's intuition was coming into play, in fact, his enthusiasm negated the need for it, it was unashamedly obvious, he was instantly infatuated.

While introductions were made a small group of three gathered behind Yoko, she turned and likewise made introductions. All were now standing and apart from one, all were able to converse with easy and reasonable English. Yang took up a position behind Mary Li to assist her by translating rapidly as needed.

The conversation flowed almost without hesitation. Liz occasionally observed Andy from the corner of her eye as he hung into the conversation with Yoko, it was an instant relationship. The atmosphere around them was tangible to the degree of excluding others; target talking. Causing unspoken moments of embarrassment and the obligation to converse with others in a superficial manner where an open cross-flow conversation would have been ideal and more appropriate.

Ultimately, Yoko Cheng interrupted the flow and suggested the party move to the restaurant where table arrangements had been made.

As the group strolled in that direction Mark lent forward towards Andy who was in front of him, "Andy, don't make Yoko exclusive, you're going to cause embarrassment for all of us."

It was a simple message. Indeed, Andy was embarrassed to hear that he had been so obvious, so much so, that he was aware of a reddening within his cheeks. Within his head, he prayed that no one else had noticed, but they all had. He whispered in reply to Mark. "Sorry about that Mark I feel like such a jerk but what a stunner."

Mark moved ahead of the group with the intention of organising the seating arrangements. "If I may suggest Mark." "Sorry Professor, of course." Yoko, speaking with a clear yet gentle voice redirected the scientific element to one end, and the observers to the other, ensuring that Yang sat alongside Mary Li.

Turning her head to address the waiter, she then spoke forcefully with confidence and authority once again and appeared to be reconfirming the meal, the surroundings and the behaviour she expected.

Almost immediately further staff appeared. The tables surrounding the party were hurriedly cleared and with much grunting, removed from the restaurant. Three waiters took position on the outer of the area while others scurried about delivering bottles and snacks to the table. For a while, there was mayhem.

"Wow!, Professor, that was impressive. We have no chance of equalling that in London."

"May I address you as Elizabeth?" "Liz is fine and how do I address you."

"Well, Yoko is my name, Liz. The trouble here is that they are stupid; the arrangements and instructions were organised and agreed upon beforehand. The food though is quite incredible here. The point is, that we need some privacy to discuss a number of matters, do we not?"

Andy and Mary Li both broke into the conversation.

"Professor Gould." "Andy please." "Ok Andy, may we agree to address one another by first names throughout our discussions and time in China."

Yoko sighed; "well, at last, that is good." Everyone smiled and Liz raised a glass to salute the agreement, all followed and instantly an air of relaxed conversation was initiated.

"You read the paper on the double mutation, Andy?"

"We certainly did; more to the point we actually replicated your tests and confirmed exactly the same results numerous times. Our only problem here is the nature of the initial mutation at King's I have never seen anything similar, therefore we carried out a large number of experiments; which continue back in London and elsewhere; to test the effect of the originally mutated spores on endless organisms in scaled temperature conditions and varied environments. Absolutely nothing until tested in water, seawater and there, a scary replicating and mutation rate was created. We were horrified until we also attempted to replicate the solar activity that helped caused the double whammy effect for you people. Activity slowed but we concluded it had little relevance. We applied Silver Iodide as with some of your own cloud seeding experiments but sudden combustion was seen at a lower temperature. It was all very strange. Regardless, it did produce an instantly good result, so yet once again, confusion was at every turn.

Some samples were allowed to develop further without radiation or applying Iodide. It was a bad mistake in some ways. Of course, we know we are dealing with a strange situation. It appears we have toxins, viruses and bacteria interacting and mutating. If the incident at King's was introduced via sabotage, it obviously means somebody out there is ahead of us in their understanding, and no doubt, they are, to some degree aware of the mutation capabilities and that is seriously threatening, globally, but I do not accept that anybody could possibly have known about the massive mutating potential." "Andy it is correct to look at every possibility, but are we really looking in the right direction? I think we need to look closer at these strange happenings. I think we must reject those incidences that simply do not fit at this stage and face the fact that we are dealing with multiple-layered incidents, possibly, and in part, being introduced from a vicious external body determined to set the world asunder."

There was an instant and abrupt interruption from Mark, suddenly he was standing at Andy's shoulder, he placed a hand between the conversing parties, in the other, and he held a small notepad before him, which simply said *'Not safe here – Say no more'.*

At Mark's shoulder, was Yoko's security officer. World war 3 seemed to hang in the air for a second. Mark spoke in Chinese. They appeared to agree. Mark passed the note to Yoko for her and Mary Li to read. Yoko stared at the message and considered its contents; she turned to Mary Li who nodded.

"Andy, Liz, and Mark. The restaurant has been thoroughly checked; please note there are no other dinners here. The waiters are not waiters, all are all security, but you are possibly still correct Mark. What you are speaking of Andy is very sensitive we will have to vacate to another more secure location, I am sorry about this. Security must be paramount but time is of the greatest importance and is against us."

She raised her hand in an instant response, and then returned it to her lap; she stood and spoke rapidly to Jonathan standing behind Mark. Jonathan turned and disappeared to organise.

Mark lent forward over the table. "I apologise for the interruption but your exchange was becoming too sensitive." "How did you know Mark?" said Liz with innocents, Mark looked at her, and instantly both Liz and Andy understood. "I didn't realise either Liz, suddenly we're both being educated yet again I think. Scary stuff a! Anyway, it was getting pretty involved." Mary Li spoke up via Yangs' translation. "Mark was correct Andy, this is big news you are telling us, great caution must be taken."

The party all slowly rose to their feet and formed small groups while security jumped into action. No more science was spoken of; Liz leaned towards Andy, "I know all this is difficult Andy and I can see you are wowed by Yoko here but please don't forget us." It was a measured comment, which impressed Andy. "I'm sorry Liz. Hell, I was embarrassing. I don't really know what happened to me there; I'm really sorry about my stupidity."

After the thirty-minute break, the whole party was relocated to a small conference room on the first floor.

Everyone settled and the discussion continued,

"The spores; well not spores any further, they had developed into microbes and multiplied at an alarming rate, by approximately a thousand per cent over two days.

Further experimentation determined the resulting specimens to be aggressively carnivorous and cannibalistic in the extreme, dominating all samples introduced. We decided to stop there; all samples were deep-frozen. Specimens and the full notes are with us for your own consideration. The natural progression here is obvious, we all live surrounded by lots and lots of water. You are the first to share this information. We should be very clear about these initial results and how to deal with them if this situation is then confirmed, and before we pass on those results or produce a paper for anybody. There is here a great deal to be considered. Currently, marine samples are being taken globally and upon our return to the U.K. initial data should be available for all of us to look at. My team is becoming convinced that we are dealing with a double, or even a triple event, this is something I have never encountered in this form."

Yoko and Mary Li sat in silence for a while; obviously shocked by what they had been told, albeit, none of them around the table were truly surprised by the strangeness of the initial results, as indeed every research laboratory dealing with the matter. They were pleased by the results they had experienced and if Yoko had not done some of the initial work, it may have been some time before the fullness of the possible reality would have dawned upon anybody else.

It was so difficult to absorb and accept a completely new scientific phenomenon; there was excitement and fear in all their minds. Just maybe they could see the way forward, but the security services around the world would have to step up and deal with the apparent sabotage that was becoming obvious in all their thinking.

The group broke after endless further details had been exchanged, the methodology and the fine details of the experiments; while the discussions continued, the table around which they were sitting was slowly being cleared and prepared for food, and it was annoying. Finally, giving in to the change of direction it was agreed that they would try to enjoy their meal before deciding the next course of action. The atmosphere around the table became solemn as the scientific element within the group began to absorb and considered exactly, what had been discussed and agreed on and the possible consequences of failure for the whole world.

As paperwork disappeared from the table and it was exchanged with a fine meal that was further mixed with the growing fears of realisation and the daunting prospect that they had all been moved towards another new starting point and that simply added to their constantly growing confusion.

It was pre-planned that the following day the whole party was to travel to Fujian. Yoko now decided that with the discoveries now presented by Andy's team the situation had changed everything; he and Yoko decided they should attend the university laboratories to carry out further investigation and prim her support team while Liz, together with Mary Li should carry out the site investigations at Fujian. Mark, Phil and Jonathan agreed with the arrangements. It was now late and with an early start, the following morning the group agreed sleep was the next best move. It would be difficult for anybody to find sleep that night.

They wandered into the reception area finalising their arrangements, the air was full of seriousness. "You coming Andy," asked Liz, "I'll be right there."

He lingered to complete his conversation with Yoko, and between their serious conversations, looks flashed from one to the other as once again, that magnetic force obviously grew between them. As they moved slowly across the area deep in conversation, it was necessary for Andy to guide Yoko around some chairs, instantly causing within him those tingling electrical pulses. They travelled along his arms, into his hands and to the very tips of his fingers; similarly, Yoko become transfixed by his touch awaiting whatever the next move would be, her professional stance disappearing into an uncontrollable blur. Both were very aware that magic was taking them over. They were the last two within the reception hall apart from Jonathan and Phil who stood together at a discrete distance from Yoko and Andy.

"I think I should go, Andy." He stood for a moment thinking through the situation. "I think you shouldn't Yoko." He looked up at the ceiling in the desperate hope of some kind of miracle, possibly holy guidance. She looked down at the sparkling marble floor. Andy spoke painfully and slowly. "Sorry Yoko, you're right. Tomorrow then as arranged, please travel home safely."

"I will Andy and you sleep well."

As they moved apart, both were aware of something being torn, of something ridiculous and inappropriate. Of something way beyond common sense. It felt embarrassing!

Andy did not catch up with Liz. He turned into bed and as normal nowadays, very quickly buried himself in sleep, hence, he neither heard the knocking at his door that night nor early the following morning, which continued gently off and on.

–

England: Eynsford, Kent:

In a small whitewashed cottage, overlooking the River Darent, William and Betty Gould sat at their kitchen table chatting quietly about their plans for the day. A little brown teapot sat before them covered with a knitted cosy. Upon a large willow plate, lay four slices of fresh bread, which Betty had baked prior to Bill rising that morning. Amy, their Old English sheepdog, who had now been a member of the family for twelve years lay quietly upon the quarry-tiled floor.

Most mornings started in a similar fashion, maybe a little outdated, but that was their way of life.

They made plans for the day, discussed their children Andrew, who was to visit soon and had always been their pride and joy; plus, Sally and Jill, their daughters and then listened to the news on the radio. They flicked from one program to another, forever trying to gather a real feeling of what was going on.

Generally speaking, it was a little depressing, often an obituary of the grand and famous or some supposedly new idea which seemed to Bill and Betty to be just another 'flying pink pig or a blue elephant.'

Sometimes a member of the government would rattle on about the great strides being made around the world to resolve the terrible state of affairs; 'flying blue elephants again', Bill would say, and Betty would agree, "pink pigs I think darling", and they would both chuckle and enjoy their little joke. In more serious moments, they were both annoyed about the sad quality of the news, the obvious censorship, the obviously incorrect or exaggerated and conflicting numbers that came with every report, and the ludicrous interviewing of people with no knowledge or over-the-top expressed emotions.

President Hewitt would again express his undivided support for his friends across the pond. Sure, once again the American continent had rushed gallantly to increase production of just about everything his European friends were now finding difficult to obtain but it was almost impossible to solve the lack of base foods that existed across the far East. Over China, India, and Indonesia and then beyond, areas of crop production had been devastated and increased hunger was suddenly the real and immediate enemy.

The United States and the Americas generally had endured their own problems in the form of successive tornados all rating four or five's. Unseasonal weather patterns were causing havoc from Baffin Bay down to Drakes Passage.

In the U.S.A., many of the great cities in the southern states now lay beaten and destroyed; New Orleans, Houston, Port Arthur and around the coast to St. Petersburg and Miami lay in a devastated state and yet the story only rated small paragraphs in the press over a three-day period.

Like others, Betty and Bill Gould listened to the news with a grim understanding of the underlying truths. They finished their tea and bread and then stepped into the world to do the best they could.

As winter was now approaching rapidly, Bill spent much of his time collecting any discarded wood or other burnable materials for he was determined that his Betty and their children when at home, would not be cold this coming winter. It always amazed Bill that so many folks still threw away such a valuable resource as wood or paper of any type. He, on the other hand, carried or dragged it home. If he could not manage that, he would break it up where he found it and over time, move it all to the store in his backyard, neatly stacked and covered.

Betty spent much of her time planting vegetables amongst the shrubs and slowly removing more and more areas of grass to increase their production. She preserved as much as she could and together they had been walking the local fields and lanes throughout the year collecting nuts, damsons and other wild fruits, they also collected seeds from anything they thought may be useful in the future, and nobody really knew what that future may be. They had a full cupboard of reserve food jars, all produce preserved in salt or syrup. Outside, to the rear of their cottage home was the largest pile of Bill's logs and recycled wooden items, which were slowly broken down further, ready for use. It was a busy life.

They may off been in their seventies, and that obviously created difficulties for them, but there were also advantages to age, they needed less and they knew more and also how to survive better than most youngsters. In a strange way, they enjoyed the closeness and challenge that the current state of everything created. They were both very pleased that they had passed the time of real responsibility, particularly the responsibility for young children, regardless of the great love they both had for their own.

—

China: Beijing:

Liz awoke earlier than she needed and made her preparations for the trip, when completed she knocked yet again on Andy's door to check he was moving in the right direction.

At last, he had answered. Liz decided not to comment on her earlier efforts. After a further ten minutes of Andy scurrying around while making idle chatter, they both wandered towards the lifts. They paused half the way along the corridor and Liz run back to call Mark and Phil, she found them both in Mark's room and together they all wandered towards that essential cup of *wake-me-up* coffee.

Mary Li and her team were already drinking coffee awaiting Liz's arrival at their table. She had but fifteen minutes to achieve being fully awake and intelligent, and then her group was to dash to the heliport for their journey to Fujian Province.

"Any problems Liz, just call straight away. Have you got everything you need?" Andy took Liz to one side to check and chatter.

"Listen to me you; whatever is going down here with all our emotions, remember that I love and care about you woman. Now you take great care of yourself, do not take anything for granted Liz, check and double-check everything you can, and write the notes. Collect as many samples as possible and take thousands of photographs."

As was now the custom between them, Liz wrapped her arms around Andy, gently patting his back. He took hold of her shoulders and lent forward placing a genuine and loving kiss on her forehead; he thought for a moment, and then placed a soft, gentle kiss upon her expectant lips.

"I'll see you in a day or two Andy, ring me please." Then Liz, Phil and her group were gone. Andy felt confident that Liz could deal with everything they needed. Somehow, they all had to piece together the confusing science that was being generated. At times they had all expressed the craziness of the situation, how the concepts kept changing, but somewhere within this horrendous mess were the solutions, somewhere there were answers or an answer; somewhere!

Andy and Mark had the luxury of enjoying another hour of chatting quietly and waking fully before Yang arrived at the breakfast table. He appeared in no hurry but Andy was now suddenly becoming anxious to get on with the job, there really was no time to sit around. He was very aware a great number of people were relying on the results of this trip, it was indeed of enormous importance, even more than his political masters realised, and potentially even more than he wanted to visualise.

Yang finished his two cups of coffee. Then informed Andy and Mark that Professor Cheng had started preparing the laboratory at around 5 am that morning. By the time the samples were delivered, she was ready to replicate Andy's experiments.

"Wow!" commented Andy. "In fact, that's really amazing. She seems incredible. She just keeps on impressing me more and more."

"Professor, if we arrive at the lab in about an hour it would be perfect; this is what Professor Cheng has said."

"Ok, in that case, I must sit and read. There are papers I need from my room; I will be ten minutes. Mark, can we all move out to the patio for some fresh air?" "No problem; ten minutes, see you out there."

Twenty-five minutes later, Andy had not returned. Mark was uncomfortable, instinct bells were beginning to ring inside his head.

"Yang, stay here. I must check out where Professor Gould has got to." Mark rushed off to the lifts and the sixth floor. As he exited the lift, he was immediately confronted by a scuffling to his left. Two large bodies were trying to contain a struggling Professor Andy Gould. Mark, assuming a security misunderstanding, instantly responded. One large body was sent firmly to the floor with the fastest of movements while instructions were shouted at Andy. "You stay very still you stupid fucker." Mark, now holding his security pass in front of himself, while the other hand held an extended stop signal. Andy, dishevelled and crutched in a corner, had responded to the instruction, or indeed, he simply could not do anything else. The large standing body straightened and stood back while the floored body regained his feet, his look expressing extreme anger, which he managed to bring under control quickly. The quartet stood off. "Jesus Christ, they just jumped on me from nowhere," Andy shouted out through his heavy panting and disorganised attire. Mark spoke rapidly to the two bodies, and they responded simultaneously, both speaking their story of the incident. The exchange continued for some time until slowly the pitch and aggression subsided into a civilised conversation.

"Andy. It appears they challenged you but you did not hear them or as they thought, ignored them, then you dashed for the lifts. I think we are dealing with a well-intended miss understanding here. Possibly, you were miles away in other thoughts professor. Could that be correct?" "I guess so," Andy responded, as he tidied his attire and swept his hair back from his face. "Yes, I think I was far away in thought; sorry, it may well have been my fault."

Andy reached out his hand in a gesture of apology, Mark translated, and it was accepted with smiles and nods. Mark translated again, what the two-security people were saying. They did not want to battle with any more English scientists. All smiled and life took on its regular face once more.

As Mark and Andy travelled down in the lift, Mark spoke; "Bloody hell Andy, we can do without that occurring again." "It wasn't bloody planned Mark, you keep your bloody opinions to yourself." Mark held back his response and they walked across the reception area in silence. As they approached Yang, it was obvious to him something had occurred.

"Is everything ok here?" "No, it bloody isn't," responded Andy before Mark could respond and he duly planted himself down in isolation, obviously still recovering from the affair.

Yang and Mark spoke quietly amongst themselves. Yang took from his pocket his authority card; he was more than a simple translator and that surprised Mark; he had not been informed fully about Yang's status.

A driver approached the group and addressed Yang. The group moved off; Andy battling to regain his composure as he begrudgingly walked between them towards their transport.

At the laboratories, Andy was pleased to see Yoko once again, the very sight of her allowing his earlier discomfort to fade away rapidly, but of course, replacing it with other mixed thoughts and emotions.

While the security story was re-iterated to Yoko, they strolled towards where the replicated experiments were being carried out. "So where have you got to Yoko?"

"Andy, we have only worked on the most virulent samples with precise replication of your procedures. I can already agree to your results." A pause and then she continued.

"You know what we are dealing with here Andy, don't you?"

"Yes, the beginning of evolution." He smiled broadly.

"That's without the sixty-five million years in between. Potentially very scary Yoko. These marine samples are now of prime importance. If we can, I think we must attempt to obtain some information from Kings."

"I agree Andy. I have already dispatched orders to our governmental department to have samples collected and analysed by all secure means under the highest priority. Unfortunately, this could cause you some embarrassment in London, but I think now your results have been re-confirmed, personal considerations must be over-ridden."

"Yoko, no problem about that, it was the correct procedure and the only decision, I'm glad you acted so promptly. If we can discover here and now what we are dealing with, it would all be a massive step forward."

Andy made the necessary secure calls to London while Yoko's team prepared endless further tests designed to observe, contain, control and ultimately destroy any toxins and microbes.

"We should take the time to talk everything through Andy, everything here is under control." Mia, Yoko's number two, a professor in her own right, was fully conversant with everything that was to be done.

Yoko and Andy took their leave quietly and made their way toward Yoko's office, which clearly indicated her status within both the nation and campus.

The authority she had already displayed; was in contradiction to her petite and attractive frame, let alone the personality Andy was beginning to know, and was obviously very considerable. Nobody, yet, had questioned her instructions. This incredibly attractive and slight female had the world at her fingertips. Her ability to organise precisely; her detached use of authority, which appeared to generate a following equal to worship were impressive. Andy felt her equal; indeed, he was her equal intellectually and scientifically. Yet he felt subservient to her every whim, word and glance.

In the province of Fujian, Liz, Mary Li and their group had been duly met at the heliport by the local dignitaries, who proceeded to treat the group with great reverence, much to Liz's feeling of awkwardness.

After endless formalities, head nodding and shaking of hands repeatedly, the great motorised caravan move off to begin their observations. The devastation of the surrounding world outside of the urban area had obviously created insecurity in the community, it was a situation, which, none of the local people understood and certainly could not resolve. The growing and serious disruption and breakdown of food supplies were obvious. People gathered in small groups, on corners and outside houses and cafes throughout the town, all unable to carry out their normal activities; some with their families gathered about them clearly displaying a kind of bewilderment. Normally in this affluent province of China, there would have been a work buzz from morning to dusk. There was obviously no wish to go back fifty years to the times of back-breaking toil for eighteen hours a day with very little reward. The coming deaths within the area had not as yet begun, but one could feel the awareness of the threat and possible reality that would follow, it could be seen upon every face, and everybody could sense it and feel it in the atmosphere and in every breath they took.

The caravan of vehicles packed with dignitaries was a positive sign of hope for those watching the parade of vehicles. A sign that somebody was going to solve their pain and confusion and something was at last happening. Next week everything would be back to normal-maybe. Their great leaders would not leave them to suffer the obvious oncoming fate; they would not or could not leave them in this situation, those days were surely gone-maybe?

As the group drove through the streets in their shiny parade of vehicles, those gathered to either side occasionally rose and clapped or waved appreciatively, many bowing in respect and in anticipation and hope of salvation.

The children occasionally running along the side of the cars as if greeting a victorious army or a popstar, their saviours. They still having to learn servility and their place in the pyramid.

Liz again began to feel the measure of what she was dealing with. She was not their saviour, hence, she felt fraudulent and insignificant and yet she could clearly see the hope her presence, together with so many officials, generated. She wondered if that was the only gift she could offer these people, then, she sincerely hoped her skills could give them real hope.

If she had spoken truthfully to these folks and made them aware of all the confusion and doubts that she felt, their hopes would have been dashed and may be completely destroyed.

Was this the obligation of leaders, scientific, political or religious throughout history? For the first time in her life, she felt the true and immense weight of real responsibility; it was almost unbearably heavy; *'God was one hell of a guy'*.

As the numerous vehicles travelled further into the vastness of rural Fujian and its surroundings, the reality of the visit stared straight back at her. Acre after acre after acre of dirty dark grey-green blackness, liken to a creeping mould lay before them as far as the eye could see, on grass, crops and trees. *'What the hell is going on here?'* She was horrified and shocked. She clicked away with the camera, close-up and panoramic and spoke her thoughts into her voice recorder. The horror before her eyes was transferred into words. When occasionally they passed a cluster of peasant farmers outside their humble dwellings, the despair and hunger were already obvious. Speaking via Yang, Mary Li spoke to Liz. "Sorry Liz, we must not stop. It would only serve our emotional needs, not theirs.

We have our work to do, that may help their children and many others. The military and the newly formed social armies that have been formed in every region are responsible for supplying social assistance and food aid but it is miserably inadequate at the moment. We must hope that improves. We must also concentrate on our task and stop here and there for samples. I guess from your reaction, you have not seen this effect anywhere else Liz"

Liz was indeed stunned by what she was seeing; she had not expected such widespread devastation. Her hands went to her face in sorrow and small tears trickled down her cheeks.

"Do we have the current fatality figures?" "We did have. Initially, as you are aware, there were hardly any deaths but as we can see, the problems are just beginning. In some areas, I gather there are now enormous rates of death, mainly generated by anaphylactic shock. China has survived many famines involving millions of lives but generally, we understand, as do the people but nobody can relate to what is happening now, nobody. Luckily, if that is the correct phrase, we could now have a scientific explanation, or indeed a few new options to consider. When you consider that such a strange variety of conditions exist in so many countries, appearing to be all caused by the same source, how and when will we ever be able to solve this horrendous situation and be able to return to yesterday's world? As you are very aware, we appear to be dealing with something capable of mutating so very rapidly. Possibly millions will continue to die. Now the evidence is saying this god-dam-thing is invading us from the oceans, the lakes, rivers and water butts. Thereafter, sent upon the wind, like a great plague of death, where it appears to drop randomly, dependant on the weather systems and local geography. Then silently creeping onto the land and affecting certain types of flora to consume and destroy whatever the mutated form decides.

Looking so different and indeed being so different in each, and every single form it takes. Giving us an almost impossible situation to deal with. Ultimately, I wonder if the world population, 'we humans', and all the other creatures, can withstand this nightmare for much longer. Everything seems to be at risk."

The vehicle in which Mary and Liz travelled fell into silence. Nothing else could be said, there was no need to see another acre of ground in this region. After endless photographs and samples were taken, together with endless notes, everything dated and locations recorded, their driver was told to turn, and they, followed by the other vehicles in the convoy, solemnly turned towards Nanping where their helicopter awaited them. The dignitaries travelling along with them, sitting straight-backed and silent, accomplishing their tasks of confidence and hope that buys their uniforms and glittering medals and chain displays, together with the shine and size of their peaked caps over pushed out chins of authority.

Once back at the heliport, it was wonderful for all not to need to consider those bio-suits once again and to pretend they could feel the fresh air, regardless of what it really contained.

They flew across other areas; flew over and stopped at Lake Poyang Hu and again stood in almost silence at the still-dying waters. Somehow, it felt that Poyang Hu would be acting as another nursery, a threat hung over the great lake and all along its shores. They flew on, now Liz was looking down upon the land below and she now knew the people's pain. With this new knowledge, she was feeling like her heart might break, both for humanity and particularly for those families she had seen, the little ones.

When at last they ended their tour, she was more than ready and thankful to once again land in Beijing. There in her own hotel bed privacy awaited her; where there may still appear to be normality, but in her mind, where constant visions flashing one after the other, she could only see the growing disaster and feel totally inadequate and insecure.

With her awareness now fully alerted she knew that this great nation, like so many others, and which, had come so far over the last forty years lay at the door of a creeping and totally devastating plaque which nobody appeared, as yet to understand.

Regardless of being amongst people, she felt suddenly so very, very alone and sad. So useless and so ineffectual. Her brain was not working properly, it seemed to be spinning slowly around and around within her skull. She guessed Andy would be feeling the same. Then she realised that everybody involved, everybody in the know, would at some time be feeling just as she was at this very moment and, by-god, even those being protected from the truth, *'from that something that was ugly and horrendous'.* They would all realise they were being deceived, not told the truth about anything.

The awful realities smashed through her being at the stupidity and confusion before her, why had she not seen things in this way before? Then she thought of her family, her sisters and parents, her horse of all things, and the tears began to roll down her now solemn and disturbed face.

As Liz, Mary Li and Phil Browning silently sipped tea in the reception area, each was trying to absorb their personal visions and their awful consequences but it was at that moment, too awful a vision for any individual to deal with, the universe may well have been an easier subject to contemplate, and was certainly more palatable.

It was not long before all parted, each to endure their own thoughts in an attempt to smooth them a little. Liz awaiting to hear from Andy, she lay upon her bed and simply closed her eyes, trying desperately to think of the green fields of home. There was nothing else she was capable of and in many ways wished she had not undertaken the days' sorrowful mission.

—

China: Beijing University:

Y oko and Andy strolled across to Yoko's office, there they moved to one of the large windows and stood for a moment staring out over the campus and beyond, the tower blocks, the mass of life and energy that existed. Nervousness lurked and a kind of depression resurfaced at unexpected moments. Yoko turned away to switch on the kettle, then she disappeared through a small door. Andy continued to view the enormous array of buildings that formed the panorama outside the window, between those buildings thronged thousands of people going about their lives. Their own small lives that may not last very long, he remaining there stock-still and feeling alone with all that awful knowledge stored in his mind, filling his emotions, and so deep in many confusing thoughts.

The kettle boiled and momentarily screamed pathetically, almost replicating his feelings, it seemed to be screaming for hours before it clicked itself off and fell into silence. He moved slowly towards the dresser in an attempt to locate the equipment for coffee production. As he did, Yoko returned, obviously from her shower. She was wrapped in yet another beautiful silk gown, white with endless detailed embroidery surrounding beautiful flower prints, obviously very much her personal style and very expensive. Her short black hair was swept back, wet and tight against her small round beautiful head. She wore no jewellery, no shoes, or slippers, exposing her tiny white feet with long individual toes, everything perfectly balanced, and perfectly beautiful.

Andy's head swam into a whirlpool. Suddenly he was not feeling very scientific and nervously redirected his wandering eyes back towards the coffee.

Yoko moved towards the window where Andy had now returned. "Are you making coffee Andrew?" "That's a first, not many call me Andrew; how do you like your coffee."

There was no answer, Andy moved back once again to the coffee and then turned towards her, she was looking out on that panorama, the sunlight flooding into the room, it was also flooding through the silk wrap exposing clearly her wondrous silhouette. A diva, framed by a mixed hallo of golden and white light.

Andy lost his concentration for a moment, totally captured by the view of Yoko's curvy figure, he could clearly see her long legs and where they ended below her perfect buttocks, then the delicious curves taking her hips into her tiny waist.

Attempting to force himself to remain dignified and professional he forced himself to return to his task with an unsteady hand.

"I guess you to be a "Coffee Solo" person Yoko." "You guess correctly Andrew; you have excellent intuition for an Englishman. I am told that is a rarity in Englishmen as it is in the Chinese."

"Just a lucky guess Yoko. Intuition, no; but I am lucky at guessing", but he wished at that moment he had guessed wrongly; somehow his guessing correctly took him closer and deeper into his attraction and desire, those powerful feelings were filling every part of him, he thought he could feel something changing within Yoko's being also. He was trying hard to be in denial of his feelings; none of this was supposed to happen, he was in enough trouble with Liz already.

Unknown to each other, both were trying to consider their emotional dilemmas, trying to convert them into escapism, seeing them as mental and emotional relief, and making strange and knowingly false excuses to themselves. In a brave attempt to calm his feelings, Andy tried to make simple conversation.

"I think we should address the issues arising from the laboratory Yoko; where shall we start?" Yoko turned, looking straight at Andy with a soft open look on her face. "A meal and a fine bottle of wine appeals to me Andrew, can I persuade you in that direction?" "Absolutely, you can persuade me. Strangely, until this new realisation is digested it is difficult to know exactly what we should say to each other and indeed, our lords and masters. Certainly, this calls for a new strategy. We still don't have anything confirmed and conclusive. Yet, at the London conference, this will turn so many heads inside out; probably this is the most important of all the new discoveries at hand, but as I just said, not conclusive." Andy realised he was tarting with every look and posture, playing to the crowd of one and without intending to, allowing double meanings to slip into his conversation. How could the sight of this obviously beautiful woman, be dismissing the serious objectives they had; he realised then that this was not just desired, nor was it stupid self-indulgent sexual infatuation or the feeding of his large ego, it was something very serious.

As his head screamed *No, No, No!* His heart and body screamed even louder, *Yes, Yes, Yes.*

In his mind, he now began to accept that saving the world was only second on his list; then he rethought and positively placed it third.

The last thought he had prior to being disturbed was, '*God help you, Gould, you are but a crazy fool. Just make sure you generate some excellent camouflage.*'

"Andrew, Andrew, where were you? You seemed lost there for a moment, are you troubled? Come, finish your coffee while I dress and let us go downtown and relax for an hour or maybe even two. I am most sure we are in need of relaxation. Let us both just be for a little while, be just us, talking about our lives and the things we like."

"Yes, absolutely. I was miles away, so sorry Yoko, but it was your fault." "What do you mean?" "Nothing, just silly English joking around."

Andy knew that earlier, being he was occasionally a gentleman; he should off looked away from Yoko, been discrete, but he also knew it was now too late and that he didn't really care anyway. His heart was committed yet again. He had no idea how to deal with his emotions, it was not his forte, and he knew he was incapable now of rejecting either Liz or Yoko, and his other responsibilities.

They strolled across the campus, through the area that was once the old palace parkland. The light was fading as they wandered slowly, the two security officers followed at a discrete distance. She placing her arm through his. His mind visualising her being Liz for a moment, then Yoko, then Liz again and back to Yoko. She was evidently happy with the position between them, but what was in her mind, he knew not. Neither of them said anything, words appearing inapt but Andy very much noticed when Yoko placed her hand over his, gripping it gently which felt like affection and paradise wrapped tightly into one great emotion and confusion.

Yoko then turned to look back to Mark and Li. "Come you two, we are a group of four, let us go and eat together."

Once again, Andy was in ore of Yoko's smooth control over a situation, but was that how Yoko felt inside or was she too feelings of paradise.

Then together all four entered the lighting of busy streets and bustling pavements, food bars and busy people, small paths and alleys leading passed busy people.

Settling in chairs outside a small restaurant, which Yoko knew well, the chatter flowed nicely. Talk of work was band hence questions went back and forth about everything and anything, London, families, the world. Memories of childhood, disasters, and successes. Each joining the conversation, causing both laughter and seriousness. Then after a dozen varied dishes, wine and the constant good and light-hearted conversation the four strolled back through the campus, Mark and a hesitant Andy taking a cab from outside Yoko's apartment towards the hotel. Andy needed so much and so badly to lean forward and wrap his arms around Yoko; he could feel her similar desire but it was not to be. Polite 'good nights' were spoken, and then the arrangements were agreed. "Good night Andy. You sleep well, let's say no more now." "Good night Mark."

Then with a heavy heart, the cab journey to the hotel was made in relevant silence.

Andy lay back on his hotel bed running the events of the day through his head. Yoko continually came into his mind but sleep began to creep upon him, for which he was thankful. Then within a few moments, he was stolen to sleep which did not allow him to hear the quiet knocking that once again that appeared at his door.

—

London: October 2006:

Beijing, on a professional level, had been a positive experience. All felt an understanding was beginning to appear; slowly but surely, wiggling to the surface, the crystal maze was slowly being conquered and although nothing followed conventional understandings, a new and surprising picture was, for the first time, developing in some minds.

Andy and Liz together with others had been forced into a world of true awareness; it was a place they would not off chosen, and they would never or could ever be the same people they were before this experience. It was not only the science; it was the politics, the emotions. They were being thrust into a world of ultimate decisions, mixed with twists and turns, on everything appearing before them.

On a very personal level, Liz and Andy had also gone through a number of emotional swings, and through those recent experiences, it was all probably to be expected. It was at times impossible to relate to the enormity of the situation in which they had so suddenly been thrown.

Yoko Cheng was due back to Beijing and only time would resolve the confused feelings which sat between Andy, Yoko and Liz. They knew emotions should stay in the background as far as humanly possible and were each committed and secretly sworn to that position, if only it was that simple. Regardless, it did concern all three of them that a further trip to Beijing was likely.

The world community needed to regain its confidence, and the feeling that humans were in control. Another Olympics was not far off, it was impossible that such an event could or would be held in these circumstances, yet in a strange way some such event was desperately needed as a flash of yesterday's normality and order. Everybody, everywhere needed, *'a-feel-good-factor'*, to feel that we, homo sapiens, were indeed going to be back in control of our destiny, that truth and goodness would overcome evil and disaster; albeit, currently a happy illusion.

On Friday morning at eight thirty sharp, Liz and Andy left Kings and found themselves walking briskly along the Strand towards Whitehall. It was a bright crisp morning matching their mood. The streets of London these days were very different to six months ago. The rush hour traffic of both vehicles and workers was thinner; shops were partly staffed or closed, and ply-board shuttering was across the once vibrant window displays, the old rush, rush, of yesterday, was different, many people retained face masks generating an uncomfortable and slightly frightening air, others had just discarded them in exchange for hope. Six months ago, the people would have carried a look of serious stress upon their faces, now the look was of dull acceptance, and uncertainty, possibly even hopelessness in some minds. This was not unexpected, as literally nobody could quite understand or take a grasp on what was happening to the world they all once knew. If the majority had known the full extent of the happenings, which they certainly did not, maybe many would have simply given up any hope on tomorrow.

There was of course that spirit of determination lurking within communities; 'second world war - Dunkirk stuff", survival at any cost, but as the enemy was unknown, it was a strange and new experience for everybody; the only historical reference in most people's minds being the historical *Black Death*. The information given was in well-practised sound bits, conflicting responses, and of course, deception.

Slowly a new breed of leader began to appear on all levels, managers and politicians; those that processed an inner strength, that walked their own paths and had the common touch, people with happiness, optimism and confidence, people that had that special something around which others could gather and rely upon.

They were the people who could be living in any community but had no need to rely upon fashionable media stories or the fairy tales spun out by all the media. Politicians of the day; simply applied their own common sense. Joined up the available dots; a commodity that had been in short supply since computerisation had taken over every aspect of the global village and confused societies, migration discontent, inequality, fear and nationalism.

As Liz and Andy walked through the great swing doors at an entrance in Whitehall, an apprehension imposed itself upon them; neither Liz nor Andy enjoyed this kind of meeting where there were no worthy or adequate explanations given.

After security obligations had been thoroughly completed, they were ushered to a waiting room where they sat as if awaiting an extraction at the dentist; it even smelt like the dentist. There were those polite nods, which said, 'Good Morning, isn't this room just awful' but no real conversation, there were the stale old magazines that few read and that were duly spread over the obligatory low casual table. This waiting area was particularly austere and a little sinister and there was an unknown something hanging in the air, or indeed, was it just that building, these people, or indeed, just the very threatening times they lived in?

At last, a uniform appeared at the doorway and called their names.

"Professor Gould and Clements please follow me."

The corridors they strutted appeared like tunnels, or conveyor belts, each replicated one after the other. They travelled on until their usher stopped abruptly and knocked lightly upon a door signed, 1013.

"Enter!" The door was opened for them and they entered. "Arr, Gould and the lovely Miss Clements. Sit please."

In the office were two other gentlemen, and a distinguished-looking woman; none were recognised by Liz or Andy; their names were presented to the others in the room.

The 'minion' feeling began to creep into Andy's psyche once more, causing tension and resentment to build immediately. Why did these dam people use the old *'wig on the judge'* techniques; at that moment he settled for the situation and tried very hard to concentrate on the issues at hand.

The suit behind the desk continued to read paperwork in front of him while speaking.

"The trip was relevantly successful I believe." A short uncomfortable pause occurred.

"Current thinking please Professor Gould, I want to hear it from the horse's mouth so to speak."

Andy immediately resented being the 'horse's mouth', it was silly and a stupid reaction, and he knew that it made him feel like a foolish youth. Liz now was also building a clear dislike for this character and now found herself glaring across the large mahogany desk feeling that this character was rather lucky to have such a barrier between them. 'The beautiful Miss Clements indeed!'

The others in the room maintained a detached yet observing presents. Andy and Liz hoped upon hope that their reactions were not obvious to all present.

"Well, basically we are dealing here with total and utter chaos."

"Chaos, total or utter, is not really adequate Professor, please elaborate further. I am afraid that as difficult as it may be, we have to find a direction, a solution. Somehow, bringing all this global knowledge together, bringing this horrendous situation to an end."

Andy paused, took a couple of deep breaths, contained himself, and continued.

"As I was about the express; Professor Clements, Professor Cheng and her department plus myself, of course, have concluded that we are dealing with numerous layers of problems, unfortunately, they appear to be running in parallel, and simultaneously. We jointly expect the situation to continue deteriorating before any improvements can truly be expected. This is all very dependent, as we all know on the level of international commitment and discovery."

Andy paused to re-gather his thoughts and pass a quick look towards Liz who was watching him closely and looking rather nervous.

"On one hand we agree that major terrorist groups or similar must be at the centre of a number of the instants around the world, if not, that the whole event we are experiencing is sabotage, created by an unknown party. There is simply no other conclusion that can be drawn and I guess you are aware of that. It would appear further that this is a very well-organised global operation which seems to of attached itself to a natural disaster starting possibly at King's, or more concerning, created at King's by this unknown body. We would suggest, way beyond the likes of Al Qaeda or similar, it must be very well organized, and to what purpose, god only knows. There is no way we are able to connect or conclude that all of these incidents are directly connected. That is in our joint and considered opinions, indeed it is the only explanation for certain, so explaining the occurrences globally, and is well outside of our domain, and in itself very serious and threatening, but that said yet again, we assume you must have already reached that conclusion.

What appears likely, is that this activity has been planned into such a chain of natural disasters over the past few years, if indeed the event at King's was a natural disaster. Simply waiting patiently; on top of this, it appears to us, that the chain of natural disasters themselves has changed in nature, intensified and been affected further, initially, maybe by solar activity, but we doubt that, and it is still only a theory. Open-air experimentation, by others, and ourselves together with the rapidly growing effects of global warming, let alone undeclared nuclear testing; are good examples; the current run-on secret cloud seeding experiments, there are just so many possibilities I am afraid. Scientifically I think we will get there, but it is going to take time and luck. It is very difficult to speak about without certainty about anything, we do need that time to analyse all results and data, and indeed time to confer with many colleagues around the world.

We are certain that the open and wide theories placed on the table by Beijing University and ourselves are beginning to show us a way forward. That the spores, which escaped from the King's laboratory were subsequently mutating rapidly and continued to mutate. Maybe affected by other factors, maybe not, and driven along the weather front. As the front approached North West China, the cloud seeding activities that were undergoing a number of new and extensive procedures, coincided with a massive and sudden reduction of solar activity, which totally changed the nature of the mutant spores yet again. Please understand, we are guessing wildly here, just maybe; there is a lot of research still to be undertaken and results to be analysed.

No doubt, you are aware of the extensive experimentation investment in that area by China over the last decade; cloud seeding seems to be involved, maybe. In fact, their investment amounts to more than the sum of all other global investments in that area of research, it may well offer some answers but much of the science is still secret, apparently even to Yoko Chen.

No doubt you will remember the miracle of the Beijing Olympics, how the horrendous weather, the smog that was happening, was then kept away from all Olympic venues.

Well, the seeding could have interacted with the spores that were carried into China. Mutated once again, or more precisely, killed off the original mutating effect and created another; this is possibly a logical element in this theory; proven only in part, remember it is a theory and until Chinese authorities allow the release of all their data, we cannot confirm one way or the other. Yoko Chen or we desperately need that information.

When you add to the whole story, all the climatic changes we are currently experiencing; mostly man-induced, we are, without a doubt, left with chaos and many random outcomes. There is currently a number of further important results, which we are awaiting. Once we have further clarity, which should be within a few days, it would be appropriate for a further meeting. We are not just dealing here with toxic spores. You do now understand it is confirmed the toxic spores are carrying both viruses and bacteria and then the global conditions are causing and further affecting those mutation rates. It appears to be a completely new scientific happening that is upon us and we desperately need to find both the source and if applicable, the saboteurs.

'*This whole period appears very much like a trillion butterflies flapping their wings simultaneously and changing basic structures, understandings and the weather patterns of the world*' and that is without evil intent."

"Mmmm! You have a poetic tongue Professor Gould. I will let you know about further meetings. What you have told me, Gould, is obviously horrendous. Further to that, security appears to be forming similar views, so at least we begin to understand where we are going."

"I am glad you recognise what has been said, but I am sorry to have to say on this occasion and from now onwards, it will be necessary that we ring you, it could be that important. We'll need direct numbers and names for instant contact."

The man in the suit turned his look away from Andy with obvious momentary shock at the sudden change in the balance of power and Andy's forcefulness, and then looked directly at Liz.

"Professor Clements, do you concur totally with Professor Gould, his statement and theories in general? Do you wish to add anything?"

Liz ignored the direct question. "Professor Gould is correct at this point in time in all that he has said, and indeed, not said. Direct and immediate contact is now vital if you wish to be kept up to date, either, via this office, or a higher one. The current level of contact is of no value to any of us from here onwards. From our point of view, if the situation is to be improved, and allow us to work in harmony, we simply have to change the availability of contact; a completely new system needs to be created, and as soon as possible.

As to your question!

Yes, I do agree totally with Professor Gould. I would like to add that from a scientific point of view, this is a long-term nightmare, let alone a short-term problem. It appears that for us, the scientific world, to attempt rectifying matters; the enemy within, so to speak will no doubt have to be dealt with by others, but we must have our space, be separate and removed from all those other issues. We would suggest that some serious political action is needed internationally; global warming etc has to be dealt with; trends must be reversed at a rapid rate or whatever action is taken scientifically it will possibly be to no avail. I say again that the terrorist element will need increased effort applied. A weekly meeting of all departments, with the professionals in attendance, not just politicians; a weekly meeting at an international level, beyond those that we are continually carrying out. In our view, and it is our joint advice, that such action is essential."

Liz delivered her comments as agreed with Andy. She took a deep breath and continued.

"It appears that the enemies within are employing biological means and misinformation, which continually confuses everything we have to consider. We receive endless reports, every day and some are never looked at, we have no time, and not enough staff. We've constantly requested further facilities and nothing has been forthcoming, you rarely answer our questions. This is all very Monty Python. Everything appears interwoven. Politics, important as it is, is very much in the way of solutions currently and that is up to you to sort out.

Everything we understand to date is detailed in those reports in front of you."

"Ok, ok; let me stop you there Elizabeth; take these cards, Gould, ring whenever you think it is necessary. I have heard your frustration and your recommendations. They will be acted upon and that is a promise. Unfortunately, Gould, we within politics are a necessity, we are not all fools full of self-interest, although admittedly there are far too many of that ilk. Keep the faith Gould. I will attempt to speak directly with the PM's office today. The upgrading of the weekly conferences is something we have been considering and working on."

Another long pause ensued.

One of the gentlemen sitting alongside the mahogany desk spoke.

He was a man in his seventies with silver-greying hair. He spoke clearly and precisely, in perfect English and yet with an underlying French accent. He held before him one of the reports that Andy had handed out initially.

"I assume these are the fullest reports available?"

The man in the suit looked directly at Andy re-enforcing the question, and implying some kind of authority.

"By tomorrow midday you'll have the updated reports." Andy managed to avoid using the 'Sir' word, which he strongly regretted using earlier.

"So be it." The suited man checked a diary to his right. "Four thirty tomorrow then Professor Gould, together with Professor Clements.

I wish one of us could express satisfaction with your investigations and the situation but that is obviously not possible. Hopefully, that will follow in the course of time. I can confirm that the general sweep of international opinion seems to be running in the general direction you have both indicated – utter confusion is a very accurate phase.

Two other small matters for you to consider Gould.

I was able to speak to Yoko Cheng this morning. Very impressive Lady! She has been asked to head the U.N. Scientific Unit, which is to coordinate and progress the international effort. She would have complete control globally and is considering the matter currently. I do not think she seemed very interested as she and her team are heavily committed but she did comment that if she accepted she would require you alongside her but I do not think it would be practical, you are, in reality, at the head of this disaster currently and should not be involved elsewhere in my view. Let me have a response tomorrow, please.

Also. There is now a new and developing incident in Africa, *'for god's sake'*, and it is clearly accepted by all as covert activity of some kind. Sinister in the extreme, and sadly that appears to be happening around the globe in differing forms that appear to confirm what you have already told me. Unfortunately, there does appear an irrational number of such incidents globally. You will all no doubt be discussing all these issues fully next week, by which time we very much hope to of gathered considerably more information. New structures are being organised right now, as said, both on international and national levels. These good people here are able to confirm that massive efforts are being made outside of the public view to create an internationally accepted model, under which we can all work more effectively. In other words, yet again, everything you have requested and expressed we have already been trying to establish for some time. Unfortunately, it has not been practical to involve you directly. You have had other priorities."

In a sudden and unexpected change of mode.

"Your work is appreciated Professors and my abruptness, I am aware is not appreciated; this I understand. We will resolve all these issues, of that I feel confident."

"Aah! By the way, I expect that tomorrow, these good people will join us again, together with Blyar Prescott, James Guest and the Head of Scientific Studies at Brussels, Michael Raimondi, who follows in his father's footsteps and who once headed up a scientific department for us. I imagine you have heard of him.

Good Morning everyone and thank you all for your support and attendance."

Having been duly dismissed, and now back on the street again, Andy and Liz glanced at one another with a look of satisfaction at how they had handled and delivered their summary report, all be it, contained very little clarity. They knew it was far from adequate but they had progressed the situation considerably; well in theory at least, and now it appeared their conclusions and recommendations were similar to others and were, at last, being acted on.

The whole meeting had only taken forty-five minutes. It was incredible how such matters could be summarised.

One more meeting tomorrow and freedom for two days and that thought seemed like a dream, neither of them could visualise it really happening.

"I tell you what Andy; that guy looked just about all in to me, I thought we looked rough and tired out, it makes me feel like we are coping pretty well and maybe we have misjudged him.

Those other three looked like a dodgy lot. Why the hell didn't we get formally introduced, I find that really annoying."

"Liz, I think the principle is that names are unimportant above a certain level; similar to below a certain level. It is simply power and action up there in the clouds; anyway, that is my guess, I don't really know.

God! Did you hear my 'sir'? Boy, I felt a real prat and as you know, I really do not like referring to people with that title. Don't you dare tell anyone."

"Ok, Andy Gould. I will tell you what; you forget about the 'honey reason' and I will forget about the grovelling 'sir' booby and all the other grovelling you did in there. Is that an agreement?"

"You cunning little fox you; and, anyway, what other grovelling. I didn't - did I?

Oh dear! Liz Ok, for now, you're winning, it's a deal; you a cunning witch." Liz generated a satisfied smile that Andy noticed but kept his counsel knowing he was a beaten man on this occasion.

By the time they had returned to their digs at King's, they were both tired and agreed to take a shower and a couple of hours recoup.

—

New thinking: The passing of time and the United Nations:

Andy had written and published a theory paper on his current view of the situation. Liz and the whole of King's were in support and worked equally hard on the paper, this was being frowned upon by many governmental representatives within the inner circle of events. Moves to replace Andy and Liz by certain officials and via underhanded means were circulating around Whitehall.

It caused a great conflict of both power and thinking. The government slowly stepping down, due to the enormous support within other political and scientific circles. Ultimately finding it necessary to succumb to the investigation, and of the new thinking, facts and concepts now being accepted as a strong possibility of why the results to date had caused such disarray amongst prominent scientists and politicians around the globe.

The fraternity at King's was in full support of Andy and Liz after reading his five-hundred-page paper on the new concepts now being considered. So many factors were now running against the tide of normality. It was an enormous credit for Kings, although generally the investigation was kept under wraps until further confirmations could be announced.

Andy had numerous meetings with M.I.5, the government's chief medical and scientific representatives and other government agencies who together with their own classified files broadly supported his views. It was the politicians that seemed to have the greatest difficulty with how approaching the public. It was essential that information and advice were shared, also tight control, but control without panic or social enforcement. It was a thin line to hold, and around the world, the balance was only just being maintained.

Michael Ramondi had been in close contact with both Professor Andy Gould and occasionally with Liz. He had become a clear and open supporter of their work, views, and approach. It explained so much of the ever-changing situation causing confusion and alarm around the world.

The updating of Andy and Liz's report was complete, all had been working hard on their Beijing notes, basically, qualifying their summarised report at the briefing that morning. The updated report now added conclusions that were more detailed and incorporated new relevant international findings that agreed with their own growing findings and feelings. The conclusion was a powerful piece of work by Andy, with Yoko's and Liz's full support and assistance. It clearly laid out the way forward by separating the issues and suggesting sound administration structures and the required additional funding and staffing.

The report contained the words random, inconclusive and ciaos, and those words appeared in numerous paragraphs, hence, anyone that read the document was left in no doubt that, this was, in the main, a developing group of theories, open to many questions and further research. At this stage, they were all confident they could not or should not add anything further, now it would be dependent upon others to take the appropriate actions and leave them and other professionals to do their work.

That evening Liz and Andy dined together, in the same Mexican restaurant where they often found themselves. Liz was now in a rather quiet mood.

She broached the subject of their relationship as the starters of Nachos arrived.

Andy found it difficult to answer her questions clearly, at this moment in time there was no committed relationship between them, yet love, respect, and desire filled both of their minds.

Yes, lots of feelings, quandaries and emotional confusion. Andy had no doubt the matter of love would develop, he wanted it to, but any such matter was bound to be awkward under the current intense circumstances. He could wait; there really was nothing else to be said, especially at the moment and yet of course he knew he must respond and wanted to respond appropriately and caringly as that was Liz's need. In the back of his mind, he also feared that eventually Yoko would be brought into the conversation and that could be a nuclear explosion.

"Liz, you know I love you, probably have for many years, possibly since you first raised your hand at my lecture and asked, 'Sir are you just guessing about that.'"

He said this just as the main course of Tamales and Enchiladas landed at the table. "Let's stay with that thought sweetheart, let's stay really close. Everything will sort itself out; you know we have so many other pressing things to deal with, probably more important even than our own feelings." The waiter hovered.

"If you are ready Madam would you like to consider the sweet menu?"

Liz answered sharply. "No, obviously not at this precise moment, thank you, go away."

Andy had known as soon as he had spoken those words and they had left his mouth, they were the wrong ones. It was way too late to take them back and now having read Liz's body language and noted her tone, the mistake had been clearly noted and was now being reinforced, the emotions cranked up tightly; hence he began to feel very edgy.

Sour cream was defiantly on the menu now. He tried a little to adjust what he had said, smooth it a little but slowly he began to feel the noose tightening around his nervous neck, tighter and even tighter and he knew he deserved hanging for his foolishness.

There would be no Chocolate Mousse or Key Lime Pie now that was a certainty. 'Sad', Andy thought, '*I fancied a banana split with loads of cream. In fact, Andy boy, if you're not careful here you'll be eating the dam cutlery and have a banana split up my butt.*'

He kept his thoughts to himself obviously and simultaneously contained his inner awkward smile.

He certainly did not need the Yoko subject to surface at this moment but all his instincts told him it was going to be launched straight at him any moment, just like a nuclear missile. He was correct.

Liz now looked angry and that anger fill the atmosphere sucking in every trace of pleasure and niceness, she raised her head to stare directly at Andy, her eyes on fire with that anger and emotion. She was obviously hurting and wanted to hurt him in return, but, all things considered, it was still bad timing as far as he was concerned; he was not going to say that again, walking on rice paper was an art, one that he was not so clever at.

"So, what's this Yoko thing about Andy?" "Oh, please Liz, can't we do this another time, let's just enjoy this evening."

Liz continued her line of questioning regardless.

"Ok, so you are right, I am in ore of Yoko Liz and a little infatuated with her; I'm sorry about that under the circumstances but she is so similar to you, she is very smart, attractive with loads of personality. You would like her if you gave her a chance." Andy immediately hated what he had said, but thought it was the best option right here and now.

Liz stared at Andy in silence for a long time, obviously juggling her thoughts. Andy awaited her response. "Ok Andy, you win. Some other time."

It was going to be one of those long silent walks back to Kings and no doubt, a night filled with endless tossing, turning, guilt, and emotional confusion. For a short while, science and saving the world seemed far, far away.

The following morning there was no sign of last night's mood or uncomfortable conversations.

The morning was fresh and sharp. Thin silvery northern corners of frost lurked for the first time, it was necessary to rub the hands together in a kind of recognition of the changing weather. Andy was standing in room four looking over the central courtyard as Liz wonder her way towards the science block and room four. A long black scarf that was wrapped around her neck also drooped to the floor at both the back and front. Her hair was obviously uncombed yet; her arms fully cuddled around herself. She looked up and observed Andy watching her, she smiled in recognition, and then understanding his thoughts, she proceeded to enact her Quasimodo impression across the courtyard causing Andy to chuckle and generate feelings of love and desire towards her. He simply loved this Liz, with her great sense of fun and foolishness, if only they had maintained their friendship as it had been, and not let love and desire come to the fore. The timing was awful.

The day continued in good spirits while further fine-tuning their report and reading through new incoming reports which were constantly arriving from Harvard, Kingston and Melbourne; indeed, the four corners of the world. In general, although expressed in a variety of ways, the conclusions once again, lead in similar directions to those that they had reached with Yoko and had presented to Whitehall.

As they again trod the path to further meetings, they spoke of families and the thought of just being themselves for a couple of days. The coming short break was well overdue. Liz was looking forward to seeing her two sisters again, horse riding and drinking too much Chablis, and then falling to sleep in front of a real fire. Andy badly wanted and needed to see his parents and check on Amy, and likewise, drink too much, but for him, it was bitter down at the Five Bells. Thereafter, maybe read a book about anything apart from the science of any type, yes, he knew he was always on call but at home, he would be able to hide; especially now security had been slackened on Liz and himself.

Yet again, usual procedures lead them through to room 1013. Inside the office, they were a little surprised to be confronted by only the grey suit.

"Good afternoon. Sit, please. A lot has happened since yesterday's meetings and others were, unfortunately, unable to attend; the situation is moving very quickly. I am afraid we must keep our meeting short. Is there anything new to mention Professor Gould?"

Andy took the ten copies from his briefcase and passed the updated reports across the great mahogany desk. "I assumed a number would be required. We also had copies made of other material we received early this morning which, if you have not received them, further supports our conclusions."

"Thank you, Andrew, it is an excellent job you are doing." With that, the very brief meeting was over, "good afternoon to both of you. Call me immediately if any further important information is available and we will speak clearly once this report has been thoroughly reviewed."

As they left the office, a voice called out from behind them, "Professor Clements, one moment if you would please."

Andy lurked awkwardly outside the office door, alone in the endless corridor feeling rather like a gooseberry. Two minutes later Liz returned to join him and then as usual they were ushered from the building and into the big grey world outside.

"Well then; tell all, what did he want; what did he have to say?"

"Security Andy, security. I just can't tell you everything; you know about national security."

"You are bloody kidding me." "Yes, of course, I am. You will not believe what I am about to tell you." There was a calculated pause, an amazed expression, everything drawn out for effect.

"Yes, come on give it to me."

"It is indeed very, very complicated; a long, long story indeed."

"What is? You are hanging me out you fox and even more evil than that, you are *'so loving'* every single second of it."

"Yes, I certainly am Mr Gould; I just *l-o-v-e* this, Oooh, give me more of these opportunities."

"Liz, I'm beginning to hate you! I am beginning to think about murder now."

"Ok. Well, he wanted to take me to a restaurant and no doubt, spoil me rotten."

"To meet who, and Liz why only you, I don't like or understand this, do I need to know something here or not?"

"You fool, you're just not catching on; he fancy's me and let us be honest; who wouldn't? He wanted to date me. Shower me with gifts I expect and then have copious amounts of sex."

"The cheeky bugger; I have a good mind to go back and punch him out. Anyway, he's far too busy to take you out, plus he looks tired and he's too dam old and ugly."

"Listen to you; Mr Jealousy lurking? *Yes Elizabeth, I think you hear jealousy, mmm!'* Anyway, he's neither old nor unattractive, plus, as we are not being serious at the moment - - I thought it would be perfectly all right, I like him. I think he is rather cute."

"No Liz, you bloody did not say yes, please, please, tell me you didn't?"

Andy stopped dead in his tracks holding his head.

"As I was saying before you rudely interrupted yet again; I thought it would be all right – to, a, to a, well, turn him down of course." Liz chuckled with endless tormenting delight.

"You are such a little fox Clements, dam you and give me a cuddle here and now."

They hung there for a while both enjoying the cut and thrust of the moment, all be it, it was necessary for Andy to allow himself to calm down.

"Come on you, we're on sanity break."

Andy and Liz had known there was going to be a few days spare prior to the London conference and both needed to see family; to let matters settle within their minds before re-gearing and presenting and discussing their current theories and thoughts. They were also looking forward to spending time listening and discussing with a wide gathering of international colleagues. They simply had to resolve the spread and mutation issues. It was what everybody was working on, but every time a new theory was generated, everything changed.

Andy headed off at the first opportunity, he spoke briefly again to Liz but there was nothing of value and new to be added, he embraced her affectionately, hanging on again for that important extra second or two. "Liz we both need this couple of days, ring me if you need to, if not, I'll see you on Wednesday, you take good care and have some fun."

There was lots of caring, but no kiss.

—

England: Eynsford, Kent. Late October 2006:

Eynsford in Kent had been Andy's family home for as long as he could remember. He had not been there for two years and he really needed to see his parents and touch base with familiar surroundings and old friends; he did not even know if Amy, his Old English sheepdog, was still alive and that was a bad thought to handle.

He kept in touch with his parents regularly, but somehow it was always a very brief conversation by phone. They were now in their mid-seventies and although they maintained busy lives, he was aware they were approaching a difficult age when a little more attention would be required on his behalf. Yes, he did have two sisters the same as Liz. Jill and Sally, who were both a little younger but that wasn't the point, they were his parents also and he knew that he would, by nature, have to find extra time for them when needed, but the current nightmare pushed everything into a new frame, and that was always at the back of his mind.

The cottage gate swung open and he strolled slowly up the old tiled pathway taking in all those old memories and feelings that rushed at him. It felt so good to be home, away from all that pressure and he immediately felt relaxed, the tensions leaking away into the ground. Outside of the garden fence in Eynsford, all looked exactly as before, no one would ever have guessed the enormity of the situation facing mankind at that very moment; he felt as if he was stepping back in time, taking part in a film, it was unreal, but boy, it felt so very good.

He turned to face the whitewashed cottage again and walked over to the little blue wooden bench with plant pots scattered at either end and still brimming over with early Busy-Lizzies, Ferns, and Antirrhinums. Most of what remained of the grass was kept short but not all over the garden, his Father had never liked everything just so. He liked areas left uncut so there was a corner plot for stingers and Buddleia and an old rotting log or two.

The essential garden pond was still in the smaller rear garden and he would get to see that later; for now, he just wanted to sit there and enjoy this rather special moment, which he knew would last too long. As he sat in the dying light, he really felt relaxed for the first time in eight long months, maybe even for the last few years. With the lack of traffic through the village and nobody to be seen, he drifted away on a cloud of momentary contentment, safe within the knowledge that here everything appeared, as it should be.

An instant haven, a security blanket, where he could feel once again, his childhood.

"Andrew, Andrew son, wakey-wakey, fancy a cup of tea lad, you look exhausted, no doubt you've been overdoing that work of yours again, either that or you're running with two women!" They both laughed in unison, Andy looking up into his fathers' kindly face.

"Ah, Dad! You look good; yes, a cup of rosy-lee, please. Where's Mum; how is Mum?"

"She's just fine Andrew. She's around her friend's place, Mable, chin-wagging endlessly no doubt; come on in when you are ready, I'll put the kettle on. Need anything to eat lad?"

"Any of Mum's cherry cake going?"

Suddenly, without warning, there was a great rush and much waggling of something at the rear end, as a large black and white furry ball was crashing and chasing around the garden, then rushing at Andy, turning, the rushing once again too leaning on the fence in a number of specially selected locations and checking for any neighbourhood dangers. Once she was satisfied that her domain was safe, Amy waddled over to Andy, her tail still wagging nervously and constantly at the excitement of their reunion.

"Well, how is my favourite girl, I am sorry I haven't been to see you recently Amy.

Look at you, don't you look wonderful."

After much fussing with each other, Andy, now with a wet ear, lead the way into the house, down the hallway to the kitchen at the rear; Amy was now firmly attached to his heel with no intention of ever letting him escape again.

"So how has it been down here for Mum and yourself; everything looks amazingly normal; is that really how it is?"

There was a pause while Andy took in the kitchen with all the familiar knick-knacks and objects of his childhood, the tick of the old railway clock, the brown teapot, and the unglazed chicken upon the windowsill that held the eggs. He remembered fighting with his sister over the chicken; his mother had taken it away from both of them.

"Dad, I cannot tell you how wonderful a cupper and cake in this kitchen feels, for some reason, I feel like crying." He tried to force himself in another direction.

"It was sad about Uncle Bert and Aunt Mary; many families have been devastated.

Are food supplies being affected around here much?"

"Slow down lad, slow down. Your Mother and I are ok; yep, there have been some sad old story's around the village but folk have a way of adjusting, luckily your grandfather educated us well, occasionally one has to stretch things; bread and pull it or air-cake but compared to some poor souls we are doing just fine.

Your sisters too, there are ok, so we are the lucky ones."

Andy's head was flicking from turbocharged thoughts to a strange relaxed state and then plummeting into a deeply emotional moment. That moment suddenly and unrepentantly developed into a release of stress, that was well overdue. Andy sat at the table bolt upright, one hand tightly upon his cup, the other tightly to his forehead, emotion building uncontrollably and then he sobbed and cried like a baby for over ten minutes.

The tears ran down his face, his nose ran heavy with mucus and he jerked with the power of the emotion that flowed from within. No words were spoken by Andy or his Father, they were not required, and both understood, just a gentle hand upon his shoulder told Andy all he needed to know.

As the moment began to pass, his Father reheated the kettle while Andy breathed deeply and cleaned his face and the back of his hand and a tissue.

"Sorry about that; how very silly, I don't know where it comes from dad."

"Coarse you do lad. Who could possibly lose so many loved ones, then sit back, and watch the people and world you know start to fall apart? Watch clever men lose their confidence when so many are relying upon them. Watch stupid people plying only their egos as if in these times anybody needed that rubbish. Lad, I know you are at the heart of all these happenings, I cannot imagine what you have to deal with son, but for better or worse, I know you care and especially when one has to block out your personal feelings to continue to act professionally. Well, it all has to come out sooner or later, that's why you're here and that's why we're here also boy."

The kettle boiled and another pot of tea was made in the little old brown teapot so familiar throughout Andy's growing. One last deep breath and Andy felt as if he was regaining his composure and yet being here in the bosom of his family reduce him readily to being a child; how could he possibly be the person that yesterday was reporting to high government upon the latest group of disasters affecting the world.

The two characters within seemed to separate inside his head; it was without doubt a schizophrenic experience.

Andy now realised it was going to take a while to be relaxed if indeed it was possible at all. The phone rang and Bill Gould answered the call. "Andrew; it's a Miss Cheng for you."

—

England. Guildford, Surrey. Late October 2006:

On the borders of Guildford, Liz sat upon Star, between her two sisters' horses, and looked out across an amazingly green landscape; she had almost forgotten just how wonderful it could be, particularly after her visit to China. In the dell and along the ridge were good size Elms and Oaks occasionally grouped and forming secret magical woods. Blackthorn and Hawthorn stretched endlessly between field after field. From their position they could view three spires, each one being the original centre of a once important village; that was the England that most hungered for but was now somewhat depleted. For a moment, the thought generated both sadness and pleasure but the company of her sisters compensated fully for any negative feelings. The three women dismounted and strolled quietly along the ridge intending to rid down to Cuddlesford, tie up at the 'The Old Farmers Inn' and solute each other, possibly with champagne, that was if they could stop cuddling and kissing each other long enough. On this overdue occasion, it was, all about self-indulgence, and the necessary catch-up conversations and sister chatter.

Liz still found it difficult to relate to what she saw before her in comparison to her recent experiences. There was certainly sorrow and death all around her according to her sisters, but fortunately, the mutations had not affected crops throughout the United Kingdom.

One cheddar ploughman's and a plate of crispy chips plus thick flavour-sum ham off the bone with eggs, which must be cooked just right; firm white and runny yellow. A steak pie with peas. Chips, in fact, chip butties in freshly baked crusty bread layered with butter from the fridge. Just giving their order on arrival was a delight. Their mouths foolishly watered in expectation.

"Sorry girls but no ham or steak pie. Spam or Cornbeef and no butter either; is that ok ladies; I'll do the best I can."

Well, of course, it mattered but nothing was going to spoil this reunion. Anyway, they had enjoyed planning their desires, which, had also made their stomachs rubble in anticipation but they would just have to settle for the new vision. As it turned out the meal was scrumptious or was it the company or just the moment; it mattered not. The alcohol flowed, the conversation took tangents, and the voices got louder, together with growing amounts of laughter.

Sometime later and with all of them a little worse for wear the three girls rode gently back home, still deep in chatter and knowing they had all indulged too much. "I hope we don't get stopped for drunken riding." "Did I tell you about Paris Jones? Well, I saw her Mother the other day, I did not recognize her but she did me. She pulled me over to one side; as proud as punch, Paris is playing the lead in the new Cats at the London Palladium." "That is simply brilliant, I'm real please for her, she was always going to be a wonderful actress, a star even, she deserves it. I'd like to see her again."

"What about the Goodhews, I've heard bad news about them I'm afraid."

"All gone; well apart from young Martin, he's now completely on his own, it wasn't fast either, it was totally horrific, and our father used to visit them. He should not have done that but as he said, how can you ignore friends you have known for so many years? Young Martin has gone to stay with some distant Aunt; I gather the poor kid has gone to bits; we've all been lucky, so very lucky." Nobody bought up the obvious subject, it was kind and understanding, I guess we will find out later what has happened to Martin.

—

Eynsford, Kent England:

In Eynsford, the 'Five Bells' time was being called. Andy raised his glass to empty it. There had been all the fine choice of bitters available as there would have been eight months ago. In London, shortages were not so obvious, particularly in Andy's world and until now, he had not really noticed just how bad things were outside of London. At least, he had met up with some old friends, James and Brian. They all tried to skirt around the bad subjects as best they could and each did their best to keep the evening light, albeit was almost impossible. Nobody it appeared to Andy had managed to escape losses, everyone knew somebody, and it added up to many. That of course was bad enough to endure but added to the growing list of deaths were the job losses and the general shortages. Rationed water and electrical supplies then added to those burdens, let alone the regular ailments of life. All totalled up to a bleaker picture than Andy had ever expected, stupidly he had expected Eynsford to be excluded, to be as it always was. Within the conversations held throughout the evening, all were scathing of the media and politicians. Why o' why didn't they act twenty years ago when the whole situation began to tumble out of control? All those relaxed regulations, were they stupid or corrupt?

In Eynsford, it appeared there was not a lot that ordinary folk could do apart from the pull in their belts and put on a happy face, and then wait for the hands on the big clock to turn.

Private vehicles were hardly ever used now days across the southeast, shopping centres only opened for limited periods with minimal staff. Public transport had been widened to incorporate most locations but reduced in the hours of service; that in its self was an excellent intervention and kept communities together, confined and just about functioning. Communities needed all the innervation that could be mustered.

Bill Spike, the landlord at the Five Bells, had allowed Amy to sit under Andy's table; it was against the rules but so was smoking and the hours he kept. What customers he could attract on a Monday night, he wanted to keep and these were times to bring back a little of that good old common sense. Sure, the habit of smoking hardly existed in public places these days but folk needed all the comforts they could find and with only six punters to occupy the Five Bells throughout that evening what did it matter in the greater scheme of things.

Andy strolled home slowly, his toe or heel catching the pathing stones occasionally, the night fluctuating from pitch black to as clear as day due to the full moon dancing and hiding between the thick clouds in the night sky. There were no streetlights. Amy waddled alongside, investigating each new and exciting smell. Her body language displayed complete contentment in being next to her best friend once again.

Back at the cottage, there was no light left on; all was still and dark. He hit the light switch simply out of habit as he entered the kitchen, nothing, not even a flicker. 'Bugger it', he thought, 'light bulb gone'. With the moon shining brightly now through the kitchen window, Andy switched the electric kettle to boil and stood there for ten minutes gazing out across the rear garden at a glowing silvery moon before he realised there was no buzz of heating water and remembered the rationed electricity. He placed the kettle upon the gas ring, took out his mobile phone and rang Liz.

"Hi And, are you ok." "Kind of. I am trying too hard to settle down and enjoy this but I am struggling Liz. How is it going down in Guildford?" "I'm doing ok Andy. I went out riding today with my sisters, you remember Rebecca and Maggie, it was great, all be it, and the head is throbbing rather badly. The family all seemed to be doing ok. I cannot wait to see my father tomorrow. Do you need me to try to get over to you; I will if you say. My father can arrange matters like that, no problem." "No, no, you needed this break as much as I thought I did. You enjoy yourself, I shouldn't off rung you really, and I'm sorry Liz."

"Don't you dare say that to me? Dam sorry indeed, I don't believe you said that. You must be struggling. I am coming over to Eynsford and that's that. Get yourself to bed Andy, we'll speak again in the morning, you sleep tight sweetheart."

"Good night Liz, I'm so sorry about this funny mood I'm in, so sorry; speak tomorrow."

Andy was surprised by the sound of such a relaxed Liz. He was pleased for her and yet he had to admit to himself, a little jealous that she was obviously already relaxed and enjoying herself, or so it seemed. He had also noticed with slight doubts the term 'sweetheart'.

He took his tea into the garden, Amy dragging herself after him. She had forgotten that total devotion was a lot of work. The night was now fresh, not cold, but pleasant enough. Amy, with some help, dragged herself onto the bench next to Andy and rested her head on his leg.

He ran his mind through all that had been spoken of since being at home and with his old friends down at the Five Bells. He ran his fingers in a constant flow through Amy's fur. His mind returned repeatedly to what his father had said to him about the mass burials that had taken place initially and the funereal fires, which had been employed when the system simply couldn't cope any longer, he'd forgotten about so many of the difficulties being endured by ordinary folk, his family and friends. He felt a little stupid for not realising how different other people's lives were nowadays in comparison to his own. Somehow, he had known it but just had not related it to his parents.

His thoughts were suddenly moved in another direction and he became aware of drinking too many pints of bitter ale; he was not used to drinking that much these days and he lent forward with the discomfort. His stomach irrupted and he continued to reach for a while and there under the moon, he felt like death itself. His head spun while jetting in, out and spinning unpleasantly.

Three hours later Andy and Amy stirred simultaneously. He was now cold, dam-freezing cold; his neck aching and stiff. They both stretched long, and slow, then moved into the house together, he shivering as he shuffled into the kitchen. Andy continued to try to straighten his neck, then he moved to the sink to rinse his mouth thoroughly removing the taste of puke and wiping his soiled clothes, he was a mess. Afterwards, moving cautiously with Amy still attached to his every move, and still wobbling he hunted out his bed for more warmth and comfort, whilst his head belonged to somebody else, he felt awful.

—

Guildford, Surrey, England:

Liz awoke early, feeling good, even spritely. She was in one of those moods where a second should not be wasted. She dragged on the nearest clothes to hand and with hair looking as wild as ever she made her way downstairs. Alone in the kitchen, she scurried around hunting out juice while the coffee percolated. It was chilly; she grabbed a coat from the hallway as a wrap-around and shuffled back into the kitchen. The coffee had percolated all over the hob; not what she needed right now and she cursed.

"Good Morning sweetheart." Came from behind her.

"Daddy, oh I'm so pleased to see you. I've been missing you loads and loads."

Her father wrapped his arms around her and lifted her cleanly from the floor and placed her on the kitchen worktop. Leaning forward, he kissed her forehead with as much affection as only a father could conjure. Pleasure and love ooze from both of them.

"So how is my pretty and clever girl? You look better than I expected you to, especially with all these terribly tragic things going on. I've been keeping a secret eye on you my little princess; did you know that?"

"Nooo. So who do yooou know, that knows meee?"

"Never you mind but who had a meeting last Friday with the ministry; need I say more my little princess? You are becoming increasingly well-known in certain circles."

"Daddy, you appear to know just about everybody in London. I simply cannot get away with anything, it really is not very fair you know, I am a grown-up woman now daddy. I hope you don't know all the details of my wild and raunchy private life."

"I've heard a few tails about dancing on pub tables but I was pleased to hear that you kept your jewellery on my girl." "Daddy! That is awful. You know I wouldn't." "Only teasing sweetheart. The moral of this story is; large glasses of alcohol need equal large pieces of jewellery. I'm only talking rubbish darling." Mr Clements chuckled to himself, enjoying the nonsense teasing of his daughter Liz well understood his game, and she loved him for it.

Liz did not get around to ringing Andy until quite late that morning. She had guessed he would be laying in late and hopefully finding his spirit again. Her sisters were staying until she returned to London. Rebecca was three months pregnant and kind of putting a family life together. That was no easy task these days and this would be the first grandchild in the immediate family. Their father was ecstatic about becoming a grandfather but for all his connections, he was still very concerned that she was receiving the right kind of care. Regardless of all the optimistic words on the radio and in the newspapers, everything was crashing; services were understaffed and technology was letting people down.

Margret worked in Whitehall but her path never crossed with Liz's, and like Liz these days, she was not allowed to speak about her work. They were lucky in that their father new many people of position and was able to pull a string or two. None of the sisters understood exactly what their father did and the whole family had been trained in discretion regarding such matters and in reality, they rarely thought about it.

Margret and Rebecca appeared together in the kitchen looking somewhat worse than Liz did; that was somewhat amazing, as she had forgotten that looking bad in the mornings was a family thing, almost a competition.

"Good God! exclaimed their father, they look like two scruffy rag dolls; nothing to do with us I hope; call the staff and have them thrown out of the back door, into the rubbish bin or taken down to a charity shop."

Grunt, grunt; moan, moan.

"Good morning girls, coffee or juice."

Liz rang Andy at about twelve-ish. A young female voice answered. "Hello, can I help?" "Yes, my name is—-," "Ah! Is that Miss Cheng." "Nooo; as I was going to say, my name is Elizabeth Clements, I work with Professor Gould, would it be possible to speak to him."

"Yep, sure thing; Andy! Andy! Elizabeth Clements for you. She silently mouthed a sorry to Andy. I called her Miss Cheng."

Andy opened his eyes widely in horror as he came rushing forward and grabbed for the phone.

"Ooh! She must be important or very pretty", commented Sally, Andy's sister.

"Morning Liz; you ok. Look, I am sorry about last night, I just felt a little down and I guess a little drunk and threw up everywhere. I was forced to see another side of life last night. I felt stupid that I had not really thought about it properly before, seeing it from their point of view. It seems it's been really tough in the suburbs. What's it like where you are?"

"Well apart from no ham on the bone, butter or steak pie, all seems the same as ever. I am not going to look too close at anything Andy. Are you sure you're ok now? Have you been doing anything or seeing anyone special? Anyway, if you are ok, shall we just meet up as arranged?"

"That sounds good. I'm ok, honest. So, early Wednesday morning then Liz."

The next two days passed slowly for Liz, she self-indulged, eating, sitting and occasionally worrying about personal and work problems.

She found it increasingly impossible to deny the reality of her involvement in this massive global affair. She found herself sitting for hours at the computer desk, tucked away in her bedroom considering matters and alternative ways to overcome the issues both she and the rest of her world were battling. The initial pleasure of her home visit faded, as her family had to change and re-juggle their own arrangements; all their good intentions being put asunder. Of course, there was no escape from the task and ultimately, she was happy to stop fighting with the illusion of a holiday break and return to Kings where she could concentrate.

Over the same period, Andy received a number of calls from Yoko. Yes, they did discuss work but mainly their chatter drifted into personal areas. The talk between them was easy and comfortable. There never appeared any pressure, no awkward questions, particularly about Liz. Yoko had managed to leave Tuesday afternoon completely free; Mia was more than capable of dealing with any appointments or issues arising from the endless meetings she had been engaged in since being in the U.K.

"Andy, we must take advantage of tomorrow afternoon. We must spend some time together, just you and me, no world, no disasters and no science. Do you want to do this Andrew?" "Yoko, of course, I want to spend time with you, if fact more than anything else I can think of. We could do a real smart lunch, stroll across a park, visit a gallery, the Tate maybe or see a film. Whatever your hearts-desire." "I am really pleased you want to spend some time together. I can meet you under your Trafalgar Square Colum at one o'clock; is that good for you." "Yoko, that's wonderful, at one o'clock then tomorrow."

Andy found it necessary to close down the conversation with Yoko at that point being he was overtaken by boyish nervousness, moreover, not capable of generating any further worthwhile words. Once the phone was back upon the receiver, joy, excitement and anticipation filled his soul. He simply did not know how he would be capable of filling time before their meeting.

"Hi son, you look happy today. That's good to see."

Andy threw his arms around his mother and landed the biggest of kisses on her forehead. "I love you Mum."

—

England: The Queen Elizabeth II Conference Rooms in Parliament Square.

London, late November 2006:

Since the early part of the season, when the first wave of a pandemic had rushed across most of Southern England decimating so many of the population initially, then proceeded to reach out its terrifying arms over most of the southern half of the country and then the world in one of its many forms, people, agriculture and beasts.

London was affected in the extreme, and a new development had taken place within the city and surrounding suburbs. Bicycles and shoe leather were now employed like never before. Public transport was now viewed by many as a potential breeding ground for disease. Hence, the use was now reducing, all be it, for many, there was no other choice, work had to be carried out and money earnt. Thousands of bicycles had found their way onto the streets, together with a lot of that old world, shoe leather. Riders typically were masked, like most pedestrians. The route from the Savoy down the Strand and into Whitehall was often biked and predominantly taxied by officials. While the semi-empty pavements and numerous closed shops, restaurants and offices, and businesses generally, had succumbed to the lack of patrons and workers, now so many lay empty and boarded. When those changes first started it felt weird, now it was just normal, a little erry, but normal.

The London conference was to begin officially in two hours, Andy and Liz were keen to attend and meet the Brussels delegation in particular who had initiated this bizarre gathering, as well as the K.B.H.L., government side and officials who were still alive. Their findings from China were, yet, inconclusive but formed part of the wider jigsaw puzzle. From that muddle of endless facts and fiction, someone else might just manage to find significant links, which could grow and consolidated the picture. Likewise, what Liz and Andy might learn from other leading professionals reporting on studies of pandemics and epidemics from around the world might lead them all to cry 'Eureka'.

Whatever the rough plan, Andy's anti-establishment hackles were already up, having been told by Mike, *you need to be open, honest and polite to these guys from Brussels. No getting up tight or I won't be able to save you; they are on our side Andy!'* The use of those words sounded too much like his mother on a bad day, when he was trying to make a point about some view she had held forever, and, which he wanted her, to change to his views, but he knew she would never budge, not even, *'over her own dead body'*.

Andy was now a coiled spring before he had even left, let alone before entering the conference centre.

The route to the Queen Elizabeth II conference hall in Parliament Square, took them past Downing Street where the gates were closed and the main residences had been sealed off for some months, inside there was filtered air keeping the occupants as safe as possible – if indeed, the PM or anybody else was actually there. Round a virtually empty Parliament Square, the taxi joined a small queue of black cabs dropping off suited occupants at the entrance steps to the conference venue.

Lurking along the pavement in both directions, and in particular, around the main entrance, where the TV crews, press, photographers and the usual dross of paparazzi from around the world. God knows how they still managed to travel so widely and so freely but they did, and they were there in force.

So much so, that is was necessary to push and shove, then wiggle ones way towards the entrance doors. It was unpleasant and threatening, the thrusting hands, their eyes and ugly mouths, teeth, tongues, and spittle spraying at them. How could anybody expect a worthy comment under those conditions; anyway, there would obviously be a press conference once the talking was completed. A press conference where sensible questions and answers could be generated; maybe not all the answers they wanted but enough to fill most of their rubbish publications.

A few characters appeared particularly aggressive and pushy in their approach. Forcing themselves violently between other reporters, shoving microphones in faces, shouting out crazy questions. It was awful.

One character amongst the throng, a paparazzi type, was being uniquely forceful and obnoxious. Olive skinned with long dark hair. Repeatedly he forced himself in front of Liz and Andy. He was smallish, dark haired and tanned, possibly of Mediterranean origin. He continually shot his camera off at both of them and others arriving, whilst thrusting out handfuls of business cards. "Just take one Liz and keep moving, don't stop for god's sake or we'll never get through this mob. Where are the bloody police and security when you need them, this is ridiculous." Liz kept her head down, blond hair flowing to either side as she grabbed to Andys coat, she was scarred of these threatening and horrid people, and in reality, so was Andy.

They arrived at the entrance just as the security staff decided to attempt to do their job.

It was a big relieve to step through the revolving doors into peace and order and stand for a moment without being pushed and shoved. "Who was that strange long haired and annoying little man? I have not seen him before, and Jesus, if I had had a gun I would have shot him." "Here, you have his card Andy, looks as if he's an Italian; God, the Italian paparazzi have to be the worst." "Liz, I hate them all, thank goodness we're not pop stars." "You are Andrew." "Shut-up and get in there you; hey, I've heard of this guy, well, I've read one of his articles anyway, conspiracy theorist stuff; possibly an interesting man this Mr Luigi Maroni, or alternatively and more likely, a complete nutter, whatever, he was very annoying."

Once inside, Andy and Liz took a deep breath and joined a gaggle of people waiting for security checks, and to pick up name badges from a table set just inside the entrance. However, there were few badges left on the table, which was strange, and only a handful of individuals appeared to be visible within the hall.

"I thought this was a bigger event," Andy said, looking around the open and empty hall.

"Are we too early or too late?" Liz offered a quizzical knowing look that said she did not really have any idea. "Here's your badge." She offered him his nametag, changing her mind she attached to his jacket, and then tugged on his sleeve gently while unobtrusively, pointing with her other hand to a name badge still on the table.

"Jim's going to be here", she smiled, referring to Jim Stapleton's named on the table. Jim, he was from the US Centre for Disease Control and Prevention, the CDC. His team had been in constant touch with Andy's lab since the first weeks of the outbreak. They had also co-ordinated with the World Health Organisation/W.H.O. in Geneva and New York. However, even these two organisations were calling on all comers for help. It had been a little-known D.G. department in Brussels that had raised its head apparently, 'ordering', all E.U. countries to send participants and supposedly requesting input from teams in other parts of the world, obviously not all had responded, probably most were far too busy.

Over load and under staffing was a big reality these days.

Somehow, Andy thought, there just did not seem to be enough people here, or enough nationalities, to support the content of the conference invitation or their instruction they had received to attend the conference – 'Research teams from across the world will offer their latest findings'. It was clear to Andy that only certain regions were represented, and that fact alone made him rather suspicious for some reason, yet it could also be beneficial leaving far more time to speak one to one with important colleagues.

They moved forward forgetting their suspicions for a moment, towards a second barrier and the serious security. Then were both totally scanned, searched, photographed and then their identities double-checked thoroughly before they entered the main area. Immediately and naturally, eyes searched around for familiar faces. Eyes meet eyes that were not known; eyes meet eyes that were slightly familiar, then Liz was first to spot the grey suit standing next to a tall gentleman in a finely cut cream suit, his silver-grey cravat matching his perfect hair, perfectly. His dark grey shoes and shirt finishing a perfect presentation. Liz suddenly realised, that this was the person who had attended at the last Whitehall meeting, together with an unknown woman.

Nudging Andy and keeping her voice down, "Andy, look who is over here to your right." He turned his look in that direction. "Look who is just behind them; Yoko and her team talking to Jim's group and straight on is Maddo Usta; now I wasn't expecting him to appear. It's beginning to look a lot more interesting Liz, so let's keep our heads down for a moment before too many people notice us and grab a coffee while we survey the scene." "Ok, but don't you want to talk to Yoko." "No Liz. Not yet." "You sure about that." "No. Not yet anyway Liz." "Coffee, come on."

So, heads down, they ploughed their way to a coffee bar and more by luck than judgement found a small table at the extreme edge of the seating area and partly concealed by information boards. They managed to win themselves about fifteen minutes observation before the grey suit spotted them; raising a finger to his conversation group indicating a pause, he moved towards them, stopping at their table with a slight bow. "Elizabeth Clements, what a nice surprise. Professor Gould, a pleasure always. Please could you join our group; I'd like to introduce you to the Brussels delegation, some of whom I guess you know, and probably know well of course. First of course, please finish your coffee and then pop over when you are ready." He bowed again and re-joined the group. "Strewth! Old Brandon Moss-Smith is in full flow; never saw him as a creep." "He's ok Andy, anyway it doesn't matter, and he is just doing his job the same as we are. He is not looking any better, is he? He's going to have a heart attack real soon, I'm telling you."

"Can't be too soon for me, he is but a *cheeky-creepy-bugger*. Come on you, let's start working."

They weaved their way towards the group from Brussels as requested.

"Ah! Professor Gould and Clements good to see you; please let me introduce you all.

Firstly, this is Professor Michael Raimondi, Head of Biological Studies for the EU. An Italian name but a very English heritage. Is that not correct Michael?"

"Brandon, you're on the button as usual; being we know one another, please call me Michael Professors."

"Likewise, please. Liz and Andy."

"Thank you. I have read with interest the recent paper published by yourselves and Professor Cheng. Have you more to report to us here." Liz stepped up with the answer. "We have indeed Michael, a very serious extension to the events we are enduring."

A pause occurred. Brandon Moss-Smith interrupted; "May I firstly continue with the introductions ladies and gentleman."

"Brandon, being there are so many of us may I suggest we will have another occasion. My apologise everyone but I am going to steal these two-good people for ten minutes of their valuable time. We will all gather later." With that Michael Raimondi, with an arm around both Andy and Liz lead them away to a quiet corner to continue quizzing them. While Andy went to the coffee bar, Liz and Michael Raimondi made small talk. Liz speaking of her recent visit to home and Michael revealing some of his recent past.

Of particular interest to Liz was Michaels chat about his father who had worked years earlier with viral mutations, ciaos and random theories. "Liz, I never knew my father or mother personally but luckily I have discovered a great deal about them and I discovered that I like them and become very proud of what I discovered. What I am most proud off is this little book; have you ever come across it."

He took a small book from his pocket, it was titled, "The Extensions of Random and Ciaos Trends" and sub-titled, (*The Butterfly Effect & the Future*) by Professor Carl Johnson.

Liz starred at the cover and title. "No, I haven't Michael. That is quiet some title for such a small book. Is it written by your father?"

"No, a Swedish academic. He translated the data from some projects my father was working on back in the sixties. They were both colleagues and indeed great friends. Strangely, this is a little work of scientific genius and it is stupidly still a band book in the UK, not due to the contents these days but incompetence. The intro explains all. I will see you and Andy have a copy each. It is very relevant to our current problems I believe, I am sure you will find it most enlightening. - - -

Ah, coffee, thank you Andy."

"Have you bought Michael upto speed Liz?" "Actually no, we've been small talking I'm afraid. Michael, from our last paper you may have picked up upon the conclusions to date and the necessary follow up of the marine sampling. Well that has moved ahead, obviously not yet complete and will not be for quite some time but the results received to date do not clearly indicate that there is a new pollution issue in our seas as far as we can determine, yet there are clear reasons to believe we are moving in the right direction. We are reluctant to say that, but circumstances demand that all current information is laid upon the table so to speak. We should have picked up clear signs of changed or infected spores and microbes but upto now, we have not found anything conclusive. That in its self creates a large question mark; therefore, we are instructing all to carry out deeper and wider sampling, as is Professor Cheng. We have set up and organised thirty new departments globally with those particular areas of responsibility. Then any results will be made available on an international base of course. All this has already been agreed I understand."

Michael Raimondi sat for a moment to clarify his own thoughts.

"Ok you two, I have heard or read most off what you've been saying and I am aware my own people are participating and supporting your efforts where they can. In honesty, one cannot keep abreast of all that is going on, far too many theories being explored and dare I say, 'a lot of rubbish'. I can only but "try and rely", as the saying goes. What really appears important is the across species development and mutation rates, that did indeed stick in my thoughts as no doubt it did all that read that report. Is there anything further you can tell about this particular aspect as it is of particular interest to me due to my father's work in those areas?"

—

Africa: Over Zambia:

Craven was tired, but he knew he had to keep focus. His cargo kept him partly alert but the caffeine pills and coca cola did the rest, those along with the occasional rift on the harp.

He checked his instruments and heading, looked at his flight plan and kneepad map and gave a cursory glance out his side window. His eyes were sore but he was convinced by the landscape that he was spot on for a "direct hit" when the time came. He should reach his destination as the daytime slipped away. He had definite need of the laser illumination from his ground support.

"He'd better be there," he thought. The glass occupants rattled in agreement, as the little plane hit more turbulence.

Below, he saw herds of antelope dashing across the open ground, and a lush green landscape for as far as he could see. He thought of his plan. The Plan, not his. He had thought about it a good deal and what he knew caused him concern. However, he had not been in this type of clandestine work for his conscience. Nevertheless, this was also the end of his career and time for thinking was growing much longer. He watched the scene below and it mesmerised him. His cursory glance had turned into one prolonged stare.

The beautiful vista, eliminating "undesirable" population segments, and how he would escape, were just some of the ingredients of the conflict inside his head. Would he be able to escape and had they told him everything about his cargo and the effect it would have? Had they hell. All he knew was that this part of a plan to eliminate "undesirable" population segments was supposed to contribute towards creating a 'new world order'. An 'order' that, his directors assured him, was being initiated by a silent - not secret -

multilateral initiative with invisible sign-up - no traceable signatures - by almost every nation, or at least a 'representative' of every nation - even if that 'representative' was not representative of the existing governments and populations. "God alone knows what's going on", Craven shook his head as he thought. An uncomfortable stirring filled his body and soul, if indeed he had one. "What the hell am I doing? My whole dam life. Crazy things. Adrenaline. On the edge. Whose edge? Always someone else with a pay cheque for me. And now the final edge. However, something is *out-of-whack* here. I am too close to this edge to pull back from it or maybe even to be able to use the cheque. Christ!" His thoughts were jumbled but loud inside his head. Some even found their way to his lips as he flew the little Cessna in circles, indecisive as to what to do next. He pushed the harp from his mouth. Execute the plan, meet with Tranter, probably die, or abort, and get to the bottom of this whole mess and turn the meaning of his whole life round in one fell swoop? Save the world, even?'

"Now there's an adrenaline-rush swansong, if ever there was one", he chuckled to himself with a newfound inner contentment, though he knew any change of plan might not sit too well with his co-worker.

—

Taiwan-China: December 2006:

At a manufacturing facility deep in the heart of China (Taiwan), rubber and plastics were used to make a variety of children's toys and baby products. Unknown to the plant management, the line producing "dummies" had been interfered with, by an agent of evil intent. The constituents of the rubber nipple now included something else. Something sinister. Something unseen. Something that would tear the heart out of any family with a new-born infant or toddler who should use one of these dummies once they were shipped.

As they rolled off the production line, each was packed into clear plastic wrapping, then boxed by the thousands, which were then sealed and stamped with its destination, to be shipped very shortly to all points of the compass. The company prided itself on its global reach.

—

Germany, Late 2006:

On the banks of the Rhine in southern Germany, the massive complex of an international pharmaceutical company sat imposing its presence across the surrounding countryside. Its huge logo emblazoned on the side of most of the buildings was a recognised sign of long-standing quality and reliability.

Both old and new drugs entered the distribution chain daily. Here, inside this highly securitised campus, something had gone wrong. Unseen, one of the most widely used lines had had an ingredient added. Millions upon millions of little pills destined for probably the most widespread use in the world were being packaged and boxed. Low dosage Aspirin was not something most people worried about when taking.

—

Africa, Late 2006:

As the Cessna flew through the morning, Craven watched the sunrise, giving him a better sight of the wonders below. He saw the blues of the morning sky deepen as the minutes passed. He flew along with flocks of birds, storks and egrets; he thought he had seen them on the television. He watched as vultures circled, tens of them intent on something tasty below. A living thing that had not made it through the night, but that was, this morning, a life-giving breakfast for these hungry birds. He circled with them and smiled. Nature is a wonderful, wonderful mother; his thoughts were deep, very deep.

As the sun rose, so did the temperature inside the cockpit. Beads of sweat formed on his forehead and top lip. Craven opened the side window and then looked at his instruments. "Where the hell am I? Sitting over northern Mozambique, maybe near Malawi's border," he thought. He had a long way to go to reach Mongu. He had to cross the whole of Zambia to get to his final destination. He popped a caffeine pill and opened a sandwich that sat on the co-pilot's seat.

Not far south, towards Zimbabwe, the horizon was dark with storm clouds; dark streaks earthwards told of torrential, life-giving downpours across the parched land.

What an amazing continent! In addition, he had only traversed one country so far. Madagascar had been something, although from the air he had seen the wanton destruction of that island nation's natural habitat. So much forest cleared to make money. He would read somewhere that around three quarters of the island had already been laid bare. Trees gone, species gone. "Man gone fucking crazy", he scolded the world, and himself for being part of it.

Below him now, the vastness, the richness amazed him. He knew his flight path and altitude had to be spot on to avoid attracting undue attention other than the Air Traffic Controllers that expected him from their radars. He wanted to get closer to the sights on the ground. He smiled to himself again; this smile was becoming a habit now. He felt good. He thought of the plan and the tasks that, until now, he had taken for granted lay ahead, and said aloud, "Fuck it!" He turned the plane gently. The Cessna slid effortlessly out of the sky. Craven didn't forget at any stage to treat his cargo with the greatest respect. Fragile, delicate passengers. Slowly, the plane descended and soon he was flying 50 feet above the treetops. This was a once-in-a-lifetime experience that he'd like to repeat under different circumstances. He had never travelled Africa, and he wanted to enjoy it. "En route to Mongu?" he considered the thought and smiled at the alternative, "I think I'm on the bloody Road to Damascus!"

—

Brussels-Belguim. Late 2006:

The oak-panelled room, dressed in fine tapestries, satin covered furniture and priceless porcelain, stretched before the three men as they entered through a heavy oak door, carved with coats of arms and emblems representing past occupancy of the chateau. At the far end of the room, four other men stood informally in the bay of a floor-to-ceiling window, looking out across a gloriously landscaped garden, which then overlooked Lake Geneva. One of the four, a tall distinguished man in his 70s, with silvered, thinning hair, a long face and fine Romanesque nose, stepped forward to greet the three.

"Gentlemen, how are you all? Welcome. We are very excited to hear what the latest developments are and how plans are progressing. You all know each other so introductions are unnecessary. For my part, I should like to get right down to hearing what you have to report," his perfect English was soaked in a rich French accent, which leant a sophisticated, controlling air to the gathering.

A shorter, strong looking, elderly American, one of the four, interjected, "Yes, I want to hear what's what right away." It was his attempt to stamp some of his own authority on the proceedings.

The seven men took their places around a large, beautifully inlaid, round table surrounded by at least ten ornate, high-backed chairs.

"Some of our number are unable to be with us on this occasion", one of the four, a younger, square-faced, dark-haired German in his sixties, added in faultless English.

One of the three late arrivals, an Italian in his fifties with dark circles under his eyes and a greying moustache, had bought an attaché case with him, which he laid upon the table in front of him as he sat down. He entered two separate codes, unlocking the case, opened it fully to withdraw several brown folders, and placed the case on the floor beside him. He took the top folder and placed it squarely to his front on the table. Then he looked up and around at his colleagues.

"Shall we begin?" He looked at each of the seated men. All bowed their heads slightly and similarly to the left, in cult-like agreement.

"Gentlemen, I shall recap priority details. Our function here is to think-tank possible flaws in our plans and procedures target the means and areas of improvement plus outline further new disasters that we consider appropriate and how they may be handled to the advantage of us all and the stability of the world."

"Firstly; the United Kingdom; there is still no clarity in Whitehall how the initiation was implemented, and that is a great credit to the operation. The spread, as predicted, has included Scandinavia and Asia; numbers still not confirmable but believed by unilateral opinion to have reached the thirty-plus million mark, obviously there is still some way to go.

Our information sources indicate that a boomerang effect is imminent from China.

As you are aware, there are a number of predictable side effects, which have begun.

We will discuss this further.

Africa is then our next area of concern and once again, we will cover this in more detail, hopefully a report will be delivered to us here while we deliberate.

From there on gentlemen - well, who knows! We are all aware of the possibilities, you have the files, we have clear plans to be activated but we'll deal with one issue at a time."

He paused, in a practised manor, which even had effect within this gathering.

"It is necessary that right here I must change directions for one moment."

There was a second, when time hung but only a little.

"Antonio", he said looking directly across the splendid table into the eyes of his colleague, "there is one file here that I believe you have not seen. Please look at this report briefly."

"Cee, why am d only one not to av seen dis report." Then he paused and looked around at the others gathered. There was an awkwardness.

"Thi is not d way we av agreed, al shod be equal."

There was a longer and more complete silence.

Antonio Galabri slowly opened the file lying before him.

Antonio's mind quickly linked the information, which lay upon the enclosed pages, and he now understood, as did his colleagues.

He was aware of the tension, of menace, but was not sure yet whether it lay within himself or the whole gathering. All others at the table attempting to retained an air of dignity. Business and protocol needed to be maintained, but not at any cost.

Suddenly from outside the heavy oak doors staff heard raised voices, whilst as pre-arranged, two giant sized gentlemen entered the room and stood patiently just inside the doorway.

Within the room, some even raised themselves from their seats, fingers being pointed to support the angry words.

These were unheard of happenings, this should never have occurred, not at this table, yet it did.

The problem was resolved by an imperceptible nod. The table spaces were then re-adjusted, whilst one person continued his ranting. He would never be seen again. His empire broken into hundreds of smaller units and dispersed.

These were six men of great power, great wealth, and position. Respected internationally, they advised and walked with governments and presidents, when they chose. They only spoke in billions; whatever the commodity, flesh, grain, pork bellies, countries and governments; nothing phased these people.

For once, this particular group was now working with one common and earnest desire. Control, maintaining that control and increasing their financial hold over the worlds finances. For their desires to be fulfilled the world must borrow money and indeed they achieved that goal but there was a limit and balance on money lent and repayment. That side of the sum had been going badly wrong for some time. Locally induced recessions had not solved the overall picture, neither had the international events that they had orchestrated. Drastic actions had been called for and regardless, now was the time and situation they had been patiently awaiting, and it was happening. It was a perfect timing, confusion and diffusion was to cover, and aid their selfish actions, which they had deduced were essential for themselves and the world.

Discussion and deliberation continued in earnest for a further three hours.

A pause for refreshment was then called for.

Six distinguished men only retired to the open balcony and there they spoke of investment and the changing of governments and that conversation was mixed with polite small talk about wives, children, and cricket.

—

Africa. Late 2006:

O ver Zambia, Damascus grew in its attractiveness. Craven was on a new and momentary high. He continued to indulge in the wonder of Africa, his little Cessna skipped happily over risings that scattered the landscape below. Enthusiastically he returned to his harp, blasting out rhythms and tunes that seemed to blend with his growingly erratic passes over clumps of vegetation or herds of Zebra and Wilder beast.

He broke his rhythm occasionally and burst into vocals, loud shouting vocals not at all in character with the self-image he knew. He did not know whether he was having fun or not but without thinking, continued generally on his course.

In this strange and confused state of mind, he had not seen the dark and ominous storm clouds rolling and tumbling, even jumping towards his location, almost targeting him alone. The landscape around him grew suddenly very dark and then a loud 'Booming Crack' filled every part of his existence and shook him, the Cessna and the cargo.

My God! He cried aloud as the little plane shook violently. The combined noises from within, together with additional creeks and groans, filling his ears momentary to bursting point.

His instinctive reactions took over, he swept upwards and westerly, it looked the only route to safety but this time he did not think of Damascus.

He was too low, far too low. "Come on girl take me out of here, steady now, steady."

He had no time to consider his cargo. Large splats of water were now hitting his screen, increasing by the second, bigger, faster and quicker.

The little lady was doing her best but she was being swept violently one way then the other, being sucked upwards and dropped again like a baby, then again battling to regain height. Like a cork in the southern seas, he was tossed and dropped repeatedly. It was almost impossible to view anything in the distance, but a short while ago he had been looking down upon the most beautiful panorama, the Zambezi running along on his left glittering and sparkling in sunlight. Now Craven was under server pressure, working on those pure instincts, whilst fear and menace grew within him. For all his experience, he had never quite been in this deep before.

His brow oozed, his whole body was drenched, and he was drowning in humidity. On his small but normally adequate control panel, dials swung and jumped, condensation covered everything, and the noise level was now doubled by the accompanying torrents beating against the outer-skin and that deafened him totally.

Then the largest '*Crack-Boom*' he had ever experienced, engulfed and swallowed him.

"This is it, this is it, he thought over and over again or was he speaking out loud, he had no idea, thoughts, words and actions were inter-tangled; it wasn't important, "fucking Damascus, you arse-hole Craven."

All went black. All went silent. All appeared still.

Floating in warm fluid, just drifting, gently drifting, downward, and downward.

Then suddenly he was back again, fighting harder than ever now.

"Shit, I want that road to Damascus. Jesus Christ girl get me out of here."

'Boom-Crack' again and once more he lost consciousness. Time was nothingness, warm fluid and drifting were his companions for a second or two once more. He could feel the little Cessna sinking and rapidly losing height again, *"Oh please no, not fucking now."* Then she took a gentle and unexpected rise, he could just see before him some low outcrops, also some great pillars of rock protruding skywards like sentries along the ridge, "we can't do this, no, no, get the fuck up you bastard bloody stupid thing."

Boom-Crack struck him for the third time, yet again he experienced an out of body happening.

As he regained his senses, the little Cessna stood face to face with a forty-million-year-old sentry of rock. It would not be an equal battle. The stick had never been pulled back so far; Craven's will was employed as never before, he was not willing to give away his life without yet another fight. He urged and nudged the front up, the rear down; he pulled and lifted the Cessna by the joy stick and then as if a miracle was happening the noise began to lift a little and then by but an inch or two left a million tons of granite behind.

Before him, a clear sky, below him the most wonderful sight he had ever seen the gates of Eden. A deep and expansive green valley spread before him which he and the Cessna, together with his fragile cargo, drifted into as if nothing had happened; it was dreamlike; maybe God was showing the way after all.

For a few moments, he sat; no blues harp, no singing. "Craven boy, you shouldn't be here; you smooth and lucky old bastard." He lent forward and checked the instrumentation, fuel was low and not everything was working but enough.

He checked his bearings as best he could and glanced at maps "Blimey, not that far off course either." He stretched his body as far as he could several times, his saturated clothing clinging uncomfortably, his fingers felt tingly but so did his head and legs, 'to be expected he thought, that's a fair exchange'.

"Christ the time, what is the bloody time." He tapped hard on the cockpit clock face, nothing. He tried several times with the same result.

That particular part of his world had stopped functioning, he lent across to his old spare jacket of many pockets, which he always took with him to check for a spare watch. As he did, so his peripheral vision was brought into awareness, he turned to look more directly and noticed a whitish green haze filling the rear of the cabin and ominously creeping and rolling along the floor towards the cockpit. Panic again grabbed him firmly, very firmly. He froze for a split second or two, "bloody, bloody bollocks" but his momentary fear was of no importance.

Damascus was not to be for Craven.

As he leapt for his life, he must have noticed the long trailing greeny white cloud across the skies of Zambia behind the Cessna.

Technology then came into play with the remaining high-octane fuel; a final Boom-Crack was Cravens last experience; God had little to do with it.

The greenish white cloud converted into a mushroom of disaster and the seeds of doom were planted for thousands, if not millions of lives, innocent or not.

Craven was but particles, his mission inadvertently completed, off target and somewhere between Kabwe and Lusaka. For somebody non-the-less it represented a partial success. A full-blooded warning, of things to come and who was in charge.

—

Brussels-Belguim: Late 2006:

A small note was passed. Then a silvery-grey-haired man in his seventies with a rich French accent spoke in near perfect English to the group of five gathered before him,

"I apologise but I must again interrupt gentlemen to inform you that in Zambia we now have the beginnings of one of the African incidents. He paused for effect. Very shortly gentleman, I imagine there will be many small beginnings. We do have, and will have much to deal with, actually, we may well have to save the world and indeed, we shall. Let us take a celebratory break gentlemen, I think phones will be ringing shortly."

Around the table, heads nodded in agreement and recognition, together with smiles of self-satisfaction, and with the future and justice served.

–

Italy. Late 2006:

A ntonio Galabri had been one of a very exclusive number, a small number. In Italy, in his home town of Milan he lived out his particular life style behind the most extensive security. In principal, he was able to protect himself and his family, together with his key staff from even the most severe of nuclear attacks but was unable to prolong his existence after greed and dis-honour occurred against his own kind was revealed.

Unknown to Antonio Galabri, his activities had attracted the interest of a young investigative reporter Luigi Maroni. Luigi had followed his life and work throughout Italy, the European Community and globally. His many positions within government; within governments of opposite conviction. His activities at Brussels. His acquisitions, his wealth and his associates. This had been Luigi's hobby in life for the last seven years; there was a lot he had not discovered but an enormous amount he had. Now something was changing in his life routines, his activities and indeed, where he was right now. It did not feel right to Luigi, he needed an update on this most intriguing of hobbies.

Luigi burnt the mid-night oil. E-mails were dispatched to colleagues everywhere, to associates of Antonio's, in his many companies, his known enemies, distant family and defunct friendships of which there were many. Not every communication would arrive these days but volume and persistence normally produced results.

He personally waited outside known meeting places and restaurants; he spoke to waiters, gardeners and delivery people.

He would not be beaten. He did not like the subject of his hobby, Señor Antonio Galabri. He considered him evil, corrupt and in particular, a blasphemer.

He was not the only person in the world with a dangerous hobby; at least ultimately, the work on his hobby was for God and may be of interest or use to others. Indeed, it could present him with the scoop he had always dreamed of; that he deserved so much.

A little status, and a lot of cash, would go down very well, yes, very well indeed. His local church could do with some refurbishment. They would be very impressed with that new roof and in time appreciate his gifts and contributions.

Luigi continued his efforts, collecting and collating, slowly linking all that arrived at his desk. He worked alone, communicated via several non-deplumes; linked and looped his telecommunication equipment and used family addresses and those of abandoned houses or at post offices.

With his day job and his all-involving hobby, he had no time for real friendships, what indeed was the point; they either died or moved away; at least Jesus was always with him. Of course, he was a normal and reasonable man and conversed with work colleagues, when necessary, even occasionally presented a smile but the conversation was always about matters he could not affect, in reality, wasted effort, paper filling and hot air. At least with such a hobby as he had, he may be able to change something for somebody; yes, it all made good sense and would ashore his place on high when his time came.

—

Africa. Late 2006:

In Mongu, the field station was a hive of activity since the outbreak of disease a week ago on the border with Malawi. Towns and villages had, according to scant news reports and word of mouth from fleeing villagers already been decimated by an incredibly virulent disease.

At first, the Mongu team treated the situation on their own doorstep as they had previous outbreaks of Ebola, and that was exactly what they thought they were dealing with. For the moment, they had no suspicion there was any link with what was happening in the rest of the world. Indeed, the pandemic that was actually taking place; no proof of it being orchestrated by "dark forces". Those cloak and dagger affiliations that had once been described by a certain European head of state.

"We have had a communiqué from Lusaka who have been in constant touch with officials in Lilongwe, asking that we send a team of at least three to a rendezvous with ministry biohazard officials in Zooboo. From there we will move closer to the border and need to don full protective gear to the affected border region with detection equipment that has been provided by the German Government," Churchill said matter of factually.

"That's gonna be one hell of a drive. Why not someone closer?" asked Muggins.

"Cause we're the best and because it's highly unlikely that any wind-borne contamination has reached anywhere near Mongu, it's all about prevailing winds and weather fronts. However, it might have already moved west from the border, we should do our own research and rapidly.

Apparently, the Germans have provided detection equipment that will register several of our typical pathogens and provide results in hours. I think it's a lab on wheels they use in military situations," said Winston holding the communiqué without looking at it once.

"What else does it say? Looks like more detailed than you've told us?"

"Well, not a problem. It just says "it is recommended that the most experienced staff make up your recon team and observe the highest levels of Level 4 biohazard procedures and precautions at all times. We cannot stress enough the dangers faced on this undertaking. That is pretty much it, apart from the last point, which amazes me, but then who knows what is written between the lines. It says, 'we must try to determine if this situation has arisen as a result of natural causes or has possible connections with the arrival of a pathogen from the outside.' If the latter is indicated then establishing the exact nature of the pathogen and its similarity to the pathogen driving the pandemics in the rest of the world, this is of paramount importance". "So, guys, we're really suddenly in the thick of it and what 'it' is exactly, is anyone's guess", Winston sighed and sat down.

"OK, well let's take stock of what we know and not do anything in haste. Got to plan properly with the small amount of the information we have – piss poor preparation and planning produces piss poor results!" "Winston", Muggins said with authority beyond his station, but if it comes from outside it would indicate something very dark, surely that would be the case. The world would, unknowingly be counting on us.

Tranter had sat on some rocks some way outside Mongu, shaded by an acacia tree of some sorts. From his vantage point, he could see all the comings and goings at the field station through his high-power binoculars, the full house to-n-throwing, even behind the windows. He could see the whole eastern horizon, the wide-open sky and the vast country reaching away from the town, which he was sure he was far enough away from to give him an adequate chance of escape without contamination being the prevailing winds did not change direction and historically, that did not happen.

He watched and waited, expecting to hear the plane before it came into view. Unfortunately, as the sun rose higher, Craven's arrival time came and went. Tranter was obviously in no hurry. So, no panic, now he had time to consider his surroundings, his escape route, and his near future moments and the luxurious days that would follow. He had already dug a hole beside a large rock into which he would drop the laser target marker he cradled in his arms waiting for the arrival of the pilotless, laser-guided aircraft with its surprise package. Some villagers walked with goats some 50 yards away and waved at him thinking him to be one of the few white tourists travelling the roads of Zambia. He waved back without overdoing it. He did not want to encourage a visit to his position.

Sweat poured down his temples from under his hat. He wiped his eyes with his hand and shifted his bum that had gone to sleep.

Suddenly, he heard a sound in the air, a sound not from the sky but of running and shouting, goats bleating and the same villagers who had just past him were now running back the way they'd come waving hands in the air in a maniacal format of sweeps and gestures of madmen. Then he saw it. A swarm of bees rolling across the hillside behind him, towards not only the villagers but also making a beeline straight for Tranter, the swarm was so massive; he was only faced by the left flank of the insects. Before he had even had a chance to consider what to do they were on him, inside his shirt, in his mouth, ears, up his shorts and covering his naked knees and calves. His screams were piercing and horrific as hundreds of honey bees stung his flesh, the barbed stings impossible to remove with a simple uncoordinated swipe if a hand. He was running. He had dropped the target marker and his backpack remained beneath the tree. He was running in the same direction as the villagers not knowing what the hell to do and not even thinking. He was dying as he ran and he knew it. All he could think of was the field station, get to that field station and that is just what he managed to do.

The first thing Winston and the others heard were the screams and shouts of villagers as they ran into town warning folks best they could of the impending arrival of the swarm. They had done this before many times and generally, the scientists were un-phased and simply pulled the windows and doors closed. Then Muggins shouted.

"Hey, look at the size of this swarm, it's incredible and there's someone running this way and from the looks of it they've already covered him. My god they're coming straight for the front door." The dark shadowy figure was unclear. Man or woman, black or white. Nothing could be seen clearly. But they opened the outer door and kept the inner door closed. Bruce put on a protective suit as quick as he was able and as the stranger staggered into the sanctuary he was waiting for him with a dust/smoke spray they knew worked. The noise of the swarm on the outside of the building was like monsoon rain, deafening, but slowly the bees retreated. The stranger lay in obvious pain, kicking and shouting, but was eventually bee free and in a bad, bad way.

They took him into the station once it was safe and gave him an immediate anti-histamine injection followed by anti-histamine cream all over his body. They had removed his clothing and slowly but surely Tranter through exhaustion and drugs relaxed and began to breathe a little more normally. He seemed to be out of danger for a moment but God had not yet, claimed his dues. He once again descended into shock and God paid him back in full. Nothing would be found of those responsible for so much death and disaster apart from some strange equipment and a dissert backpack, which reviled no information, and was soon to be distributed amongst the local children for games of fun and adventure.

The swarming had been exceptional, so was the intuition of the bees sensing a miss-hap, something of danger, something to threaten their world.

Slowly the invisible death slid away from Mongu leaving behind its awful disaster and creeping with the aid of local wind currents towards devouring and destroying village after village and town after town.

—

Taiwan – China. Early 2007:

Around the globe, exports and imports still happened, just a lot less. Just a lot slower than before the world of politics and science had been pushed to the edge of disaster.

In the busy port of Chilung in northern Taiwan, men scurried to and throw, doing the best they could to fulfil the hungry demands of a struggling world.

At six o'clock on a misty and grey morning, vehicles were beginning to move, rusty cranes beginning to swing, grunt and lift. Voices shouted instruction through megaphones across an iron, concrete and watery world.

Collars stood up high against a chilly breeze from seaward, caps were pulled down tight; backs hunched and gloved hands smacked together. The instructions, often not reaching those intended due to the groans and screeching of metal against metal.

Most consignments arrived eventually at the correct dock and likewise at the correct far off distant shores.

Today was a little different. Not many knew it was but history in the making, and that later the world would be informing them of that fact.

Sixty-two great containers standing silently awaiting movement. Great steel boxes of death; some faded orange, some yellow or rusty-red. From a distance, they could look attractive, close up, simply lumps of functional metal. The forty footers were packed to capacity with rubber and plastic goods; all intended to service the needs of the world but within some of those great iron boxes was sure death on a massive scale and sorrow beyond believe.

As America lay sleeping in relative comfort it had no idea, it was to join the rest of the world on its run in with evil and great disaster. It's relative isolation and its position as a world base of wealth and power had to date protected it to some degree and although it's efforts in supporting Europe and Asia were admiral, plus it's security excellent; there was possibly no avoiding the oncoming planned disaster.

The sea lapped against "The Huang He" as she slowly moved with the force of the tide while taking on board her deadly cargo.

Once loaded, she would be taking her time dropping off the cargo. The captain and most of the crew knew nothing of their place in history. The paperwork was now in charge, allocating a deadly surprise for many communities and countries on route to the U.S.A., the bulk of her cargo was strictly allocated to those two end ports of call.

Even while the 'Huang He' sailed forward on a lonely and empty sea, the paperwork was changing and the final distribution details being organised. The want to satisfy and respond rapidly, or not, was so much in the favour of deceit and deception and that would be employed in the most deadly and effective ways.

—

London & United Nations. February 2007:

One o'clock on Wednesday appeared amazingly quickly for Andy. He was in a strange mood and an even stranger mental place. He stood at the foot of Nelson's column seeing himself apart from reality, as in a dated black and white movie.

Before leaving for his ronde view with Yoko, he had changed clothing three times, dowsed himself with deodorant and aftershave, and cleaned his teeth four times including an endless gargle each time. He certainly was excited and nervous, yet did not really know what the hell he was playing at. The professional side of his nature was edging him further into a situation, that in some ways he had created. *'Was this just escapism, love, or infatuation'.* Under the current circumstances, his head should be where it was before ever meeting Yoko. How strange life was, the moment you thought you were in control, that you had the measure of the things in your life, you were instead lost within self-indulgency and arrogance. Life then had the obligation to punish you in one form or the other. As he stood pondering the conflicting thoughts, Liz's image was constantly there, wounded and terribly hurt. He could not stand that thought and yet the thought of Yoko certainly filled one part of him. He juggled his desires, love and commitment and ended up staring at Yoko's ankles and then her beautiful shoulders, her eyes. Her way of being with him was so very natural, as if they had known one another for years and yet, so were the ways of Liz. He knew he could not and would not resolve the matter and decided that just maybe, he didn't need to. "Yoko, how wonderful you look." They embrace each other with obvious wanton passion and then strolled across an almost empty Trafalgar square arm in arm towards the beginning of the arranged afternoon events. Neither spoke of work or the solutions to world problems, science or commitment to the problems in hand. They ate, made love in the pre-arranged hotel, and spoke of gentle things, poetry, childhoods and families. There was laughter and fun. They made loose plans and without pain or conflict expressed their confusion about how they felt and about others in their lives. It was beautiful, honest, open and easy. Somehow, they would find a way to be together.

On Wednesday morning, Andy sat in room four at the Kings College labs, looking somewhat dishevelled and awaiting Liz to appear from the women's dorms on the other side of the complex. He had spoken to others from very early that morning and generally found himself back in the right sort of place mentally to continuing for filling his function in life. The four cups of strong, thick expresso were doing their job.

Liz arrived in a flurry, scarf flowing, hat pulled down so far, she could only just about see where she was going. "My god, it's dam cold out there Gould." She buzzed over to where Andy sat and threw both arms around him and then kissed his cheek tenderly. "You feel ready for the action?" "Err, I think so. I've been having some serious thoughts pop into my head." "Likewise. In a nutshell, this is it; massive growth rates and subsequent rapid mutations, each seemingly affecting different organisms, the life span of each is relatively short. Maybe we are looking at something very different here, possibly a transfer between organisms. At what stage and how does it initiate, plus there appears to be this other international involvement as we know, maybe terrorism of some kind, a quest for domination by possibly America, China or Russia for example, or *a-l-i-e-n-s*. I know that is being dealt with by the right people and it is not now our concern, but by god, it still pushes into the overall picture and confuses; it is really annoying. It simply does

not fit the profile of what is occurring; there is something real evil
lurking behind the scene! I think we are still allowing ourselves to be
hassled and confused by this, and our own historical experiences into
considering this issue as *one happening*, maybe it is and there is a lot
of work to do still but suddenly I'm not so sure any of us are focusing
on the reality of the situation. Are we certain that we are looking at a
pandemic that started at Kings? Sometimes I think these evil forces
created the whole dam nightmare. All of us have been driving on the
same side of the road." "Mmm! That is quiet some question Andy. I
have struggled with the, *'it doesn't fit and doesn't fly'*, regardless of all
the thinking and research, but have not been brave enough, or clear
enough to say that out loud as yet." They both sat staring at the floor
in thought. "Liz, this isn't about you or I doing research any more,
this is about thinking out of the box, pushing the joy stick in the
other direction and going around the sun rather than living on a flat
earth where Gods may strike you down asunder."

"Ok Andy Gould, let's run with this for a while. Some folks are
not going to be happy when they find out about these thoughts."
"They won't find out Liz, the only other person I am inclined to
speak to is Yoko and she's sound." "And you fancy her, don't you?"

The straight question was a shock and a dramatic change of
direction, he was not ready for that or thinking about such matters,
he had push himself into his work mode where nothing else had
existed, it hadn't been an easy journey either. Now suddenly without
warning, issues had been switched on him. He felt guilty and a little
embarrassed that once again Liz appeared to of seen how Yoko was
affecting him.

There was an uncomfortable moment.

"Andy, let's forget about that now but I do want to speak about you and I at some time. I think we should deal with work issues now. I know I brought it up but it is un-miss—able and I am hurting. Everybody has seen the effect Yoko has upon you; everybody, like really, everybody."

"I am really sorry Liz, this shouldn't have happened, it's stupid of me, I feel like a fool. I know this means nothing at this point in time' but I love you, yet I cannot for some reason deny my feelings for Yoko. I know it's crazy, I've never been in this position before, not ever, I'm so very sorry that I've hurt you."

"It's your nature!" "Ouch, ouch!"

—

The United Nations Assembly Hall. Late 2007:

M ichael Raimondi had been approached to address the United Nations Assembly regarding the current global position from the European prospective. Due to the assemblies' slow and indecisive actions, which in his view placed, the whole world at extreme risk, and even possibly, extinction, he initially and unexpectedly declined to speak, unless of course certain proposals were allowed to be presented.

Many in the know believed it would be the end of an impressive career, they were proven too be wrong.

Malcom Magarba, the current general secretary, personally provided support, no doubt after reading the address himself and discussing endlessly Michaels proposed address.

Michael stood and paused for quiet to concentrate minds and his own confidence. Michael's tie and collar felt tight and uncomfortable, his legs were shacking and his palms wet with sweat. When all felt as well as could be, and ready, he began his edited and slow address.

The assembly twitched with a kind of nervous silence in expectance of an address to update the European state of affairs.

"Ladies, Gentlemen, Nations of Earth.

There appears to be a great risk to us all, our lives, and the way of life so many of us enjoy. Together, with the many wonderful cultures that co-exist in our world.

Solutions to our problems are not yet totally clear and the pursuers of evil that appear to have decided to run amongst us for their own gain are not yet uncovered.

Yet, I believe a victory is in sight.

That victory desperately needs your help, your urgent and dedicated attention.

I believe it will not be long before those evil creatures that have either created or used our misfortune, and watched the world suffered, but only for their purposes to gain greater evil power and control over our existence, will indeed be revealed.

Meanwhile people continue to starve and die. Harvests across many lands are being devastated and you, you with the power, sit here in relative comfort contemplating what should be done, and then what you might be having for dinner tonight.

I think that maybe you should all just go and suck on a turkey heads and shame upon you all.

Before speaking briefly of the state within the European Union as intended and the horrifying problems that are destroying our world and possibly our species. Let me propose that some changes to this assembly are desperately and urgently needed. Many of you here have spoken of the need, indeed for many, many, years, yet, with so very little action; indeed, no appropriate and worthy changes have been seen recently. When this great assembly was created in 1945, it captured the hopes and dreams of the world. It has indeed improved many aspects, solved many issues, but, we are facing new issues in this global village, this assembly has become bogged down with protocol and regulation. The over use of vetoes, have defeated progression and the harmonising of internationalism, it has covertly increased national self-interests. The ignoring of mandates, have possibly even deteriorated justice and equality to a large extent. The power base of only five nations, does not produce progression. The response to so many conflicts around our world, has not been consistent.

It is time for a new beginning. That is, if we are able to overcome all our current dilemmas, then maybe, and only maybe, a new way forward could save us all.

Those changes are simple. You all understand the need. All be it, the journey may be long and difficult. Our world could be dying, due to the lack of decisive action and the evil we see being allowed to weave its wicked web."

Delegates then turned to look at each other, confused by what they heard and shocked by how he had presented his case. Michael could feel the discomfort amongst the assembly, possibly the disapproval; but bravely he pushed on.

"These basic suggestions which in the main come from within this assembly; (he lied), and approved by your director general could start a new era in the worlds history.

The use of the veto should be slowly reduced. Percentage representation within this assembly with equal voting rights. Representation from every nation, should be sworn, and committed, in fact dedicated to the cause of the United Nations alone, our world, this planet. Financial obligations, both negative and positive, must be clearly set, agreed and enforced. Payments forthcoming and paid in due time, and set against qualified national accounts, confirmable by the financial authorities of the U.N. There has to be benefits accompanying commitment.

A peace force should be employed directly by the United Nations, representing and their loyalty sworn directly to the United Nations, for the common good of all. The United Nations ethos can only be directed towards peace, harmony and sustainability. Firmness invites problems, but behind that dark cloud, we should find a blue sky of hope.

Diplomacy is without doubt of great importance, but there are occasions when diplomacy becomes cowardly, when it reduces action into empty bubbles.

There is more, but these are the basics, the basics that you have discussed and proclaimed.

Malcom Magarba has agreed that these changes should be placed before you all. Our world can and should be different, everybody here knows and agrees that."

Michael paused, he was sweating profusely, but he was in flow now, he reached up to loosen his collar and tie, confident of his task, he had the determination of his father and the backing of the secretary general and knew there may never be another opportunity for such bravery. That there may never be a situation demanding such directness. It may well be self-sacrifice, but if it changed a little something, it would be worthy. He took a deep breath and continued.

"As to the situation within Europe, well, let us be honest, you know that situation, it is more drastic than we have ever known in the history of man. So, I will not bore you.

This has not been my intended address, I have spoken way beyond my brief and position, but I will not apologise for that, but I will thank you for your patience and hope for your agreement followed by gently yet decisive actions.

It is but a plea for common sense from you who have the power to change our world for the better. It will not be an easy task. It will take time but while you consider those great changes, our world today, needs some rapid actions, now. The environmental issues need rapid agreement and action. Not just polite agreement and talk. This current pandemic of disaster is threatening us all, we may well overcome, but if recent history has any value, there will be another sooner, rather than later. What we are currently experiencing appears to be scientifically new to our species. Our lack of serious attention to the environmental issues we are all aware off appears to be punishing us, together we must act before these disasters destroy our world, and sadly through complacency.

The world we know could indeed be dying; all science is agreed. Just think seriously on that fact for a while."

Michael stood down, trembling a little and still soaked in nervous sweat. His hand holding his notes continued shacking. He could hardly believe what he had just done, what he had said, it was like a dream in which he played the lead role, probably as the joker.

The assembly sat in complete silence. Not a sound was to be heard. Translators had stopped talking. Paper upon desks lay still. Delegates gave occasional uncomfortable glances between one another, but few words appeared spoken.

The assembly felt awkward, surprised, shocked, and a kind of, air of shame, seemed to be lurking.

Michael felt very small and yet, with a strange feeling of satisfaction. The assembly felt extremely large and an air of shame or gilt clearly floated above all gathered.

Every delegation starred directly towards Michael Ramondi now, stunned and shocked into that silent thought.

Michael stepped down, and then walked slowly away towards the exit, head facing downward; it was a long, long walk, his legs just managing to maintain their function, footsteps uncertain, as if walking upon jelly. His mind was now a blur, he felt dizzy, and the sweat ran gently down his face, and then dripped upon his shirt and jacket front. As he reached the exit doors, he began to hear what sounded like a single and lonely clap; he let out a long shaky sigh, and then pushed opened the exit door. Through the closing door he began to hear more claps, all delegations were now slowly rising and joining the applause. Unbelievably there were cheers and shouts as the simple and passion felt words hit the consciences of nearly all of those gathered.

Tears ran down his cheeks joining the sweat and he found himself standing at the opened door, unashamedly sobbing away the intense tensions; he really knew not why.

He looked nervously through the glass panel towards Malcom Margarba, he was standing and looking towards the door Michael had exited via and was clapping slowly, he nodded knowingly towards where he knew Michael would be standing. It spoke volumes.

Michael Ramondi with a handkerchief in hand walked away, passing further claps and pats on his back, maybe he had achieved something after all, but as the cheers faded from his ears and the tears and sweat dried upon his face, it was a stiff drink that was required, probably two or three.

—

London. 2007:

Michael Ramondi had flown in from J.F.K. New York to London Heathrow where he was to meet once again with Andy for a brief further update, all-be-it, he was exhausted.

Liz had joined the party in a small and surprisingly stuffy chat room.

Michael looked all in and pale. "Greetings Andy and Liz, has anything improved? Well, that was the most difficult speech I have ever given. Actually, it was not really a speech was it. I just concluded that was the most important point to be made, regardless of any consequences and I guess there will be quite a few." Both Liz and Andy smiled in sympathy, feeling very glad they had not had to deliver a speech in the United Nations Assembly Hall. They shook hands, then determined a hug was called for, and then all feeling a little emotional, settled to discuss the general situation.

Andy spoke up, "A sad refection Michael that your presentation only made the second or third pages, although we have already heard that it has caused a lot of discussion around many a governmental table, and it's scared the pants of a lot of people. Others in the know cannot stop singing your phrases. Boy; we both think it was brave, simple and yet brilliant."

Liz interjected, "On the scientific front Michael quite a lot seems to be happening, mostly its good news. There are reports coming in that clearly indicate a lull in the growth of the mutation rate. Also, in the rate of deaths worldwide, but of course, we do not know yet what this means or the whys. Also, again, and unfortunately from Beijing, Yoko's marine studies are taking a long time to analyse and others are still not in full operation for god's sake, that is bad news. But, we are hopeful. Back at Kings, we have re-analysed enormous amounts of the data coming in and to be honest we still cannot confidently identify trends or see clear patterns. It is still pure ciaos. It's not science like we've ever known it."

Michael simply nodded his understanding, while all displayed their frustration, all be it, they were excited by the reducing mutation rates coming in from just about every scientific laboratory around the globe.

Andy joined the brief and rapid exchanges, "I tell you the thing that is bugging me; that's these dam happenings everywhere that seem to have nothing to do with science. I have had talks with both M.1.+5 and the Interpol guy's from Naples. Only short chats but they wanted to know the whys and what is that have led us to separate a large number of incidence and place them on the terrorist table. I am currently awaiting a call from the headquarters people from Lyon who also want to talk things though."

—

United States of America. Los Angeles, June 2007:

The 'Huang He', had taken three times as long as normal to reach her final destination. She was old, rusty, slow, and had encountered endless problems on route, now she slowly moved towards 'America's Port' as it is known, Los Angeles. It was a massive port covering thousands of acres but to the crews surprise she turned slowly towards Long Beach, which was unusual.

The captain followed his orders.

The delivery of that deadly produce would soon be unloaded and distributed across the states. Happy little drivers, singing or whistling as they sped the motorways and back doubles to delivered their cargos of death.

Warehouse managers happily signing for their overdue consignments and rapidly organizing for their further distribution.

When everything was in place, ready for those happy mums, the disaster began. Due to the delayed arrival of the Huang He, the dummies of sure death, were quickly spread across the southern states, and duly purchased by those happy mothers.

America had fared well as usual until this very point but their nightmare was now to begin.

Within the following weeks thousands and thousands of babes and toddlers fell victim to those little comfort dummies. The authorities worked endlessly to isolate the culprit from wipes, foods, and dry milks. While they searched tirelessly, the problem grew and grew. The media jumping from one product to another, causing mayhem from home to nursery to hospital. Emergency centres were established to deal with the growing problem, a problem the states where not very well equipped to deal with, or coping with very well.

—

U.S.A. President Clinton Gage. Mid-July 2007:

Every media source covered Clinton Gages speech. The B.B.C., France 24, Euro News, C.N.N. and Sky News ran the article endlessly like all the others. The great American system was challenged to the extreme.

"As president, I am humbled by the current dilemmas we find ourselves in. My heart felt sympathies go out to all who have suffered losses, the mothers of our nation are crying, we all cry with them. My sympathies go out to the pain within this global village of ours, and all those that are suffering.

Words alone are never adequate." *(He paused)*

"Mankind will not be cowed by the pain we currently feel; ultimately it strengthens our resolve and our belief in God to overcome the evil of these unforeseen and horrendous events.

All the resources of our great nation will be available in the effort and endeavours in resolving these problems and assisting all who are suffering. With the good will of god on our side, we the American people will overcome.

God bless the peoples of this earth, our home, and all Americans.

My wife and I, together with this administration, will work and pray endlessly in resolving the horrors we are currently enduring, and when the perpetrators are caught, as they will be for certain, we will return to normality and the weight of American justice will fall heavily upon their evil heads.

We will overcome that problem and the awful pandemic that is upon us and we will indeed prevail. May your God be with each one of you."

England, Kings College. Room 4; Late June 2007:

A ndy and Liz both sat on soft chairs, legs stretched before them in room four. Both feeling drained mentally and with no energy.

"Liz, I think it's time that we somehow look once again at everything we are aware of, not just the science, but the whole picture. We need to be clear about where we are upto, what we need to eliminate and what we need to deal with. A large number of these issues belong in other hands; Interpol appears to be winning as regards the confusion of terror. Let us look again at the matters on our desks, and as simply as possible. Let us list the real issues at hand. We have been dragged into a maze. As things now stand I think we could revert to dealing with only our own area of expertise."

Liz responded slowly and deliberately, also displaying the tiredness she clearly felt, "Ok, I guess it would allow us some clarity Andy but we both need a couple of hours before we attempt that." "Yep, let it be, my honey baby." He smiled lovingly at Liz and both closed their eyes immediately. Within moments, they were sound asleep.

"Liz, Liz, come on, here's some coffee. Let's make a start in a couple of minutes."

"Ok, ok, ok. Oh, that was lovely. Did you sleep?" "Yep, certainly did. I am feeling good now; I will start that list, just the initial notes. You drink your coffee and when you're ready, ok?"

Andy worked hard scribbling endless scrawly notes, occasionally looking up to see if Liz was any nearer assisting him. Eventually she stood and stretched; "ready as I'll ever be, I guess."

They worked at it for an hour, and then agreed they were ready to scribble down a positive list of what to reject and the major areas where they felt their time and the team's time would be used effectively. They both knew that this was the time to re-organize; it was now or never.

The door opened and Sarah called to Andy. "Yoko's on the phone Andy." That news changed Liz's attitude instantly and Andy could feel the immediate tension. Regardless, he went to take the call.

"Yoko, how very good it is to hear your voice, I've missed you. Is there a problem?" "No Andrew, no new problems. I was feeling a little down and needed to hear your voice as it happens. Can we find any time to be together?"

Andy was standing and pacing a little, while looking out across the quiet road outside. The hairs upon his neck stood brisling and he felt awkward, as he turned, he saw Liz leaning against the doorframe, obviously unhappy.

"Yoko, let me think about what can be arranged." Liz turned and marched away, not really looking angry, more hurt, wounded, sad yet defiant.

Andy was annoyed with himself, *'Hell, hell, hell and bloody hell.'*

Somehow, he returned to a working state and alone produced a pathetic schedule of what needed to be dealt with knowing that expanding it into clear detail needed Liz by his side and that at this moment he was full of doubts.

Team 1) Work on supporting the marine research, which seemed hopeful.

Team 2) Maintain work on the Chinese situation.

Team 3) Continue to analyse the incoming data looking for trends.

Team 4) Continue to map the spread of both crop failure and death rates.

Team 5) Keep the team on the science, sample testing.

Team 6) Grow and re-organize the admin staff more affectively. Re, secretarial, project leaders.

He created a list of the 'now recognized' instances they should no longer be involved in, all be it, important data exchange, must be continued on all incidents, but many were now clearly seen as evil sabotage, and there was still the unresolved issue of the original incident at the Kings laboratory.

Reject the African issues. (A French team were investigating)

Reject Scandinavia and Russia, as all was regenerating fairly well there but maintain constant data exchange.

Copy in Interpol with all updated and relevant information but do not maintain close interaction re obvious sabotage. Apply this to other law enforcement agencies.

Italy and Brussels' was in hand with Interpol. Treat as per '3'.

The United States. Not directly about mutation spread. Treat as per '3'.

There were many issues to define and a separate department would be needed.

At one stage all the happenings appeared to possibly been off the same source but things had now moved on and it was time to separate matters of concern.

Was it crime and science, did it need control or retribution, *(plus then there was Liz, Yoko, mum, and dad, my sisters)*.

'Oh my god. Andy Gould be a scientist. Concentrate man. Oh, I love you Liz but I think I love you a little more Yoko.'

He stood holding his head, stamped his foot and swore profusely, complete confusion suddenly filled his mind for two minutes. *'Fuck the stupid list, I'm going to Beijing. It's all, just too dam much for me.'*

Andy felt he was actually losing it. This was the last thing he needed, and something he had never experienced before. He knew carrying out that task was vital to remaining in control of the real issues he and his main team could contribute their skills too. He resolved that he would leave those actions to the team, and that his time would be best spent reviewing the science, whether at Kings or Beijing.

—

Beijing, China. Science plus love equals confusion. July 2007:

Andy Gould fluctuated between clarity and confusion, which was not really within his daily control; he had never been here before. It was noticed and questioned by grey suited gentlemen. He managed to convince them he was indeed on top of the job, on top of the science. His rapid re-organization at Kings proved to be an immediate success; all changes and demands readily complied with and fitting rapidly into the new system. His staff delighted and relieved.

Liz maintained professionalism, yet distance. It actually improved their working relationship in many ways.

On arrival at Capital International, Beijing, Andy immediately felt a sense of relief. He had been prescribed medication to assist his general state of mind. Beijing felt like the holiday he deserved.

As arranged, he travel straight to Yoko's apartment, she wasn't going to be able to meet him but the hour journey allowed him to lay back. It felt like the first time forever that his head was strangely clear and relaxed.

At Yoko's apartment he located the key as instructed, entered, poured a stiff drink, sat and shortly fell into a relaxed and beautiful sleep.

"Andrew, Andrew, time to wake." He woke feeling strange, as if entering a dream. At that moment it was everything he desired. Yoko nestled in next to him and they sat there for some time saying absolutely nothing. It was wonderful!

Later that same evening, after a lot of intimacy and overdue closeness, they went to eat late.

As they strolled slowly towards a favourite eating-place, Yoko's arm linked through Andy's. "Andrew, there are matters we must talk about." "Yoko, oh please no science, not until tomorrow." "No, no, no science." "That sounds good. Ok, so what shall we talk about, it must be happy things, I really need happy and comfortable talk my beautiful little lady."

Yoko paused, thoughtfully, then looking up and straight at Andy, she spoke slowly.

"Andrew, *(she paused yet again),* do you love me, it that what you feel?"

"Oh yes. I really do Yoko. I haven't stopped thinking about you, and us."

Yoko continued to look intensely at Andy.

"Well, there is some big news, a little Yoko and Andy is on route."

They stopped dead on the sidewalk, Yoko still looking straight up and into Andy's eyes, and then reaching out and gripping his arms, holding them tightly. Andy felt as if his head was going into a spin as he tried his best to return her eye-to-eye contact. He simply couldn't open his mouth. It was stuck firmly closed. He gulped a number of times, his mouth and throat dry, a little sweat forming on his brow.

A *'bloody hell',* eventually passing his lips.

Yoko continued looking at Andy, obviously judging his response, there was hope in her eyes.

"*Bloody hell,* once again, (then another pause), that's fantastic, wonderful and amazing. It will change our lives, but so what? Yoko that is gigantic-enormous news. A bit of a shock I have to say, but it's great, I am frilled and also, *'very wowed and gobsmacked'* and *'amazed'* Yoko Cheng. Bloody hell a father me, Yoko wow, about your baby, no, about our baby, wow, me a father!"

They walked on in silence along the hot sidewalk to the restaurant, Yoko pulling herself in close and squeezing his arm; Andy turning occasionally to softly kiss her, he was floating and staring into the future, in a dreamlike state.

The world was changing, his world, and he had no idea how he would deal with it, but in that moment, it was pure ecstasy.

—

Around the globe. 2007:

While politicians, science and health services fought to resolve and contain, the people of the world endured. They endured confusion and worry; they endured the lack of services and certain food supplies. Those where agriculture had been devastated, knew hunger. In a large number of cities around the world, there were protests, in some, looting and violence. Where a virus had spread rapidly, they experienced deaths, so many; it had quickly depleted local populations. Global finances dived, regardless of the efforts thrown at the issues in desperate attempts to stabilise the national and international massive downturns. The deviations, from the full and true story had been harmonised between every nation, the media was tightly being controlled, everywhere. The emphasis had been firmly moved to local issues. Issues that each and every community across the world needed to be dealt with. The real enemy was hidden behind endless double meanings, fake news and complicated instructions, together with new laws. Of course, there was in some areas, abuse, and that violence, was balanced by vigilantes and those incidents served to occupy local energies and thoughts.

Everywhere, politics had been polarised, presidential terms extended and democratic rights limited.

Where applicable, personal isolation laws were being enforced, and businesses closed whilst the varied forms of the virus and toxins run their course. Then, the awful devastation, or a new mutated form had moved the situation onwards, allowing authorities to claim they had dealt successfully with the last issue. Where agricultural devastation had occurred, it was the same story. The residue of every incident, lingering and left behind destroyed societies, confused regions and great cities in disorder.

All this was then confused further, by the random and strange incidents happening almost everywhere, some reported nationally, some only locally.

Laboratories and governments' laboured to find cause and cure, but as they progressed, so did further mutation. Every available chemical and medical formula known to humankind was being tested to discover solutions.

Overall, in most countries, food supplies remained available, even if rather meagre.

Hence, the average person could not make clear plans; authority was in exactly the same position. Therefore, most people were inclined to shrug their shoulders and take care, as best they could and they changed their habits and existed on the basic of routines, supplies, and services. The short-term nature of each viral form, allowed the larger part of each country's infrastructure to survive and function at varying levels. Thereby, regenerating, leaving people with regional and local issues to deal with and occupy their concerns.

—

The world moves on. London. October 2007:

As Andy's flight journeyed to a stop, the outlook across Heathrow was dismal, grey and damp looking. He was never the less in a good mood. He had worked hard whilst in China, talking most days to his team at Kings in the United Kingdom. Liz had been devastated about his decision to stay and work from Beijing, and although initially, they had managed to speak and work successfully across the void, he was very aware he had treated her badly. He knew she was looking to relocate, and under the difficult circumstances, it was perfectly understandable.

Yoko's pregnancy was progressing well and both remained thrilled with the prospect of being parents. Andy had never mentioned that particular situation to Liz, as he knew well that Liz's pain would have been excruciating. There were times when in private, he had held his head in sorrow for the pain he had given her, and knew that his love for her cute ways, intellect, personality and great looks, would never die. It was simply fate and bad timing that he, like the fool he could be, should full deeply in love with two of the most incredible women at the same time, it had been unresolvable, and the pregnancy had decided for him. In some of those lonely moments of guilt and sorrow, he had actually cried, and then foolishly dreamed of having two partners.

In Kings, now the securest of facilities, there were endless deep-frozen samples of viruses, bacteria, fungi toxins and protozoa. Those samples had been collected from around the globe and currently, they defied human attempts at understanding how they were interacting. That tests and experiments were being replicated in every major facility around the world. All would continue the work. On the ground, samples were still being continuously taken, and each sample needed the data recorded. The incidents of mutation were at last slowing and reducing, and the world beginning to recover, all be it, would be sometime before social, and financial stability would be re-established. All those involved were seriously scared and concerned by the new and currently unresolvable issues. Generally, it had been agreed and accepted that the birth or creation of the problem lay somewhere intertwined with growing environmental changes across the globe. Most of the earlier theories were now dismissed, due to the ultimate lack of evidence, or having been clearly disproved, by the tireless work in science laboratories. Andy and Yoko had changed direction in view of those conclusions, and whilst their research teams and laboratories continued to explore, test and record every aspect of the information and samples collected and received. Those reports were continually being checked and then authorised, by either Andy Gould or Yoko. Once authorised, they were dispatched internationally. Behind the scenes and unspoken off to most members of their teams, they personally began to look beyond the obvious for answers, way way beyond!

Liz, unknown to Andy, had been approached by WHO, to undertake the setting up of a department at a remote research facility. There to work with Pacific scientific and environmental groups from Samoa, Canada and New Zealand. The invitation immediately appealed to her, particularly under her current circumstances. She had noticed she could only just about remain professional at the King's facility, as her ability to speak and interact with Andy was reducing to an inadequate level.

The research station was actually in Samoa, and she investigated thoroughly with growing delight and interest. An administration centre had been established in Apia on the island of Upolu. She had already located some beachside properties, which, sat behind long white beaches, edged with palms, simply looking idyllic. There was little she could find dislikeable, that was apart from the risk of cyclones. After further consideration, she readily accepted the appointment, sold her U.K. property amazingly quickly, and organised further financial support from her father. For Liz it was a no-brainer, she had to change her life. A beautiful tropical island, white beaches, and a beachside property, which her father had already offered to buy for her, being that was what she wanted. The subject matter she adored, old friends who also work on the island, and the challenge of setting up, building, and leading something really worthwhile, totally in her own right, it simply appeared perfect. When she had plucked up the courage to inform Andy, he was verbally shocked. All things considered, the conversation had gone well, and Andy, although heartbroken in reality, had enthused. "Andy the potential is enormous as regards the range of projects, things I can truly enjoy, bury myself in, it's a dream job. Actually, subjects that I have always majored in. The increasing acidity of the oceans. It is all part of this growing environmental issue, carbon dioxide emissions being absorbed by the oceans, but I guess you are with that." "Yes Liz, it is interesting, I agree." "Anyway Andy, there are also a few people I know, mostly working with a Canadian research group. I am actually feeling very excited. I don't see that you need to replace me from outside, there are a few excellent people who can step up and support very well, you know that." Both of them had feelings and thoughts turning and tumbling over in their minds, but they were all, unspoken.

"So, when are you off Liz?"

"I would like to leave in a week's time, I know it is rather quick, but if you can live with that. Everything here has been organised, I have emailed you all the details you need. Is the leaving time going to be ok with you?" "Of course, Liz, of course. Please make sure you stay in touch, we deserve that, I would hate not to, and your opinions are always going to be valued with this dam situation, you know that; don't you?" "Yes, I know. Thanks, Andy, I am sorry everything turned out as it did." "So am I Liz, so am I. Well, good luck. I do love you. I wanted to say—-." Liz broke into his final sentence. "Goodbye Andy Gould."

Then, unknowingly to each other, they both held heads in hands and sobbed quietly in private.

—

A forward reflection. March 2008:

Whilst the world, partly unknowingly, suffered strange and new disasters, secretly too begin with, the situation slowly moved towards financial freefall. Capitalism rightly took the blame. The foolish relinquishing of banking regulation, advocated by some very interested parties, causing crash after crash. Their great marketing skills employed amongst the politicians of the day and financiers appealing to their own blind greed supported the deception. The great financial loses, reportedly starting within the subprime mortgage market, rapidly burying those true underlying causes. 'The world community had been compromised like never before'. Some powerful people had withdrawn their support for yesterdays, disintegrating world system and the fear of oncoming eco desires. The recognition of the balance of global G.D.P. between the few rich nations and others; the rich in reality, only affecting it by approximately 30%. The rest of the world was a very big market, and their desires, ambitions and needs had to be maximised by selling them material goods together with; *'alcohol, tobacco products, tranquillisers, recreational drugs, easy mortgages, vehicles, holidays and all those other coloured glass beads,'* which they craved.

Ultimately, it was the unspoken hope of the alternative view, that the oncoming environmental issues and global disasters, of which there seemed far too many, were now being fully recognised by public opinion, and that would overshadow and halt the push towards more deregulation and unsustainable capitalism.

–

Beijing and London. Late November 2007:

A ndy had returned to London to administer the departmental changes needed after Liz have vacated to Samoa. At King's, it seemed empty without her presents and assistance. The reports and data continued to pour in, and after a number of governmental meetings, Andy decided he must retain his working routines between China and the U.K. It seemed the most effective way to remain abreast of developments particularly now the whole department had been reorganised, and of course, he was soon to be a father.

At one of his meetings at Whitehall, something was said that raised his suspicions that he had not been fully informed following the intense investigation on the initial escaping material from his laboratory. Whereas, the investigating teams had worked independently, apart from endless questioning. Their conclusions he felt, had never been fully passed onto his team, and subsequently, there was lurking doubts whether they concluded it to be the result of an unfortunate or foolish era, or caused by some other more sinister body. As it had happened, he had found himself far too busy in his professional and personal life, let alone the endless meetings in Whitehall and attending a number of parliamentary enquiries, all of which he felt he had satisfied adequately.

Whilst he was in London, Yoko was invited to the U.N. to discuss directly, both Andy's and her own current position. The separation between them was the worse of feelings, for their current attachment to each other now appeared to dominate their every consideration. Yoko was subsequently asked to stay and head up a major team working on the science of the strange and mutating virus. She had declined, saying she needed time for consideration and authority from her political bosses. The U.N. were keen for her to accept and prepared to wait for her clear decision. She decided not to mention the offer and the possibly drastic relocation it would incur upon Andy until she had thoroughly thought through the pluses and minuses of the situation. She had understood that Andy had just lost the closeness of Liz and realised that her ongoing work schedule, planned, together with Andy was important.

—

B.B.C. World News. Early December 2007.

B lare Prescott, the United Kingdom prime minister has clearly indicated today that his scientific and medical advisers felt confident that a downturn in the spread and mutation rate could be seen. The virus known as 'MUT.D 1' was clearly at the top of everybody's list. All major scientific bodies and governments had similarly concurred with the priority listing.

'Still speaking about the science.'

The renowned Chinese scientist Professor Cheng, who has been foremost in working with Professor Andrew Gould of the Kings College facilities in the United Kingdom, where the pandemic appears to off originated, has been offered the directorship of the UN Science Faculty. She was reported to of said to be excited about the offer but was considering the position carefully due to her own personal and professional commitments.

—

In Eynsford, Kent, England, Betty and Bill Gould were carefully sawing up an odd pile of wooden items. Old pallets, a discarded chair, together with a stack of broken draws which Bill had gathered on one of his reconnoitring wanders around the streets and lanes of his little village.

It had been a difficult few weeks, very 'make do and mend', but that had not worried either of them. As long as their girls and Andrew were happy enough and enduring, which they seemed to be. If anyone was a worry, it was Andrew. He was always finding his way into the middle of some issue; he always had, from a young age. They had received a call from him a while back when he was in China. They really did not know what he was doing there, apart from seeing this, *'Chinese Yoko woman'*. They also wondered why he was not using any of the technology that seemed around these days, particularly with all these viruses and problems all over the world. "I love our son dearly Betty as you know, but I'll never understand him." "That's our Andrew; you know it Bill, if he does find trouble, then it finds him. I would love to see him nicely settled down happily with a good wife and giving us some grandkids. Oh well, wish on Betty Gould. By the way, what happened to that Liz that he was so fond of?"

Although now, there was not now a great deal of decease across London or the Southeast, the aftermath and enormity of what had happened, lingered on, particularly for the older generation and the vulnerable. Folks that had been affected, but had survived, still suffered greatly and that together with so many deaths had left families, communities, and businesses vulnerable. Many of those businesses had been devastated and the basic structures of society were trying hard to re-establish themselves, but from Betty's and Bill's perspective, there was still a long way to go. In fact, they thought it unlikely they would see a return to yesterday's normality.

"Come on Betty girl, let's get inside, it looks like it is going to rain yet again." They tidied up, as indeed their generation always did and made their way into the kitchen, both rubbing their hands for a little warmth. "Shall I turn on the news Bill?" "No, don't bother Betty, it'll only be more depressing rubbish and you can't believe a word they say these days."

—

An evil intent:

The C.I.A. and Interpol, together with the cooperation of M.1.5 in London had been following the money, phone calls, email, and text calls of thousands of suspect people and anti-social groups. They had tracked flights, commercial and private, and sieved through the endless number of accusing equations they received on an hourly basis.

If the theories that they were considering, were anywhere near correct, it reduced, at last, their task massively.

If, as supposed, it involved people of great wealth and power, actually, people of unbelievable wealth and power, they would, by their nature be very well hidden under endless layers of underlings, legalities, bank accounts and paperwork. *'Needles in hay stacks'.* Normally, those people were never found and never exposed, but in these circumstances, international law enforcement was very determined, even secretly prepared to break laws and they appeared to be finding their way through the mire by removing just about anybody they could implicate, and thousands of people had been safely locked away.

The first, second and third world, were all exposed to a threat of decease and devastation. Even corrupt dictatorships and revolutionary regimes were secretly on board of the effort to turn the tide of so many global disasters and they were all aware their futures were at risk and very much, out of their control. For those particular people, it was obviously a dilemma when offered advantageous financial offers as repayment extended well beyond their time on this earth.

—

Samoa:

L iz walked slowly along the beach just outside of Apia. The sand here was soft and warm. The sky, as per normal, clear blue, as was the sea alongside the shoreline. The palms swayed gently in a soft south-westerly breeze, it was all simply perfect and lovely. Her mind flickered from one thought to another. Most of her thoughts were easy and soft, at peace with her surroundings, only two things gave her a little agitation; no not agitation, one gave a severe sharp pain, the other juggled and tested her thoughts, and she tried her best to dismiss them from her mind.

She failed. The pain was Andy, bloody Andy Gould. He just would not disappear from her thoughts, day-time or night-time. *'If only he really knew. If only he would think clearly, he'd understand we should be together.'*

Although she communicated with Kings regularly, it was by email or video link and impersonal, just reports, data and science flying both ways. It appeared that neither of them had either the courage or the time to deal with any personal possibilities. *'Oh Andy, you are such a fool!'*

The other half of Liz's thoughts, which generated importance, were possibly of more value.

All be it, that she had relatively easily established the beginnings of a well-facilitated laboratory and administration offices, she had been enjoying the work with her other colleagues which involved a number of exploratory sea trips. She had not had the opportunity to sail for a long time, and although most of the team had travelled by the well-equipped motorboat, she had chosen with two others to take the available yacht belonging to the Canadian team.

When the mission had arrived, and engage themselves with their monitoring deep down, of the evolving, changing, and degrading reefs, Liz, remained on the surface and had then engaged her attention to the greeny-blue covering of the sea, which she knew as an algae bloom, an H.A.B., and quite dangerous. She had never really seen that particularly species before. She gowned and masked herself as she found it fascinating and carefully took many samples, whilst many questioning thoughts ran through her head.

She questioned the crew why had they chosen to dive and research that particular site, and were they fully aware just how dangerous these algae were, and increasingly so. It turned out they were not fully upto speed on the latest risks, and they had been concentrating heavily on the growing deterioration and destruction of the reefs, all be it, they dived fully covered. They appeared shocked by the information Liz then gave them and agreed that she should fully bring them up to date. The whole situation of these teams diving at that site, seriously bothered Liz for some reason, but she could not quiet grasp the science and feelings charging through her mind but somehow, she knew there was something wrong as she cast her eyes over the surface.

—

Beijing, China:

"Look Yoko, I think this UN job is wrong for us. I do not really think that it will engage and excite you any more than current projects. A new and different challenge, maybe, but you would be dealing with the same issues and, without hands on the possibilities you now have and love. In honesty, I do not really fancy the States myself; we have good lives now in both London and China. What could be better than this, that is indeed the only question for me, and anyway, where do you want our little one to grow up?"

Yoko was thoughtful for a while, court in her natural desire to travel the world and take on new adventures. In her mind she was listing all her happenings and adventures; she was a star on the front of the world stage, and at the very heart of a dramatic scientific challenge, a new committed romance and she knew she was definitely in love with Andy, a baby on route, her first child, another new adventure. Yes, her life was more than full, every aspect kept her busy, and she love it all, but still somewhere inside was a hunger for more.

"Andy, what if, I attempt to negotiate a, 'come and go arrangement'. If they cannot accept my terms, well, that is the end of it. It would be a very challenging job Andy and I differ from you, in that I like travel and lots of new and varied challenges. Of course, I want to spend most or even all my time together with you, and shortly our child, but you know that is never going to be possible with what we do, our lives. With your blessing Andrew I would like to talk to them about taking the position, but only on the bases I outlined." "Mmm! Ok, what about this, wherever we are, we agree that we must spend our time at least 50% together, and with the U.N. work, you are allowed to divide your working time between the U.S., China and the U.K..” “What the devil, I agree to try it Andrew. Let us see what we can negotiated. What fun this all is!” Andy threw his hands to his face, 'Oh, my god.'

—

America, U.S.A.:

In America, as in many other countries, the mutating enemy had spread its evil tentacles' in every direction and was affecting thousands of square miles of agricultural land in various ways. In one particular area, the great herds of beef cattle had been almost depleted, and there was nothing they could do about it and that was, apart from attempting the awesome and almost impossible task of the clean-up. Those issues, together with the deaths of millions of babies and toddlers in each town and community, had left the United States in a desperate position.

It had taken some time to follow the paper trail, due to the surprising ingenuity of those organisers of evil. Once they had achieved that, there was production plants and staff to investigate, and of course, after all that effort was carried out amongst ciaos everywhere, the trail seemed to simply dry up and then the confusion was restarted.

It was the same story everywhere as regards low dosage Aspirin. Anybody that relied on an occasional usage or regular usage to thin their blood was in serious trouble. If it didn't kill you, working was still impossible, hence more death and less people to hold the remnants of society together.

—

Zambia, Africa:

In Zambia, Africa, and spreading from the epicentre, some way from the western capital of Mongu, then carried by both southeasterly and northwesterly winds. Causing, those tentacles of mutating death once again, to be sent on their ominous journeys, to Angola, Mozambique, Malawi and Zimbabwe. The scanty medical services failing immediately. There were no answers.

Within the Mongu Scientific and Medical Laboratories where Churchill, Winston, Bruce and Joel Undama, laboured many long and sweaty hours, attempting to discover, if by some kind of miracle, an antibody. They had very carefully taken many samples. Then after their methodical observations, quizzically looked towards one another, and shook their heads; "they are actually nearly all different, is that possible, I don't think I have ever seen anything like this. I am not surprised this sneaky little bugger is getting the best of everyone. How does this happen, I thought I understood mutation, but at this rate? Let us get our heads down and catch up properly on the science guys. It looks like we are going to be doing a real 24/7 routine. We really can't be of any help with the medical stuff; let's forget it." Everybody stopped and looked seriously towards each other in turn. "We can't do that, just ignore what they pay us for, that's crazy man." "Look here, the bloody world is in crisis. Let us use our dam brains, and do what we were train to do. It is ridiculous just wasting our time. We can't help most of the people, there is zilch that we can do there. We might be able to do something, come tomorrow, if we can pool our brain power and look at the science, come on, let's do it."

Sadly, Sonny's little food store up the road from the 'Sleepy Time Hotel', would not open again officially, and nobody would see his friendly smile, but his shelves, full of stock would suddenly be emptied.

—

Beijing, China: 2008:

Andy and Yoko had been busier than normal. Yoko had found the U.N. were prepared to be amazingly flexible as regards the terms of her working with them, and the details had been agreed upon, with the official start date left open. Andy was disappointed, regardless of them agreeing to most of the conditions they had discussed, but he could see difficulties ahead.

They had decided to take a working holiday together, as Yoko's pregnancy was quickly reaching full term. A full support team was already in place for the occasion, and two experienced midwives allocated to travel with Yoko wherever she found herself.

Andy and Yoko had been working closely for some time and from Andy's point of view, they formed an essential and professional unit which should not off been placed at risk by the new appointment. Yoko had known his feelings, and to his surprise, had continued with the process. On the emotional level, he was very obviously, besotted by Yoko, and that together with the thought of their oncoming child, hence he made the rare choice of holding his tongue.

Their short break was a sudden decision. They needed some self-indulgent time together, regardless of having to stay in touch with all those important issues; luckily it was all carried on computers. They took with them a midwife and personal assistant. They too would also be able to enjoy the change of scene. The choice of where to go was almost hopeless, and in the end, Yoko had decided to travel to Wuhan where she had family. Staff had booked the 'Hilton Wuhan Riverside', on the banks of the great Yangtze River. Executive suites with all the trimmings, very-five-star. It was not really Andy's ideal, but he also needed a change of scene and Yoko was excited about the opportunity, and that was all he wanted to achieve. Yoko was suddenly busy organising many little trips, East Lake, Jiufeng Forest Zoo, and the Botanical Gardens. The maternity nurse was not impressed, but Yoko was acting like a mother to be, and nothing would change her plans.

—

Brussels - Beluim. January 2008:

Helicopters arrived one after the other. The whirring and clutter, drowning out all other sound. They each dropped out of a grey dismal sky, floating dangerously to either side as the strong wind demanded. Around the small castle, security, each in dark navy-blue suits, scurried to their allocated observation points, obviously each well-armed. Everywhere one looked, there were scanning cameras, large spot and floodlights, poised for the night work. A number of the security personnel held tightly to the leads of their large Alsatian dogs.

Six very high-profile people, all with coat collars standing up high against the freezing wind that blew fiercely around the location where the castle stood at around 4,000 feet. If it had been a fine day, the views across the surrounding area would have been excellent.

It was not a heavily populated region, and the decision to change from their normal ronda-view, had been driven by the current emerging circumstances.

As one by one, they were each escorted through the grand entrance arch, and then inside to the warmth and luxury that their secret hideaway offered, everyone began to settle down into a well-practiced routine of serious international issues, finance, security, and service.

After each had automatically rubbed their hands making a symbolic gesture about the weather, the refreshments having been served; the customary observance of polite conversation completed, there was an edgy awareness of the need to talk officially. Of course, coded conversations flew between these particular people continually. Rarely, friendly little chats, but brief conversations involving millions of everything, and affecting how countries would be governed, who would be elected, and how banks, energy supplies, and religions would behave.

One of the men, a tall distinguished man in his 70s, with silvered, thinning hair, a long face and fine Romanesque nose, started to speak to the exclusive gathering.

"Gentlemen, we are yet again gathered to speak face to face, it is a good habit in the circumstances, with great value. Let us move towards that very grand table and talk, I have no doubt we all have our points to express and matters to discuss; gentlemen, if you would please." The self-imposed leader of the group of six, a man of unimaginable wealth and property, sat as he started to speak, the feeling around the table was a little less formal than tradition normally demanded. "Gentlemen, Africa is a success and our grip increases. Our little blood thinners are certainly doing their job. The U.S. is scrambling to control our little virus, infant mortalities, street violence, rape and looting. I am of course sharing my knowledge and sympathies with them. They are at last learning some new respect. I was also pleased to note, that the C.I.A. is in complete confusion and its normal disarray. Our little surprise package is currently being introduced to those places where the weather patterns have failed us." He sat back for a moment to take a difficult deep breath, yet managed to remain dignified and in control. "As you are very aware, not many understand our purpose, nor should they, but the day will come when we will be unknowingly appreciated and thanked.

Currently, a number of our little operations, are being traced, and tracked, but they are not the brightest, hence, no worries, but they are catching up slowly, and that is a little concerning, but of course we are also very confident in our plans, aids and our invisibility cloak." Once again, he paused, looking a little more uncomfortable this time, then he breathed deeply, doing something quite unique in these surroundings, he loosened his tie, coughed, then continued.

"I have received a report from inside the U.K., from M.I.5, confirmed also via M.I.6, D.1 and the O.S.C.T., so conclusive, that they have discovered and now conclude that the initial incident at Kings College in the U.K. was a covert operation by an unknown group, and not caused by the unfortunate accident as was initially accepted, and believed. So, well done to them I say. If a little slow." They all gave signs of pleasure, either nodding, smiling or a light chuckle.

"Gentlemen, we here gathered, possess the key to all matters in our civilisation. Money, property, and hence total power. That of course being, the status quo we are fighting for, it must be retained and fully restored. We are all very well aware, that the status quo has been under extreme threat, environmentally and politically. A new order is not in our favour, and many will lose control, and in an unknown future, suffer, due to the natural order being disrupted. I think we all understand that nothing is one hundred percent, but stability is a very important and worthy option, retaining our authority is vital to our cause and theirs. Anyway, enough of these ramblings. I hope that we all here still understand our mission, and remain in support of those agreements, plans and the actions taken.

Now let me update you all on any new incidents you may not be upto speed on."

The conversations continued for another four hours, issues raised, folders opened and then closed, and ultimately, commitments reconfirmed.

—

Samoa and Professor Elizabeth Clements:

L iz, although deeply into marine biology in which she had majored, she had now fully researched the latest science on H.A.B.'s, with increased and growing interest. Both the Canadian and New Zealand research groups had held back until they found further information. On the bases of her discoveries and growing concerns, she had rapidly re-organised the facilities at her laboratories. Then she had further spoken to her colleagues, requesting their assistance in gathering more samples and setting up further tests'. She also wanted air samples upto five hundred metres at a minimum, from around the original algae bloom and any other sites where such blooms existed locally. The sampling flights were to follow the local air currents, sampling at ten-mile intervals, initially to a maximum of fifty miles. They were big demands, with the need of significant financial funding, which thankfully, had been confirmed, but in stage payments. Of course, she was not entirely happy with such a foolish control demand, but it allowed her to begin to test the growing theories in her mind. The whole process had taken a lot of time and effort. In reality, she wanted desperately to speak of the theories to Andy, and surprisingly, Yoko. She trusted their knowledge, but she decided to hold back until more testing had been carried out and double-checked, or was the holding back and speaking to Andy, just a personal issue, an emotional block. After many hours with her team, all their eyes were tired, and strained, due to viewing endless samples and the level of concentration employed. They were all exhausted, but continually surprised and excited by their endeavours. The samples, had been gathered from across the whole region, with many research groups assisting in the operation, and now that she and others viewed the results, they were convincing her, that her worsted fears were correct. It was the air samples, which finally and totally convinced her. She continued to feel excited, as that realisation had settled in her mind. She wanted to shout about it, out loudly to anybody and everybody, but knew she must consider all the factors carefully before that could happen. More than anything, she wanted to speak to Andy. Regardless of those desires, she went through her discoveries once again with her team and then decided to call in just about every scientific brain on the island. It was a great discovery and she felt rightly proud of her work, but she needed to obtain the agreement of sound and critical scientific minds, she must not allow her excitement to allow some critical aspect to be miss read, or overlooked. The following day, she generated enough of a gathering to allow her to present everything she had discovered to date. It was not a standard formal presentation, just people she knew, key people, which actually reflected numerous countries from around the globe. She had organised to use the local church hall. Standing in the pulpit and feeling a little nervous, she called for silence. "Welcome everybody, we are all known to each other, so no need for formality. We have some very important slides and video for you all to view later, but if you will allow me to chat you through our findings, which, if you concur with my team and I, it will be what so many of us here and elsewhere have been hunting for; the source of this awful mutating nightmare." The gathering went completely silent and many looked one to the other. Expectation or doubt appearing on everybody's face, all be it, many of them had been fully involved throughout. "So, I see I have your full attention." She flicked her blond hair behind her ears, took a deep breath and continued. "In brief, as you all are aware of ocean acidification, due in the main, too pollution and rising temperatures I shall not speak or complicate this matter with all the involved details as yet, as a detailed paper is currently being assembled, and indeed some of you here are assisting in that endeavour. As some of you may be aware, there has been serious and growing concerns due to the increasing acidification, which has not been anywhere near the top of many agendas. What yesterday, was considered a low priority, has turned into something quite unexpected. The rapid and increasing effects of global warming, oil spills and the general and horrendous amounts of pollution has tipped the balance of safety against us. H.A.B.'s have become seriously dangerous according to our recent research. Due to the warming, small as it is currently, together with those other polluting issues, the reproduction cycle has shortened the germination rate and the division rates dramatically increased. The range of toxins currently being produced have increased, the toxicity level, has dramatically increased according to all the tests we have carried out. There seems to be an interaction occurring with plastic Nano-particles that is, like so much of what we have discovered, we need further rapid and intensive research.

All of those observations are severe enough. Recently, we have confirmed that the airborne rate of dispersion has also increased, one thousand-fold, and to a far greater dispersion height than would have been expected, and certainly never recorded or even suggested previously. Initially, we were only carrying out capture procedures upto 500 metres, but the percentage was so high at that level, we increased the capture upto 1,000 metres. That together with the changes in the worlds' weather patterns, the scenario has produced a serious enemy. These findings need to be modelled rapidly, and I have already made enquiries with highly respected teams. The weather and incident mapping is not yet complete, and I have to say, there are some very large queries that have been indicated and need answering quickly. The main reason for saying that, is the location from where the initial infection chain was thought to of started. Once again, there will be full details in the paper when it is completed. These discoveries, could answer the increasing death rates found over the last thirty years of dolphins, seals, manatees, even alligators and whales have officially been recorded as victims of toxic blooms, plus many more specie, but those reports have never been seriously investigated politically. Of course, we have known about the problems in fish, shellfish and other lower species, and kind of ignored it on an international level, but mammal deaths, wow. Now humans and human culture is being seriously attacked and millions have already died, harvests and communities devastated, it is the H.A.B.'s, it is the airborne algae blooms carrying toxins, bacteria and viruses. We have observed toxin intensification taking place under laboratory conditions; it has been almost unbelievable. We have confirmed H.A.B. spores and Protozoa infected by bacteria, those bacteria were further infected by virus. At this moment we must accept that a new and formidable new relationship has been formed." Liz paused, and sipped at a glass of water. Those gathering before her seemed stilled and concerned, or was it dismissive and unbelieving. She was not too sure, but she was confident of all that she was saying. She had done the science; rechecked, and check again. Her team had confirmed the conclusions. She had included lead members of other research teams to observe her testing procedures and they now were among those standing before her. She had only one regret, and needed only one further confirmation, and that was from Professor Andrew Gould. She had total respect for his scientific abilities, his natural skill to see past the obvious. With his stamp of authority, and if possible, Yoko Chengs', her work would immediately be accepted seriously, and internationally. "Sorry about the pause everybody. To continue for a little further, then afterwards may I suggest we take a little refreshment and openly discuss this threatening diagnosis? The result of this revelation is multi layered, fraught with problems. Our ability to control H.A.B.'s is currently very limited. Our ability to reduce pollution, in both the oceans and the atmosphere is slow and limited. We are unaware of the science of the constant mutation rate. On top of all those issues, we do not fully understand the ongoing effect of these H.A.B.'s, their life span or dormanting, regenerating and reproducing abilities. Actually, it is not mutation, as we normally understand, it is also about epigenetics. It changes directly the D.N.A. structures, or the biochemical switches, the methylation pattern. Remember, viruses have D.N.A. I hope you are following my thinking here. There is still a lot to be discovered, but to date it explains why we have been struggling. Everything is pointing to pollution levels. In the sea, air, and on the earth, plastics, oil products and chemicals. Oh yes, I forgot complacency. Also, remember please, alga produce an estimated 50 to 72% of the oxygen we need on this planet, yes, it is nearly, *forget about the Amazon and the Northern Forests'*. 'Of course, I am being a little flip with that comment.' But, you can see the point I am making. We do have a big, big problem.

Before we break, I want to emphasise exactly what I am suggesting here. This is something very new. We are aware of interaction between plant and mammal, normally via insect interaction. With this situation, we believe currently, that due to the pollution of the land and seas, together with global warming affecting both air and ocean flows, mixed with the increasing existence of H.A.B.'s, new toxins are being created, which are feeding the relationship with the virus and bacteria. The alga spores are being distributed both higher and wider by those developing and warming weather patterns we have been recording, carrying the new toxins, virus and bacteria to all corners of the globe. We have allowed the creation of a major across species threat that we suspect is generating across all our oceans and more particularly, germinating in the coastal regions and the estuaries of the world.

Thanks for listening, help yourselves to refreshment, and ask away with any questions, or tear the science apart if you can, I really do not mind. Feel free to view the slides and other material evidence on the tables, along the left-hand wall. Obviously, I would very much appreciate any helpful contributions, and if you would like to receive a copy of the pre-released full paper when completed, please complete the contact forms on the end table. Thanks. Arr! One last point to mention; we are going to want a lot of help with establishing more sampling, testing and general research. If any of the teams here can assist further, please make sure you speak to me, or one of the team. In my humble opinion, there is futuristically or currently, nothing more important. Nothing anywhere!" As Liz stood down at last, the whole assembly stood up, then applauded politely and began to mingle, the noise level rocketing suddenly due to the depth of the concerned discussions. The following day Liz felt simply exhausted and too hot, in the end, she decided to cabbage and ignore the endless phone calls. She simply had to. As she sat cuddled on the sofa trying to watch films to break the endless circle of thoughts going around in her mind she realised that the issues could not be put to rest mentally and she resolved to call Andy Gould.

"Andy, this is Liz. How are you?" There was a long purse, during which both of them dived into the emotional depths, together with a natural awkwardness of wanting and confusion. "Yep, I'm good Liz. How is going on that desert island of yours. Feet up, lazing on your hammock with lots of cocktails." "Actually, no Andrew. I have been working like a beaver. All that lying in a hammock stuff is just a dream at the moment Andy. Look, I have something real serious to discuss with you and Yoko if she is there." "Ok, fire away Liz, I am all ears and as it happens have some down time right now, so what's the problem?" She ran Andy through the whole story of the research she had tumbled into, and the resulting discoveries she had made. Andy Gould listened intently and in total silence as the results were fully explained, each discovery given in some detail. "Are you still listening Andy?" "Yes, yes, of course Liz, to every amazing word. If all this stuff holds up, it is a revelation, and at last, there is something real to work on. It sounds incredible. Nothing showed up in all those ocean samplings we organised, it looks like we made a mistake there, looking for the wrong things and maybe in the wrong places. Look Liz, this is really important, how do you want to proceed from here?" "Andy, what I would like to suggest is that I send you the incomplete paper we are working on. There are still many gaps, much unresolved, but if you and Yoko and both your teams can find the time to review where I am upto, tear it apart if you can, just check it all out before I go public, it would make a big difference. We cannot get this wrong. For all the work that had been going on, all the deaths and destruction, this is the first time we have found something that really fits, possibly something very real to work on. I can also send you samples that will amaze you. I think that London would arrange delivery. What do you think?" "Ok, do you want me to speak to Brendon, or will you do that?" "No, you can arrange that, quickly please and confirm the situation, and I'll get this paper over to you tomorrow, and then follow up with all the photographic data. Does that sound like a plan? Oh yes, I'll include a full contact list of everybody that has assisted on this, some you'll know of course and a copy of the proposal sent to 'Complex Dynamics', I think you know of them. If everybody ends up agreeing my findings, then some serious modelling needs to be done and rapidly. I have the backing in place already, ok?" "Ok Liz, you've worked hard on this, I can hear that. I am sure that both Yoko and I will move this to top priority, promise. Do you think we should travel to Samoa?" "*No Andy*. I have so much to do and follow up. I will settle for top priority. We'll speak very soon." Liz finished the call abruptly. The very thought of Andy actually arriving in Samoa was too much for Liz, let alone with Yoko alongside. The conversation with him had been hard enough, luckily, it had all been about science and work, world changing, but now that was done, emotions immediately started to appear and she hated herself for that understandable weakness.

—

Andy and Yoko. Science and a baby:

Yoko, Andy and both maternity nurses, Al and Lanfen were edging on panic. All the signs were there and Yoko felt strongly that motherhood was at hand. Al and Lanfen agreed, hence Andy went into action and ordered a helicopter flight back to Beijing.

Andy was determined to stay on top of the situation. There was not even a slight thought of science in his mind; he was scared, and very excited. Yoko on the other hand was still occasionally mentioning work, different aspects popping into her mind, all in-between hot sweats and strange feelings and movements going on inside herself.

It was a long journey, all be it, comfortable, apart from the level of noise when they remove their ear protectors. Yoko, between her awful sweats, chatted endlessly at Andy trying to discover the latest news from Liz, about her important discoveries. "Have you organised with Brendon about the collection of materials from Samoa?" "Yes Yo, all done, we are just waiting now. I have to find more time to read her report, but that will have to wait now, it is you and baby that are top priority right now. Just try and relax, close your eyes and take those slow and deep breaths, please, please." "Yes, yes Andy, but it is all so very important. It is you that must calm down Andrew, and be responsible for both of us now. I will no doubt deal with this little problem, it has happened before a few times you know. I am so very excited about all our little problems, but now I am worried about you. I am just 'tickidy-bok' as you Englishmen say." "No Yoko darling, its 'tickety-boo'." "Yes, yes, yes, Andrew Gould, it sounded fine to me."

Andy was told to sit down and strap himself in. "Take deep breaths Mr Gould, we have everything under control here, you no need worry." Andy closed his eyes tightly, trying to force any sense of panic to disappear, as he took slow deep breaths and could feel strange pains in his body.

Eleven hundred kilometres was not so far really by air, but for Andy Gould it felt like a journey to the moon. By the end of that journey, Andy's mind was full of dizziness and blurring. He had turned his phone off, and now found himself pacing a corridor, the end of the flight a complete miss, now surrounded by white walls and apron-clad people rushing in opposite directions. In that odd moment he turned his phone back on, only to find many missed calls and half a dozen calls from Liz and one message, 'Andy, I guess you are busy with that report I email to you, but please let me know when these samples are going to be collected, asap. Time is flying and we might just be able to help millions of people, its real important Andy.' He just cannot find it within himself to open any of the dozens of emails; he turned his phone back to off.

Walking quickly after somebody looking official and trying to use his few odd words of Chinese to discover where Yoko was. After a difficult exchange, he ended up in front of an English-speaking matron, much relieved, he asked for Yoko Cheng. "Master Gould, yes. You sit and wait, keep out of the way, out of my way. We busy. No problems, not long wait, ok?"

—

London, Whitehall:

In his secure London office, Brandon slammed the phone down hard with frustration; he stared at the ceiling breathing heavily. The R.A.F. had dispatched the plane to Samoa after crazy complications. He wanted to know, *'what the hell was going on'.* He knew nothing of Andy Gould and Yoko's little surprise package soon to arrive, and frankly, he could not afford to care either. He had been annoyed by the amount of time Andy was spending in Beijing. All be it, the department was working well and new updates were still being presented regularly from both Kings and Beijing, but none of those reports were truly taking the situation forward, and it sounded like something big had been discovered in Samoa, but he didn't know what is was. The annoyance and frustration were driving him mad, let alone the constant calls from ministers asking questions he could not answer. He had emailed twice to Andy Gould demanding some answers, and yet he had received no replies recently. He had done likewise to Samoa and Elizabeth Clements, who at least had replied briefly, *'Brandon, please be patient. I want to be sure of the science before Andy or I respond. It could be far too important; we must not act hastily. If my research is agreed, yet again, and after my own team has double-double checked everything, then we have found the cause, 'Not the solving', as yet. Regards, Liz Clements.*

P.S. Side issue at the moment, (and being the science holds up), what are the security services coming up with – how the hell did this all start at Kings, do we know anymore? Something very strange there Brandon.

—

France24-International News:

To follow immediately after the news is a special report covering the disturbances now occurring in major cities across the globe. Many public and government representatives across the world are concerned that contradictory statements were now combining with false news and conspiracy theories. The inability to understand and discover exactly what was happening everywhere has become intolerable, both for the public and authorities, and particularly due to the obvious press restrictions, which, have been internationally imposed.

In the British parliament yesterday the Prime Minister, Blyar Prescott was haggled by a number of members of the U.K. parliament demanding full and qualified information about the numerous disasters occurring across the United Kingdom and the world. He responded saying that, 'a full report and analysis was being produced and would be available shortly, hence it would be inappropriate, due to security issue, to comment further at this time. I can confirm the bout of unsubstantiated occurrences appear to be subsiding and deaths decreasing, whilst the situation is being fully monitored and contained by our experts comprised from the N.H.S., the armed forces, security services and our foremost scientists. We are constantly reappraising the situation based on those professional opinions.'

Answers are being demanded globally. Protests and disorder issues were currently growing and governments are concerned that such actions will destabilise and undermined the current international scientific and security efforts.

The majority of the news was inadvertently or very successfully, driving people towards those locally presented events, with personal disasters, and overly expressed emotional families sharing their pain on televisions in every country around the globe. Generally unknown to each other, some of those people suffered serious food shortages, some agricultural collapse, others awful respiratory deaths. For some it was all about outside aggressors attacking their nation, or a strange new flu virus. There was no consensus on the cause, and no realistic solutions being presented.

—

The B.B.C. World News:

In the French parliament today questions where being asked about why there had been no credible explanations or answers forth coming, concerning the protests in Paris against the lack of transparency and the restrictions being place on journalism on the current global situation that many believed was happening. The small bands of protesters have caused significant disruption and stretched police resources. The French Prime Minister commented; 'The protests have subsided and order has been restored. I thank both the police and the public for their patience. A report was currently being compiled, and would be presented to the French parliament shortly. He commented, 'it would not be appropriate therefore to comment further at this moment'.

The French President is to address the nation tomorrow at 5pm, when he is expected to give a fuller explanation on the current disturbances in Paris together with details on the potential global pandemic.

–

Alcazera-World news:

The current plague of false news and conspiracy theories spreading around the globe is beginning to cause serious concern for many governments, which generally fear a situation is growing out of control. Many have commented that the stories circulating of wide spread terrorism are generally false and people should view government websites for the true regional situations to place their concerns at rest. False news and conspiratory theories are currently ripe and considered the scourge of the world.

–

World governments rejoice:

From Samoa, an immense amount of organisation was being generated. Modelling requests had been forwarded to W.H.O., together with further requests to old colleagues at Portsmouth and Sheffield Universities in the United Kingdom, and Autonama Uni in Barcelona. All were more than interested in receiving and working through Liz Clements paper on the expanding and deadly abilities of H.A.B.'s around the coastal regions and oceans of the earth. The supporting endorsements of both Professor Andy Gould and Professor Yoko Cheng had further generated their rapid response. In London and Beijing, laboratories had been quickly re-organized, to accommodate the need for the confirmation or denouncement of Liz's discoveries. Everything was then rapidly confirmed, and further research procedures were quickly established; all designed for further investigation and the search for rapid solutions.

Andy Gould had initially work with the Beijing team in their laboratories alongside Yoko,

both of them confirming and checking the science. He knew he should be back at Kings to oversee the same work being carried out there, but he was happy his team were more than upto the task, never the less, his instincts were driving him in that direction.

With a troubled head and heart, Andy spoke of his decision to Yoko. She had known that would have to be the situation. In this time of their greatest pleasure, life was not serving them well. Yoko resolved to speak about delaying her arrival in Geneva and her new post at W.H.O. Andy booked his flight back to the U.K.. On the evening of the booking, they took Ava Rose to the park and walked slowly around in relative silence. "Yoko, I have been thinking seriously about our impossible life situation. I have decided that once the new Kings research team has been thoroughly checked and established fully, I am going to resign, that is it for me. I want us to be together with Ava, a real family. We have enough money between us. When we are ready, we could set up our own private research laboratories. I think we would find funding easily. We could take on occasional consultancy work; we could set up home in more than one country. What do you think?" Yoko was very quiet, as she listened to Andy's idea. She loved his suggestion, and yet something still held her back from immediately throwing her arms around him in celebration.

"Ok Andy, I love the idea, I truly do, and yet I am thinking that we cannot step away until this awful plague has left the world. I must admit to being confused. Currently my head is saying that I want everything, including the escape. Just to walk together by a river with our little one. Watch her first step and listen to her first word. Hold her close and feel her beautiful baby warmth, see her smiling and giggling. Oh Andy, what should we do? I say again, that I love the idea, truly, truly, but can we really do such a thing. Will either of us be able to stand apart from the needs and excitement of our work, the work we are currently so very involved in?" Yoko stopped walking and rocked the buggy looking down at her baby, then lent forward to adjust AvaRose's blanket and ran her finger across her sleeping face. When she stood straight once again, a tear rolled down her check. "Oh Andy, you know this is impossible. Both of us have so much to do, so many commitments." It was now Andy's turn to stand stock still in thought. He immediately knew that he was currently talking about the impossible. In reality, he knew it even when he felt the first words tumble from his mouth. He lent forward and gently kissed Yoko's tear away. "I love you Yoko Cheng, you are perfect. Let us work towards a plan. Yoko we must be together, all of us, or what is it all about. I have thought a lot lately about America, the U.N. job,

Kings Uni and Beijing. It will drive us mad and drive us apart. I now know foremost, I want to be with my family. Yes, I, like you, love my work, and I do not think either of us could be happy without it. We both have a need and a hunger for it, there is so much to discover, to learn, to give, but we must be together. Let us just think on that shall we.

—

All situations change:

Liz Clements had said nothing to Andy about her pregnancy. In fact, when she had arrived in Samoa she had only female intuition about the possibility. Now it was very real and an obvious happening. Each day she became larger, ate more, slept whenever she could and of course thought more about what Andy and she had shared, and indeed lost. Constantly she thought of contacting him, but she knew that would be unreasonable, particularly as she had heard via the scientific grape vine about Yoko's baby, and slowly she began a resolve that he should never know the truth via her own tongue and that she must push the memory of their relationship into history. She would try never to speak with either Andy or Yoko, therefore would only speak with others at Kings or Beijing.

As best she could, she threw herself into preparing for single motherhood and science, and that was truly enough for any human being.

The time was flying by so fast, each day bought forth-new discoveries, in both her body and her mind. She had gathered an impressive team on Samoa, and all her projects were now, well-funded, she had been both lucky and cleaver.

She had a wide range of interesting and clever friends, a beautiful home, occasional fun and more than enough to occupy her mind, yet her heart still needed healing.

Liz shunned notoriety, she preferred to work, and with her birthdate approaching rapidly, her efforts in the laboratory were reducing quickly. Ultimately, she had no option but to past on the reins to those around her whilst she spent endless frustrated hours caring for her condition.

Andy Gould and Yoko Cheng resolved their dilemma the only way they both felt they could. Yoko would not take the W.H.O. position, albeit, she would go there in person to discuss her position. Andy would await her return in Beijing, rushing between the university and little AvaRose. At times, little Ava would go with her father to the university, were of course she quickly became a celebrity, with all desperately wanting to care for her.

The time passed quickly while Yoko was in Geneva and then New York, and for Andy Gould, life had changed beyond believe. It was not just time, for he found himself living in a blur, never really being able to concentrate on most things long enough. It frustrated him. Hence, his delight of the agreement with Yoko. He had never been in such a position before, he had never realised just how much his brain had needed to work, the work that but some short time ago devoured him and gave him his greatest satisfaction. Regardless of the personal confusion rolling around his being, there was these days always AvaRose, which never failed to fill him with delight. He had housemaids, and baby carers, but when possible, he wanted to deal with all her needs, somehow it substituted his work and smoothed away those confusions a little.

Yoko had firstly attended the meeting in Geneva with Dr James Ryan who desperately wanted her on board his W.H.O. team, but after hearing her situation, was reluctantly happy to suggest she should also speak with his colleague, Michael Simson at the W.H.O. offices in New York. Yoko knew Michael Simson, so had readily reorganised her arrangements and immediately flown there. Yoko's conversations had developed well for both parties. The talks had concluded she would not take on the permanent role offered but agreed to take on particular specialist projects and to officially become their lead consultant on viral pandemic infections, the V.P.I. The initial conversation had been difficult. Ultimately, both parties warmed to each other and arrangements were found to suit both parties, on her part, she felt sure that Andy would find it satisfactory.

"Thank you for your understanding, and I am so pleased Michael we could find a way to compromise." "Ms Yoko Cheng, we are most lucky to have you on board. It is for us to thank you. Anyway, I think we are possibly obtaining two great brains for the price of one." The two colleagues laughed, then stood and began to shake hands, then Michael Simson withdrew his and lent forward to embrace Yoko, it was a happy moment for both colleagues. "You pass my regards on to your husband Yoko, and travel home safely; we will speak again very soon." She bent and pick up her brief case, feeling relieved and satisfied, her mind immediately reverting to AvaRose, Andy, and home. She strolled out into the New York sunshine and took a deep breath, this stunningly beautiful Chinese woman, with a brain edging on genius felt like a million dollars. Her flight was already organized, so there was nothing much to do apart from speaking to home and maybe grabbing some gifts. She desperately wanted to hear Andy's voice, and if she was lucky, too hear her little one giggling or even, screaming in the background. Either would be a delight.

As she balanced her brief case precariously, and then fumbled with her phone, she slowly wondered forward, intent on speaking to Andy and telling him her good news, and then she tripped on a slightly high pathing slab. She started to fall forward, taken by the weight of her briefcase, and with some force generated by somebody behind her also falling forward, the whole incident due to the crowded footpath and her precarious juggling. Both people were sent sprawling. One falling to the left on the path, another to the right, it was Yoko unfortunately, falling to the right and into the path of the then swerving, hooting and breaking vehicles. There was that horrid sound of crashing and crushing and skidding of taxicabs, vans and cars, people screaming and shouting. Vehicles flying and twisting across the road at awkward angles in their attempts to avoid the unavoidable collision, bonnets into bumpers, metal glass and plastic parts flying in all directions, then the awful realisation that somebody was lying to the edge of the road. It was Professor Yoko Cheng. She lay still, a pool of blood spreading below her still and damaged body, her hand still gripping the phone. She was heard grunting, whilst her arm twitched furiously.

Folks around the scene rushing to help, making emergency calls, sobbing. Some uncontrollably turning away and covering their faces due to the sad and bloody vision before them. Others holding back as the ever-growing crowd and back-up of twisted vehicles grew. Drivers shouting at drivers not aware of the hold up. Yoko's briefcase had been flung high into the air with all that metal and plastic, then crash down to the road surface and bursting open.

The valuable contents within, flying in all directions, almost symbolically ending so much promise, and so much hope for the future. Her brilliant mind slowly closing down as further twitches were observed, a little gurgling as blood trickled from her nose and mouth. Her love and dreams fading into the great abyss of the unknown, so ending her story and the journey she so loved with Andy, AvaRose and their wondrous and exciting life and future.

As the ambulance crew fought their way towards the scene and then bent to check for her vital signs, she jerked violently, and then remained completely still, laying amongst the blood and surrounding panic and chaos. All those important words, all reflecting enormous skill and great thinking on those endless pieces of paper flew away amongst the chaos of the awful and sad scene. Loves lost, dreams ended, hearts broken.

—

The world goes into action:

L iz Clement's pregnancy had almost become a non-event. In the last few weeks, she had concentrated, as best she could, on the efforts to organize and resolve the next stage of her discoveries, and those were going to be the toughest of solutions to be generated.

The satellite program, which was already in place, all be it, low-key, was expanded, both rapidly and enormously. They needed to know clearly the global situation of H.A.B.'s. She had also initiated conversations globally with prominent engineers and scientists regarding new and imaginative ways of controlling those dangerous blooms. She had concluded that, all be it, there were very few realistic options currently for oceanic use, the obvious and main problem was generated via coastal and estuary discharging of surplus nutrients via fertilisers and human waste in the widest sense. Chemical and aeration options appeared impractical, and although the brief she generated covered all possible means of control, her preferred choice to progress, was ultrasonic alga control.

At her extended facilities and laboratory on Samoa, and using just about all the scientific, technological and engineering skills within the communities on the islands, in the generating, and trialling of method after method of control and research. Communications were dispatched globally, concerning and enforcing the awful effects of nutrient run-off's into the rivers, seas and oceans. Then how that situation together with the rising global temperatures were changing oceanic layer flows and subsequently weather patterns, causing the H.A.B.'s, (dinoflagellates), to become more readily disbursed by air. After which, then mutated at increasing and unpredictable rates due to the embedded virus's within the bacteria.

In full, it was a powerful communication, backed by much undisputable science and scientific icons, pleading for action and greater effort. Within the communique, she offered numerous alternatives to control discharging and run-off, all were untried on the scale required, and hence a massif amount of testing and imagination would be required. Her thinking being globally based, to encourage competitive and rapid action, together with those creative applications. In her communique, she favoured the ultrasound as the possible solution; that due to the readily available applications, such as the facilities on, and under the seas, in commercial and military vessels, together with the wide range of fishing applications, which included tow-fishing, so allowing shallow water applications. Tweaking was the possible solution. She knew that if only sound engineers and scientists could discover the correct and most practical wavelength, these H.A.B.'s could be destroyed, or, at least controlled with no bad environmental side effects apart from being cautious of the ongoing production of oxygen.

At that stage, Liz began to realise and accept, at last, the whole situation had moved way beyond her scientific skills, importance and possible input. She had done her part, she had been lucky in her discovery, and the world had benefitted. Now the baton had finally been moved onward, as governments, particularly of those countries, which had been badly affected, began to work in unison to ban and control hundreds of activities, products and production plants.

Great projects suddenly appeared to swing into action. Deep valleys selected for filling with human waste and rubbish were located, and redundant mines and cave systems were employed at great expense. Investment into amazing and relevant inventions and science was suddenly found and rapidly applied.

Ultimately and reluctantly, Liz resolved to allow her pregnancy to take priority, and she finally began to relax into another world, a smaller world, all be it, of great personal importance, that of soon becoming a mother. Once in that position, her excitement grew day by day, which of course, was combined with discomfort and inconveniences, whilst some parts of her were being driven towards strange instinctive responses and regardless of the support of many good friends and her own self-reliance. Even so, inside her soul, she felt loneliness, which she was unable to shake, even whilst overindulging herself with sardine and marmite sandwiches, washed down with fresh coconut milk mixed with cola.

—

Brussels - Belguim. Mid 2008:

I n a secret location, an important meeting that could affect the world was in progress.

Of course, there were many important meetings in progress. Men and women with good brains all around the world were struggling within their specialist areas of responsibility and government. Each contributing those skills in a global effort to regain stability and normality, aimed at survival.

Some of those people were formed by a particular group of men, men of great wealth, and of course great power, which moved with them wherever they stood, and everywhere they travelled. They smiled easily, displaying the manors of civil and moral men, yet their reality lived in shadows and cunning calculation. Their bond was simply to increase their wealth and power, supported by a deep belief in their importance. It was not intentionally corrupt or particularly dishonest, for within business, and as far as they were concerned, those were seen as the rules of combat. Ultimately, the winner takes all, and it was a long game, in which they played with the highest level of skill, and always to the very limit.

Of course, there could be seen as a form of logic within their aims. Most people around the globe simply wanted a peaceful existence. A system that would provide them with the opportunity to support their loved ones, their communities and their countries. Just enough was good enough. That needed planning and balance. These grand men of power and wealth saw their duty as the work, almost of god. They had deleted emotion from their clear and logical minds, as they alone understood the reality of the world and most importantly, survival. Their power had been granted to them by success; total success, which they had achieved through their own efforts. As long as the system was driven towards need, they were in control, and control must be preserved at all costs.

"Gentlemen, our missions and endeavours must now be curtailed. We have achieved a great deal aided by our friendly pandemic. Our services are in greater demand than ever before, and via those means, the attempted limitations on our very important control, have been very successfully, dismissed. Confusion will reign for a short period of adjustment and ultimately vanish into the mist of a new era. A new era that will ideally suit our purposes and maintain stability across this world. Through our efforts, Pharmaceuticals have trebled and the demand on financing grows each and every day. Politicians are doubling their efforts on popularity, and indeed, so they should, while we will assist and help, each one of those struggling lambs to achieve that very worthy goal. Hence, I raise my glass to each one of those lambs and say to them, thank you."

There were subdued chuckles and smirks around the table. Some raised a glass, others preferred to give out a little hoot or to pat the table with their approval. That had to be done with some care, as before them, sat fine crystal glasses, valued at roughly £1,000 each, containing Chateau d'Yquem, and when they each took a sip of that exotic liquid, it was costing them a mere £100. In the centre of the great table lay cheeses like Pule and White Stilton Gold, which they nibbled at their convenience whilst nodding their approvals and agreements.

The distinguished gentleman with the silvered haired, remained standing, his knees wobbling a little due to his age and its accompanying problems, and then steadying himself against the edge of the table, he once again spoke. "Gentlemen, I think I do not need to say this, but as you know me well enough, so I will continue. Time has taught all of us here that clarity and security is everything. All those that have been involved in our little games and endeavours must be dispatched; excluding limited first-tier personnel. We all understand the rules and routines. We must all deliver our reports on the actions taken, and they must be on the central desk within seven days, not one second later, but I assume such plans are already in situate. We all know what must be done. All of us expect this from each other. There are no exceptions, albeit, always with some sorrow. If any problems are experienced, we must communicate that immediately to the inspector. I hope this little prompt is very clear and adequate. Now, in front of each of you is a full, up-to-date report of our activities and the resulting effects. This you may review whilst we are gathered, maybe throughout the afternoon and while we take tea on the balcony, then I shall destroy them before us all as per our rules. The full information will be forwarded in the usual secure manner. Before we move on, are there any further and immediate questions on these particular matters, or shall we go immediately to the rundown issues in the US, and what indeed, we will do with these Chinese friends of ours? It does appear that more team members are needed if we are to continue to adjust matters in our, and the world's favour, hence I suggest we seriously discuss who we can consider, and who would be fit to join us at this table." With a look of relief, he lowered himself onto the Toscano carver and waited for his colleague to take the lead on those other matters whilst he recovered his strength.

—

Motherhood and peace:

As Liz Clements began to give herself seriously to the prospect of motherhood and the strange endeavour of actually giving birth, she also strangely allowed herself to relax, picking up the occasional book to read and refusing to answer her phones, excluding of course family and friends, of which there were far too many. She decided to ban any mention of science and cancelled all journals and newspapers. When able, she wandered the few yards to the beach, or sat quietly at a favourite bar close by, or on the patio, either too fall asleep, or bury herself in reading sloppy romantic novels and adventure stories. There were many friends that also popped into check on her condition and engage in chatter. Most of them finding it immensely difficult to avoid the big issues, and subjects of yesterday in which Liz was their leader.

Nobody really knew this new Professor Clements, apart from her family.

Her father had flown over to support her; it was a long flight via Australia and a one-way flight arranged by her sister Angela. It was all she needed. They both scurried around, relieving her house cleaner of most of her duties, and then as she once again fell into a slumber, they would leave the maid in attendance and stroll to the town or countryside. The family were excited by the prospect of another Clements and asked no questions about fathers'; Liz thanked her lucky stars that she was born into such a family that only cared for her wellbeing.

Andy Gould only occasionally crossed her mind these days, and although her thoughts of him were never that far away, she had come to terms with their separation and his new life with Yoko Cheng and their new baby girl, AvaRose.

It had been one of those extremely long days; Liz had found herself tidying and then feeling too hot, then a little chilly, and maybe a little agitated. She had told her father and Angela to go for a walk, she felt fine, and she had lied. Now she was having cramp and backache, *'boy o boy what next'*, it was forty weeks, so she knew it was about the right time for the big show to begin.

When her sister returned she had advised her of the happenings. "Sounds to me Liz like it's all about to start sister. Call that midwife; no, don't you worry, I will do it. Where is the number? Let us all stay calm. Have your waters broken?" "I don't think so, but I think I peed myself a while back, maybe that was it, I keep dribbling." "I reckon that was your waters braking Liz."

Liz's father strolled, hithering, and dithering, touching things he had no need to and looking worried and out of his depth. "Dad, just go sit down somewhere, stop worrying and panicking, we've told the midwife, everything is under control. We will call you when your services are required. Pour yourself a drink, read a book, go on, out you go." Liz and Angela chuckled. They rarely saw their father like this; he had always been a man in control.

The evening had drawn in; Liz had calmed a little, "I think I'll be better off on the bed sis."

She had quickly fallen into a restless sleep and was waken at 4-30am with extreme stomach cramp. "Angela, Angela." Angela sat up from ware she half lay in the corner of the bedroom. "Has it started?" "I think so. Oh my god, what do I do now?" "You remember everything you have learnt, that would be a good start Liz."

It was not to long before professional help arrived in the form of Safina, short and round with a great big smile, which never left her face. "Out of the way Mr Clements, go on, shoo, shoo, back to your newspaper." Safina gave out her instructions. Angela, tea please, off you go." Her knowing confidence generated peace and calm. She had checked the timings and then sat down satisfied to read a magazine awaiting her tea.

At 9:30am, Talia had arrived to assist Safina. Contractions were on schedule. "Ok my darling, I think we can start the pushing game."

Liz looked at her in horror, then groaned and gave out tiny little screams as mother nature continued her job. "O, my god, O my god. Fucking hell this isn't possible, push it back, O my god." "That is wonderful Elizabeth, nearly there darling, nearly there, one or two more great big push please, then relax for a moment." Liz, gripping tightly at Angela's hand, sweating and swearing profusely gave that last, 'hopefully', big push, followed by more relaxing and yet another last push. The wondrous product of Liz and Andy's love then decided to enter the world. A blood stained, slimy little thing, which, they all instantly fell in love with. Once clean and cradled, with his tiny arms and legs kicking in all directions he was placed into a soft white shawl, from there, he appeared to look around in a knowing way, already old and wise for a new born.

"Hello my sweetheart, I am your mummy."

She held him close and looked deep into his eyes, and then kissing him gently on the forehead, after which she took his wee fingers and kissing them. He is so hansom, so tinny. Oh, my goodness, he looks exactly like a miniature Andy." It was, as expected, and the love just kept flowing. She had unwrapped him a little and simply could not look away from his beautiful little face, his fingers and toes. 'How did he fit inside me?' Turning eventually to Angela, "Sis, I have a little boy, and is he not just amazing and wonderful. Do you want a quick cuddle with Noah Andrew Clements, then,

I must give him his first feed?" Tears rolled down Liz's face, total joy and total love, she simply could not remove her eyes from him even when she had past him to her sister. She felt it would never be possible to ever look away from little Noah. The two women had tears of delight running down their tired faces, which, were joined by streaming noses, and strange incoherent noises derived from giggles and sobs.

Mr Clements arrived at the doorway, hands held to his head and in his sleeping shorts, "I have missed it all, haven't I. Why didn't you wake me girls?" "It happened to quickly Dad and you have only missed the messy bit. Come in and see your grandson, he is such a wonder, and yes, I am fine. It was a bit painful and I have to say. I do not think I want that experience again any time soon. He gently took little Noah from Angela, he cradled him gently and nervously, and then joined his daughters with the streaming wet faces. "Boy, look at us lot, what a load of softies, just look at him. Lizzy, he is truly gorgeous."

Still busying around the four, were Talia and Safina, who then joined the joyous group, wet faces all. Liz suddenly felt extremely tired. She retrieved Noah and nestled him to her breast. The other women arranging pillows around her. "This is your moment Liz, you enjoy, I think we need tea, and father something stronger maybe." Safina gently swept back Lizzes bedraggled blond hair. Is there anything you need right now mum?" "I think I have all I shall ever need Safina. Thank you all so much. I couldn't have done this without you all." Nobody bothered to respond.

Elizabeth Clements was a natural. She adored her new role in motherhood, nothing seemed to phase her, and with the luck of the gods, Noah Andrew was a perfect baby.

After two weeks, Liz began to glance once again at the hundreds of emails on her computer. Mostly, her colleagues and staff had efficiently dealt with post and email, for which she was thankful. Everything, had been correctly filed into their folders, and where a response was urgently required from her personally, a copy had been left for her attention.

She rapidly realised that the future would have to be very different. Her interest in the global drama appeared minimal. The science still intrigued her, as did any messages from Andy Gould, she simply could not resist viewing each one, all be it, she never responded to any. Although, she was emotionally locked into the father of Noah, each mention of his name jumped on her heart and she knew that life had to continue without his presents and that it must remain that way.

It was a strange experience walking near the sea with young Noah in his buggy, the great bag of babyhood goodies swinging at the back of his buggy, then stopping when meeting a colleague or arranging to meet at one of her favourite bars to discuss responses at the highest levels in world society or immensely high-profile scientific institutions.

All this, whilst warm breezes blew in from the Pacific Ocean and palms swayed gently under blue skies, there was the wet season, and indeed, it could be very wet. The thought of tsunamis bothered her, as did the centipedes and the horrid dogs found around most of the countryside villages. It was all about adjusting, pluses against minuses. When she had bought her bungalow, she had been well advised, all be it, she had paid top dollar.

She simply loved the simple life and the beautiful and easy people, one way or the other she had found her paradise. Between May and October, she would often stay down at her Fala at the beach and concentrate on science, whilst back at the bungalow's, now extensive facilities, research continued in earnest. Or, once again, at that favourite bar she would remove her laptop and work slowly in between changing and cooing to Noah. Then turning to enjoy chattering to friends and colleagues, whilst one hand still typed away at the odd email response. She was determined to remain detached from the big picture, and Samoa gave her that possibility. She knew she would only give of her mind and knowledge. She had truly found where she belonged, and how she wanted to be. Now she knew exactly what she was prepared to give away in her life and it was no longer her soul. That now belonged forever, to Noah.

—

Life moves on. Eynsford, Kent, England:

B etty and Bill Gould strolled slowly down the lane in Eynsford towards the Five Bells public house. Life for them continued as normal and in their own particular way. They watched their money carefully and consumed very little beyond their basic needs. It was Bills birthday and he just fancied a couple of pints of good English bitter. They had both changed into good clothes and washed behind their ears before wondering towards the Five Bells. In their generation, that is what you did, wash up and smarten up.

"Do I look ok Bill?" "You always look good to me Bett, come on now, what do you fancy to drink?" "I think I'll stick to my sweet sherry with a dash of lemonade, and maybe a packet of pain crisps. I don't want those favoured things Bill." It was summer, but not too hot. Their daughters were to meet them at the Bells to say 'Happy Birthday' to their father and they were both looking forward to the gathering. "It is a shame Andrew couldn't make it. Never mind, his life will settle down once he manages to come to terms with looking after young AvaRose and the death of Yoko. *'By George'*, he has had a rough time of it recently, that lad of ours." They both sat in silence for a short moment in thought. Of course, they had worried about their son, his life style and his loves and work, and they wanted desperately to see their new granddaughter and Andy settled and happy once again.

At that moment, Jill and Sally Gould entered the bar, talking six to the dozen just inside the doorway and not even noticing their parents. They had left the children and husbands behind as today was about their dad, direct family. Jill was the first to rush over and wrap her arms around her parents "Hi mum and a very happy birthday daddy dear. My goodness, you look like a couple of young whipper snappers." Bill and Betty laughed. "Where are our grandchildren, and of course, how are my lovely girls?" Sally spoke up. "All the kids are at home with dads today, it's just us today. No Andy I guess?" "No, I am afraid not, he is back in Beijing. He is not too happy these days. That brother of yours has to get his life in some order. It is a real tragedy what has happened but hopefully we will be seeing him and young AvaRose in a couple of weeks; just cannot wait to meet her. Your mother and I offered to fly over to help, but you know him, stubborn as a mule, always has been and always will be. Andrew has some serious thinking to do about his situation, he was so happy with Yoko and although we only meet her twice, she seemed lovely. We took to her, as indeed you girls did. We worry about him all the time I'm afraid."

The birthday session flowed on happily and then they all strolled back to the cottage a little more relaxed and where amongst them, Amy took over the star roll.

—

Guildford, Surrey, England:

In Guildford, the Clements household also continued their daily routines. Liz's father and sister had both returned to the family home. They had both loved it in Samoa, being with Liz at that special moment, meeting the newest member of their family, little Noah. The island had also captured their hearts, her friends and colleagues had all welcomed them and new relationships were readily and happily formed. Even dad Clements with all his years of diplomatic travel had fallen in love with Samoa and had resolved to return, as soon as he could arrange it. Her father and sister had returned to the U.K. with heavy hearts leaving behind Liz, young Noah and the island, together with all those new friends.

—

Kings College and Whitehall, London, England:

Andy Gould had maintained a close involvement at Kings although that was not his initial intention and his colleagues had welcome that. The exchanges between Beijing and London were maintained at a particularly high level, together with numerous other strong connections around the globe.

On a political bases Andy still attended many meetings in an advisory capacity when in London or when recalled by Whitehall. Often working with updated information and papers published by Liz Clemence.

He never attempted to contact Liz directly; he found he simply could not. Emotionally he wanted too on numerous occasions, but he found within himself a solid block that regardless of his need, he simply could not make the approach. Between thoughts of Yoko and AvaRose, his family, London and Beijing, all piled on top of serious scientific work he found for the first time in his life, that a lack of confidents was creeping into his mind. It showed itself in the questions he asked and the unresolved dilemmas that circled around inside his head. Those thoughts often leading to, *'Oh Liz, what is happening to me'*?

—

Africa:

All across Africa, life was returning to a *kind* of normality. Where the pandemic had course deaths of people in their thousands, also, in the odd places where the cattle were depleted and the lakes polluted. The towns and areas where horrendous explosions had been experienced and yet, the people of Africa saw small signs of hope. Unfortunately, the tribal conflicts, which had been created, continued, causing unnecessary deaths, political unrest and horrid mutilations amongst the waring people, let alone the results from the huge number of unexplainable disasters. The people were hardy and they saw seasonal disruptions regularly, drought, floods and decease, albeit, nobody had ever seen before, those strange and deadly happenings. But on this occasion, as with all those horrid occasions of the past, they would with luck, recover.

In Zambia, at the field station just outside of Mongu, Sam and his team had survived the mysterious and horrendous explosion that had occurred. Thankfully, a westerly breeze had saved them from the greeny-white mist that had covered, then floated across the towns, villages and savannah, killing in its path, thousands and thousands of people carrying out their daily lives and then having been hit by the asphyxiating toxins' carried within that misty cloud of death. Man, women and child, together with their beasts, all died horribly. Across that large area of land, it would take years of confusion, sorrow and regeneration, before any kind of normality would truly be seen once again. Sadly, most of the world had hardly noticed the African horrors. Certain people with financial interests were rubbing their hands together, and placing marks on maps showing a whole variety of incidents across the continent, which were now a little more desperate for their assistance.

—

The United States of America:

There had been immense amounts of fear from east to west. The United States of America was in turmoil. Apart from the awful deaths of toddlers and babies in all states, there had been random explosions in shopping malls and other strange deaths occurring. Somehow, it had generated riots and looting in many cities, particularly in the south. Fear had turned to hatred, and hatred into accusations and blame, one race against the other. A large number of cities had experienced violence of the worst kind. The National Guard had been called out on numerous occasions, and once again people were killed, guardsmen, police officers and public. Senators gave great speeches on law and order, enemies across the sea and the American way of life. The reality being, those words changed very little.

Baby dummies and low milligram dosage Aspro products, had been recalled around the world and destroyed. The random explosions across the states ceased, as in other countries, but the violence continued in a crazy random manner. The Whitehouse was in despair, the stock market had plummeted. Financial institutions globally were struggling to maintain confidence. Agriculture had suffered badly. The people of America were in shock at the devastation that had been sent upon them in so many forms and constantly demanded clear answers and explanations, which, were not correctly or truly given, as nobody knew all the answers. Somehow, the country slowly began its journey back to some kind of normality, everybody wondering what had happened and how, caused by who and what.

Within the most powerful nation on earth, they were only but confusion and accusation.

The solution to their ills was in sight. An English Professor Clements had managed to isolate the main issue leading to so much pain and the president at last could wipe his brow and speak of the solutions being in sight and how every appropriate action was being taken to resolve and stabilize the awful devastation that had occurred. "We the American people are working with Professor Clements, the W.H.O. and directly the U.N., in harmony with many international agencies. I have instructed our foremost universities and scientist across our great nation to afford any assistance requested. We the American people, together with gods help, will overcome. God bless America."

—

Beijing, China:

Andy Gould had been run ragged with supporting Liz's scientific discoveries; together the endless needs of a single parent. He had many other responsibilities, all be it, his duties at Kings College had been reduced he had ultimately, retained overall control, hence the work undertaken needed his overall leadership, which meant meetings in the U.K., at Whitehall, press interviews and international discussions, writing and checking scientific papers and voicing advice.

At Beijing University, Andy had also maintained an active role with Yoko's team.

The team, and of course Andy, had been devastated by her loss and nobody had allowed themselves the opportunity of truly grieving, there simply had been no time for such a luxury.

When rare moments appeared, the whole team would dive into grieving, normally alone in some quiet corner. Andy grieved when back at home after fulfilling his duties, which included his precious time with AvaRose, who was a total delight. Her giggles, and desire for affection was contagious, her smile was sheer magic and her soft skin and smell, intoxicating. Beyond all the activities in his busy life, AvaRose was by far the most important. When occasionally, she mentioned the word mummy, it felt like a stake being driven through his heart. There was nothing he could say to AvaRose, when the word mummy was mentioned or inadvertently she had called for mother. Normally, he would move on preparing her for bed, talking to her gently and attempting to smooth away any pain within himself and that lurked within his small and beautiful daughter. Only then, would Andy Gould say good night to aids, and lay back into sweet and sorrowful memories, normally interacting with tears gently rolling down his tired face and ultimately falling to sleep where he was, and then remaining there until first light.

—

Realism. Italy and the global community:

Around the globe there was a new energy driving governments and agencies of all types to double their efforts, all hell bent on resolving their particular aspect of the many requirements to place their country and the world back into a controlled and civilised position.

Scientists and engineers were hard at work in applying their skills on the deadly H.A.B.'s that were polluting the oceans and the very air that all creatures breathed.

National and international police and security services were chasing and following leads, and then hunting down perpetrators. Holding stations were being created for the hundreds who had been connected directly or indirectly by email, phone calls or bank accounts.

Running in parallel, there was a flurry of strange deaths being investigated after intense observations of strange air and car crashes, also over doses. Famous people were disappearing from public life and governments across the globe.

In particular, and as a good example, was the happenings in Italy, where following the sudden and strange disappearance of Antonio Galabri, billionaire, financier and politician had started a massive chain of events and wide spread investigations.

Regardless of his enormous wealth, together with his great industrial and political power, many of his business and political associates, family and friends had simply disappeared from the face of the earth. The whole incident fading initially into the mess that was Italy's social and ministerial situation. Then the unexplained death of a minor paparazzi journalist had been picked up by Interpol. Luigi Maroni had via his incredible research papers that were found in his small flat in Milan and then started an unstoppable chain of events and discovery.

Luigi Maroni's strange death; i.e. found hanging from a beam in his small apartment, under which there was no means of mounting and performing his own hanging was strange enough, but then as the great collection of reference paperwork was viewed in horror and almost disbelief for it clearly linked into the disappearance of Antonio Galabri. Suddenly, link after link was being made and as the web of deceit rapidly spread into a global conspiracy of some kind, arrest after arrest was being seen to happen.

For Luigi Maroni, his dreams of fame, wealth and international respect had vanished, yet his endeavours of his hobby had assisted the world in pursuing a network of corruption and evil, the likes of which nobody had ever imagined.

Similar incidents began to appear in other countries but regardless of those efforts, there was within the global security services a feeling and understanding that the network of evil would never be truly closed down. Wealth and power had too strong a hold within society.

As the evidence mounted, so did the realisation that somehow a group of very influential people had been controlling events over past years. It was being surmised that they, through their own scientific resources, which were very considerable, had detected the growing threat to the world of the horrendous development that H.A.B.'s were beginning to have on the environment. Then used that knowledge to apply their own plans to improve their deteriorating hold and control of events. No finite proof could yet be established, regardless of the worldwide effort.

It appeared to some authorities, that the undefined group had upgraded their discoveries by orchestrating numerous disastrous events globally to promote and reinforce their own power, services and control.

Maybe, it was just the endless fight of good against evil. The constant search for balance, equality and harmony. A battle that would continue forever.

Good seemed to of found a way forward, out maneuverer evil to some degree, or at least, enough, and good was now fighting back with weight and numbers on their side.

While Professor's Andy Gould and Elizabeth Clements had contributed a massive amount to the cause, their own lives had been put asunder; ultimately changed forever. Yet change is the state of all matter, rarely disastrous, just different.

—

Time moves on:

T he world had at last recognised or been possibly forced into the value of true human unity and harmonious action. While the United Nations at last led a gigantic and very aggressive drive for improvements environmentally of pollution on land and in the oceans and estuaries around the world. It had also, inadvertently ignited a common global desire for action. Massive changes of global responsibilities began to be noticed; the sharing of wealth was for the first time in history seriously being directed towards the environment and extending equality.

For most peoples, there was but a shrug of the shoulders as they carried on re-establishing their lives. For those folks around the globe which were generally oblivious too much of what had been occurring due to the severe censorship and sad lack of understanding by authorities. The television, as normal, was switched on to accompany them while they ate their meal. Masks had generally disappeared and normal social services and transportation were now beginning to be maintained, all be it, massively reduced.

Generally, there was an acceptance and agreement in principal with the actions happening globally. That had taken a long time to develop and very few accepted those dramatic changes that applied within their own lives. The words were clearly out there and a new and exciting ethos was growing in acceptance.

Professor Andy Gould had ultimately set up his own research laboratories exactly as he and Yoko had planned. One operation in China, the other in the U.K.. He was still a very busy man, assisting in major environmental projects and developing new and exciting testing regimes to defend the planet against endless horrendous possibilities.

It was five years on from that awful year and a half. His hair has turned grey and his shoulders a little humped but his enthusiasm for his work and indeed, the love of his life, AvaRose, had never diminished. She was now in her fifth year, pretty in the extreme with great big dark eyes together with black as night curly hair. She was already fluent in English and Mandarin, so had now decided she wanted to learn French. She charmed everybody that met her, with giggles, smiles and cute but clever chatter, often standing with her head to one side and hands on hips.

Professor Elizabeth Clements was without doubt an international star of science. Now being nominated for a Noble Prize for Science. Shadow writers contacted her every week proposing books about her life. None of those matters interested her. She remained working within her Somalia laboratories, from where her notoriety gave her work priority on the world stage. She shunned interviews of any kind. She had bought a small yacht and together with young Noah Andrew and indeed any one of her wide range of scientific or Simian friends, she indulged herself occasionally sailing the islands.

Day by day, young Noah grew more and more like his father, and although she was very aware of that development, it did not bother her. They, being Andy Gould and herself, had not directly spoken for years, all be it, they were committed to reading one another's scientific papers, asking questions and giving responses, always extremely interested in the others work.

Hidden feelings lived on within both of them, they were both aware that some years back they were on the edge of deep and sincere love and that the wind of change had somehow blown them off course. Both understood that the intense period through which they had travelled had taken over normal and natural responses towards each other. It had taken years to return to their normal states-of-being and in both cases, it was the children that had allowed, or indeed, forced that to happen.

Somewhere, in both of their souls, there was sorrow, mixed with confused love, and lurking close by, was still the feeling of hidden desire towards each other.

Global investment in both direct science and particularly environmental sciences had doubled over the last few years. Politicians and religious leaders, together with the masses had at last began to adhere to common sense and the new global ethos, which with luck, might just save the future.

In Japan, a new and worrying virus had been discovered and was being investigated. Yet once again, it appeared to of been generated from the oceans.

Professor Elizabeth Clements was called upon to assist. Ultimately, she had no option but to call on Professor Andy Gould.

Elizabeth Clements struggled for days over the necessity to making direct contact with Andy Gould. Whilst the struggles were irrational, she had to recognise that the memories flooding occasionally through her mind were real and even worse than that, there was emotion involved, even affection tainted with memories of love. For the whole period prior to finding her courage to make that call, she was flustered, irrational and then quiet and thoughtful.

When the day came, the confusion and awkwardness was under control as she dialled the digits. "Yes, Andy Gould." She was taken-a-back by the abruptness. "Andy, this is Liz." Everything went silent for a couple of long seconds. "Liz is that really you calling me. I'm sorry for the sharp response; it has been one of those mornings. How very lovely, it's been far too long, my fault I guess. This Twitter age is not good for real talking, just sound bites. How are you anyway and how can I help? Liz, I have to say immediately, it is simply wonderful to hear your voice. All be it, sounds a lot deeper and gruff nowadays. Have you started smoking a pipe or something?" "Boy, you haven't changed, but yes, I smoke a pipe and drink bottles of whisky every day. It is also good to hear your voice. Is life good for you and, I think I am correct in saying, little AvaRose, maybe not so little now." "Correct Liz, not so little, but she is a wonder, a true delight. Work is endless, as usual."

The conversation was flowing easily as the past years of no contact vanished into the ether. Liz decided to push on with her mission. "Andy, you may have heard of this problem in Japan, maybe not. I have been contacted by a colleague requesting our assistance. To be honest, I was unsure if I should become involved or not. Like yourself, I have endless projects rolling at the moment, but they convinced me of the importance. They spoke of you being invited. It sounds serious and I think we really don't have much of an option if what I already know is correct, will you take a look at the info gathered to date and have a think about it please." "Liz, if you say that it is important, then of course I will. I have no knowledge about anything-exceptional going on, so I am interested. Just send it over." "Thanks Andy. It was lovely to talk. I have been rather foolish, I should have made contact, I'm afraid it is just life getting in the way. Silly really!" "No Liz, it is really my fault, not yours, I am but still an idiot. Look, as soon as the data arrives I promise I will make it a priority, ok. Let us speak real soon. Liz, truly it is great to hear your voice again. Let's both commit to that. You take good care, soon then." The phone went down. There was silence once again. Both stayed exactly where they were, frozen to the spot. Somehow lost in a maze of romantic mist that raced through both of them. Time had just vanished.

After many digital exchanges, a meeting was decided on. Although the importance and seriousness of another global threat was looming, there was something else looming of equal importance.

Andy had the flights booked. It was going to be a long journey, particularly for AvaRose and Maryjane, his long-suffering secretary, child carer and general helper in all matters. Regardless of the urgency, he had requested stopovers', AvaRose came first, there was no if's on that decision. The whole exercise was to take five days before they arrived at the Tanoa Tusitala Hotel in Samoa. He had sent his arrival details to Liz and she had replied with meeting arrangements.

Books of every kind had been packed, together with digital games and iPad. Maryjane had packed swimwear in anticipation of a long and enjoyable holiday, maybe a trip to remember without the normal load of endless work. She had scanned every source of information about Samoa; she knew every possibility for entertaining AvaRose, the best beaches and the best play areas, particularly those with a relaxing and convenient little bar area.

When that long, long journey was ultimately over and they all three entered the Tanoa Hotel, they were all exhausted beyond believe. Andy carried AvaRose through reception and almost immediately, straight to their rooms. With a thumb firmly in position and a nodding head, AvaRose slept soundly over Andy's shoulder. Very shortly after settling the little one, both Maryjane and Andy also went willingly to their rooms.

Late the following morning a re-energised AvaRose charged haply around the large room she shared with her father. She had discovered how to open the balcony doors and was then jumping up and down beside her sleepy father demanding to visit the pool. "Ava, ok ok, let me put some trousers on and you can find my glasses for me. He pulled himself upright, sweeping his fingers through his greying two-tone hair that currently reached below his shoulder line. He shook his still sleepy head, then swung his feet to the floor and yawned. "Come on you horror. You will have to lead the way as my eyes are still half closed." Ava Rose grabbed his hand and pulled him towards the door, appropriately dressed in her pink plastic sandals, matching swimwear, rubber ring, deflated, sunglasses and hat. "Let's find Maryjane first coz she will want to come with us. Come on sleepy daddy, you silly old thing."

Two sleepy adults were dragged through the hotel, passing sniggering staff, which kindly opened doors to aid their journey towards the pool area.

Painfully they established a gathering area, chairs, umbrellas and a small table upon which hopefully coffee would be placed. AvaRose, jumping excitedly and demanding air be inserted into her rubber ring, then with a great splash, was in the children's small pool.

It was not long before Andy notice the top half of Liz wondering her way behind hedging running parallel with the pool. Andy stood, waved and called her; she waved back and sent a smile in his direction. AvaRose had seen the wave and climbed from the pool and ran towards the opening in the hedging. "Hello, who are you? Are you a friend of my daddies, let me take you over to him, follow me", then turning towards Noah, "hi, my name is AvaRose, what's your name and can you go swimming with me, it's awfully good fun."

Andy looked towards his daughter and Liz but could not take his eyes from the small lad still holding hard to Liz's hand. "Mummy, can I go swimming with Aba please", "err, what is your name, Aba-what?" "No, it's AvaRose, o' never mind, now come on, let's go have fun Noah, we can be friends. That's my daddy over there." Looking up at Liz with head to one side and hands on hips. "Excuse me, but does Noah have any trunks?" "Well, young lady, he does indeed but not here, but I think the hotel should be able to help us out with some, shall we go and ask them?"

Andy had still not been able to take his eyes away from looking at young Noah, and then he forced himself, lent forward with a genuine affection rushing through his body, and cuddled Liz in welcome. Privately, they both tingled with endless emotions. "It's really great to see you Liz. You look simply wonderful. Arr, sorry this is Maryjane, secretary extraordinaire and mistress of everything she does, and this Maryjane is the amazing Elizabeth Clements, who also happens to be extraordinaire and potentially a Nobel Prize winner."

Andy knelt to one knee looking deep into Noah's eyes and gestured to shake hands. "We certainly cannot forget this handsome young man. Did I hear your name was Noah, if so, that is a very fine name? I am very pleased to meet you, Noah, then they shook hands and Andy fell immediately in love.

"Daddy, I think you must find some trunks and things for my new friend."

Maryjane stood ready for the task, "ok, lots of coffee, cakes and juice and then off to the shops I guess." "Can we come with you Maryjane?"

Liz and Andy sat and contemplated the obvious reality of young Noah's parenthood.

"How old is he Liz?" "About eight months younger than AvaRose." "I had no idea." "How could I tell you? It was all about timing Andy. He is wonderful, my total joy in life. No doubt, the same as AvaRose, she is so bright and pretty, just like her mother. I guess things have moved on more than we ever realized. Hopefully, we can both enjoy watching them and getting to know them, after all, they are half brother and sister and luckily, instant friends."

The next few days flowed with an intensity formed by happy children, beach picnics, and delightful evening meals, and of course work. As usual, Maryjane was an instant success with both children who now behaved as if physical joined, therefore allowing Liz and Andy to rediscover each other and consider the threatening issues growing around the Japanese coastline, the Pacific, the Sea of Japan and the East China Sea. They needed to attend a conference in two months including initially, Chinese, Russian, Japanese and both North and South Korean representation.

As Andy Gould and Liz Clements sat in on a video link conference with colleagues from the Japanese science fraternity all began to feel the increasing threat that was building in their thoughts based on the research already carried out. It was an horrendous realisation that yet once again something beyond the established science was growing before them. Andy and Liz glared at each other as the latest research was presented to them. "Boy o' boy Liz, this is Bioscience all over again, or rather Biohazard; Zoology and Botany appear to becoming one." As all seven participants starred into the video link somewhat scared of the obvious thoughts that travelled to the fore of their minds. Somewhere in each of their hopes was another realisation, but that hope had been dismissed by the facts.

Liz Clements spoke up breaking the silence that had settled over all seven great scientific minds. "This is all extremely worrying. May I suggest we all need to thoroughly rethink our positions after this discussion. We must move with caution before we express, suggest or declare any information. Hence, each of us needs to produce a summary of our initial procedures to present worldwide. May I suggest two or three days maximum; video conference once again to compile a unified set of clear actions. Then once again go out to the world. At least we have our recent experience to refer to and many processes in place. In that, there is considerable hope."

In agreement, the video call closed.

Liz and Andy arranged to meet the following day at Lano Beach. Maryjane was to take the day for herself and she indeed needed and deserved it. Both Andy and Liz Clements were naturally inclined towards late mornings that allowed both organising their daily duties and answering any urgent email. Andy was still feeling a little fatigued after his long flight, all be, he had attempted to spend time with AvaRose; to somehow engage with her endless energy; plus pay attention to the drastic issues he was here to discuss. If that was not enough for any human being, seeing Liz after such a long time was regenerating his love and appreciation for her, yet that was giving him further problems with guilt and loyalty.

Andy found Liz and Noah at the bar sitting at a rickety table overlooking the beach. She looked quite relaxed and simply gorgeous. Under a large straw hat with a flimsy vest above baggy shorts, her long legs spread out and her very long blond hair blowing gently in the breeze. She and young Noah working hard at a colouring book, fruit juices set before them.

As Andy and AvaRose approached, she looked up and smiled broadly. "Good morning Andy and a very good morning to you AvaRose." Noah looked up at the mention of Ava's name and ran to greet her, taking her hand. "Shall we go to the beach? Mummy, can we go and play on the beach please?" "Off you go, but you stay where we can see you all the time. No going in the sea until Andy and I are with you, ok."

"You look very delicious Liz; can we organise some coffee here?" "No problem. Do you want anything to eat? I have to say you don't look very delicious, you look exhausted, but thanks for the kind words."

Once coffee was placed on the table, Andy began to relax a little and in an unexpected moment, he took Liz's hand and stared at her intently, then lifted her hand and kissed it affectionately. "Boy, this is strange stuff." "I know. Do not say too much. We are nearly adults now. Let's just try and start saving the world."

—

Epilogue:

Professor Elizabeth Clements and Professor Andy Gould fell hopelessly in love.

Liz Clements had decided she would never again engage in promoting herself on the world stage, Noble Prize or not and she had formed the company, 'CL Research Laboratories Ltd'. All research and papers, would only be presented via the company name, nothing personal ever again, and countersigned always by executive, and scientific directors. She had also established an admin department, including P.R. and funding.

Professor Andy Gould continued working between Beijing and London for the follow six months, but seemed to spend more and more time in Samoa working alongside Liz Clements. He learnt to understand and respected how Liz had created her new life style.

Their relationship grew to such a degree, that AvaRose ultimately stayed in Samoa, while her father dash around the world reorganising his life style so he could work and live alongside Liz Clements.

Both Noah and AvaRose remained inseparable and it would appear that both are destined for scientific greatness.

CL Research Laboratories rapidly established themselves throughout the world's scientific community and are called upon by governments regularly. They managed to retain the principals and ethos that Liz had created.

The troubling issues within the oceans around Japan reduced in severity and appeared to of vanished. Regardless, CL Research Laboratories continue their work on the incident whilst monitoring that and many other possible Bioscientific problems.

They continue to monitor, advice and progress the problems caused by H.A.B.'s across the globe. The United Nations and many wealthy nations currently contribute heavily to the enormous efforts made to improve the environment and their efforts continue to show significant improvements within the problems now recognised with H.A.B.'s+1 as they are so called.

Public information is now made readily available and accessible via the U.N.'s and other national websites on such issues, and international credence and credibility is slowly being establish for a universal ethos of harmony and equality, together with the introduction of 'open-sharing' of all scientific and health related knowledge. That is a new and significant commitment, so meeting the developing global ethos. A number of pharmaceutical giants have, as numerous people are aware, been taken into public ownership. Many moves are going ahead to reduce global enterprises' on the bases of national control being the preferred shape of the future; that is of course about globally harmonisation, not nationalism. There are many other major changes occurring globally in the attempt to harmonise more and more of the worlds' activities. There is a long way to go before a new world order of worth is fully established and there will be pain and gain, with a lot of raised voices and unfortunately, spilt blood, but in a meaningful way, the journey has begun.

Liz and Andy have embraced the growth of a new world order that they see developing and both work quietly on their many projects in an environment they both love, together with their three children.

They have been able to establish a charity to which they personally contribute all surplus funds. To date that charity, 'Harmony'; has funds available at 194 million US Dollars, and is growing day by day. Long term their intention is to invest in non-profit generating science, pharmaceutical and general medical institutions that distribute freely their intellectual property.

———— ◉ ————

"ANDY, COME ON IT'S nearly nine, today is for sailing, strictly fun and pleasure; I don't want to hear one word about work.

You two just hurry up or you are not coming with us, and also you will have to do homework all day in your bedrooms, no food or drink, think about it, so make your minds up. We're not waiting for you."

And the world rolled on.

—

P.S.: Please note that a full and factually dated list of all the incidents associated with this issue globally is available on our website and can currently be downloaded for those interested. It contains every link that confirms those facts used as the bases of this story. Please be aware that the information may at some time, be removed and that remains out of our control.

———— ◉ ————

The End.

—

Dear Reader, I hope you enjoyed the story.
Obviously, 'A Conspiracy of Events' is a fantasy, a fantasy of
possibilities.
A journey the world appears to currently be on; and beyond all else,
a warning, needing endeavour and a serious change in our ways.
'Well, maybe not a fantasy after all'.
Buried within the story are serious questions and queries about all our
traditions and habits.
Forever questioning the need for change. 'An adventure of mind and
spirit'.
We learn with difficulty, and hope with intensity, openly or secretly,
constantly attempting to balance the drifts of opinion, feelings,
experience, and knowledge against the practical needs of that
particular moment in time.
Then failing or succeeding, and hiding within our own shadows of
doubt.
All thoughts become a balance of good and evil, of timing, the decision
of saying yes or no, normally set against the practicalities of survival in
that very moment or for the unknown future of all.
The total intricacies, interactions and details can never be fully seen, or
expressed clearly,
so availing to one that single and correct direction.
Only suggestions from our own experience and thoughts echo through
our minds.
There are simply far too many variations for any human to absorb and
guide them
forward on the one and only course of action.

*Therefore, it must be as you alone perceive, or as conclusive facts seem to
dictate in that year of your life,
at that very moment in time; and even then, all may well change.
The results of your truth and discovery lie forever within destiny, fate
or the phases of the moon.
'Ride the Wave and Fly with the Wind', while eating humble pie, and
recognising the inadequacies,
for your life is but an adventure of mind and spirit, born of stardust,
and when we work together we may just be able to create a new and
worthy world.
John Brooks.*

—

Comment:

If you have enjoyed the story, **'A Conspiracy of Events'** then maybe, you'll find and read **'Garrtellia'** available from late 2023, initially in softback and published by L.R. Price, or read the first book in the trilogy, **'The First Rays of Sun'**. Currently available in Ebook and Softback. Also, published by Draft2Digital is **'Incidents of Slavery'.**

I would very much like to hear your comments or criticisms, being of course they are polite. It seriously helps one to improve the writing skills, which hopefully are improving. Criticism and comment on the story flow and grammar are most helpful.

Thanks for any comments, John Brooks.

Email: johnbrooksy@outlook.com

—

Please Note:

This story is a work of fiction and there is no intention to associate in any way via facts or truth to any named persons, titles or organisations used or indicated throughout the work.

Please be warned, that within this story there are described acts of violence and intermit sex which form part of the storyline and do not wish in any way, or intended, to offend.

—

The Author:

I was born in South London, in the United Kingdom, in 1946, and worked most of my life in the display, promotion, and design world, as well as for five years as an artist and loved every moment. Family life took over and stopped this period of self-indulgence. For most of the journey, I successfully ran my own display and promotion companies until a disastrous fire destroyed the company, and due to insurance averaging, reduced life back to basics—house, cars, wife and money were all gone. 'Oh dear!'

In these later years, I spent a good deal of time enjoying Spain, with the thoughts of writing and maybe starting to paint once again. I live with my partner, Lesley Anne, in a small village set amongst the hills and orchards of Almeria enjoying each, and every day.

Writing books is an all-consuming affair. In the beginning, trying too hard was a huge problem; it simply produced an unworthy result but with the good fortune of time and the help of capable friends reading the progressing chapters, *The First Rays of Sun* was completed and published in 2019, then the further two parts of the trilogy, *Second Dawning* and *Innocent Reflections,* and decided to place all three under the single title, *Garrtellia.* All be, the full trilogy, 'Garrtellia', is to be released in late 2022 in softback. The further array of completed stories yet to be published, include; '**A Conspiracy of Events**', '**Does Fortune become You**' and '**Incidents of Slavery**' which is now available as an Ebook. **All books will be available in both Ebook and softback.**

Whilst writing mainly through the night with adjacent cups of coffee and cigarettes at hand was and is an endless shameful pleasure. Continually, living the characters and situations, constantly asking oneself, 'what would happen now, what would I do', was enlightening. It was and is still enormous fun. I sincerely hope you too enjoy the journey. John Brooks.

—

Appreciations:

I would very much like to thank the friends who have taken the time to read the drafts of all stories.

I appreciate that you have given your valuable time, opinions and comments. Writing is a lonely job in some ways, albeit a pleasure, but without your endeavour and comments, it would have been more difficult to progress, improve, and finish the task. Deserving special thanks are Lesley Anne Selvage and Lyn Williams. In particular, Tim Guest for his ideas and initial input. Plus. I would like to thank Grammarly, AutoCrit and Microsoft Word for their amazing programs.

Thanks a million for your help guys, love as always. In addition, I would like to thank Janet Steward, Joy Fairburn, and Rosemary Johnson.

Love and thank you all.

Don't miss out!

Visit the website below and you can sign up to receive emails whenever john brooks publishes a new book. There's no charge and no obligation.

https://books2read.com/r/B-A-CMJZ-AIXLC

BOOKS 2 READ

Connecting independent readers to independent writers.

Also by john brooks